A Home Subscription! It's the easiest and most convenient way to get every one of the exciting Coventry Romance Novels! ...And you get 4 of them FREE!

You pay nothing extra for this convenience: there are no additional charges...you don't even pay for postage! Fill out and send us the handy coupon now. and we'll send you 4 exciting Coventry Romance novels absolutely FREE!

SEND NO MONEY, GET THESE
FOUR BOOKS FREE!

MEADOWSONG

by

Phyllis Ann Karr

FAWCETT COVENTRY • NEW YORK

MEADOWSONG

Published by Fawcett Coventry Books, a unit of CBS Publications, the Consumer Publishing Division of CBS Inc.

ISBN: 0-449-50209-0 .

Printed in the United States of America

First Fawcett Coventry printing: September 1981

10   9   8   7   6   5   4   3   2   1

Prologue

1802

He wore no sword. They had been out of style for a
generation, but one would still have been practical
for a beruffled young gentleman (however threadbare his finery under strong light) who walked the
London streets alone, with a slight limp, in the small
hours of the night. He had no pistol, and he did not
even carry a cane. He swung a leather case, alter-
nately letting it float free for a moment by the loop
that attached it to his left wrist and catching it again
with his long fingers as it began its downward arc.
The case was about two feet long, but it had neither
sharp end nor heavy handle. It rather clearly contained nothing but some light woodwind instrument,
oboe, flute, or clarinet d'amore, and no doubt it
looked less formidable than an umbrella would have
done.

He had almost reached the end of the last dark
street before Lincoln's Inn Fields when he felt the
footpad's sudden attack from behind—a strangling
arm about his neck and a knee thrusting up into the
small of his back.

He planted his feet firmly and bent against the
attack. The pressure left his spine as his assailant
was forced to return both his own feet to the ground,
but the arm round his neck tightened, and a second
arm groped for a hold over his broad chest. Quickly,
while he still had some liberty of his arms, he jerked
open the top of the leather case.

How long could a man remain conscious without air? He shook the top of his instrument far enough from the case to get the fingers of his right hand firmly about the polished wood. He had rehearsed this moment often enough in imagination—holding the bottom of the flute tight in the case, he began turning the headjoint, unscrewing desperately, while one strong grip bound his arms above the elbow and another choked the air from his lungs and throat...

The headjoint came free into his right hand before the world went completely dark. With just enough freedom of play to avoid his own flesh, he turned the headjoint in his hand and thrust backward into the solid body against him.

The footpad screamed, loosed him, fell away, crumpled to the street. Gasping and trembling, the intended victim staggered back to lean heavily against the nearest building. The body of his flute, still in the case, swung loosely from his left wrist, but he kept his right fingers tight round the headpiece, and his face turned in the direction of his assailant's fall.

But the villain lay groaning, almost motionless. By the time the young musician regained his breath and some of his steadiness, his erstwhile attacker had begun trying to pull himself forward through the dirt, and that was all. The musician stepped closer and prodded him with one foot. The criminal whimpered and rolled like dead weight.

I ought to finish him at once, thought Tony Beverton. But he did not. He felt sickened as well as proud. Standing well back, he found his pocket handkerchief, wiped the blade, reinserted it into the body of his instrument, and gave the headjoint-handle a single turn. The injured man inched forward perhaps half a foot during this time. I must surely have hit his vitals, Tony thought, feeling the back of his own coat and breeches cold with the man's blood. He'll die soon enough without my needing to stick him a second time. Nor am I under any moral obligation to pity a blackguard who would have had my life along with my purse.

Skirting the footpad, Tony continued on his way, across Lincoln's Inn Fields by starlight. Once safe in his room in one of the venerable old buildings, he locked his door, lit all five half burned stubs in the branches of the dented silver candlestick with the Beverton family arms, shed his blood-stiffening garments and put on his dressing gown, poured a generous draught of brandy and let himself fall into the old, fraying satin armchair.

So he had proved his manhood! What else could he have hoped for, lingering at the tavern more than two hours after the performance, to talk music and consume spirits, then scorning coach or chair? True, the walk was short, but various stinking and vice-ridden sections of the town were not so far removed from this area. The Cock and Bull itself, despite providing an upper room for the Gentlemen's Concert and Operatic Society, was not much better than a common stew.

He might have used it as an excuse that because he drank nothing stronger than coffee before a rehearsal or performance, therefore he must prove his stomach afterwards. But in reality he had long been looking for such an attack upon his person as had come at last. Well, he mused in grim satisfaction, flexing his fingers in the candlelight, wine and usquebaugh may dull my tone and slow my hands in the production of music, but they do not impede my technique in this other game!

He sighed and kindled a small fire in his grate against the chill that clung to his rooms although it was almost May. When he could postpone the necessary task no longer, he withdrew his flute from her case. She was still a beautiful instrument. She had taken no injury in the scuffle. Her polished boxwood gleamed richly in the firelight and her four keys were unbent and responsive as ever to his touch. It was perhaps incongruous to think of a long, pointed instrument as feminine, but he loved her like a sister or sweetheart nevertheless. He called her Cynthia. He unscrewed her headpiece again and slowly drew out the blade.

He had wiped it well, there in the unlit street. Only a few thin streaks of crimson here and there still stained the almost two feet of double-edged Toledo steel. He rubbed it completely clean with a fresh rag and applied a new coat of the light oil he always used to help protect it from the rust-threatening moisture of his breath. He swabbed the inside of the main joint with equal care, lest some trace of blood might have been left in the bore. Nor did he omit to clean the leather case with rag and rod.

He had had Cynthia, and her case as well, made to his instructions two years ago on his return with George from the Grand Tour, his head afire with thoughts of dark, stiletto-wielding Italians. She had cost him more than half a year's worth of gaming funds. Applying to his miserly elder brother would have been more troublesome than useful and, outraged by the rates of the professional shylocks, Tony Beverton had chosen abstinence from the gaming tables, meanwhile perfecting his musicianship and joining more than one society of musical amateurs to occupy his time. Before Cynthia was paid for, he had come to prefer music to gambling.

He did not feel the satisfaction he could have hoped to feel in her baptism of blood tonight. But he still loved Cynthia, though he burned the handkerchief he had used to wipe her clean.

He drank brandy and filled half a memorandum book with notes for his opera, in an orgy of work that enabled him to fall into bed at last, an hour before dawn, and drop to sleep more preoccupied with where to find a competent librettist for *Balin and Balan* than with his own evening's adventure.

He dreamed of himself and George as the two knightly brothers. George, parsimonious as ever despite his early inheritance of the title and fortune of Wyndmont, had refused the expense of plate armor and was plastering his body with sheets of manuscript music instead. George had arranged the tragic battle as another of his practical jokes; Tony knew perfectly well whom he was about to fight, but for the sake of his own opera he could not refuse the challenge. He himself wore no armor except on his left leg—for the rest, he was naked but for a helmet which seemed to hamper his vision. George had no helmet except a sort of large eggshell which made him appear bald. He was grinning widely because he knew his younger brother was not allowed to recognize him. When they advanced on each other, George dropped something small and hot down Tony's greave, and a second later something exploded inside the leg armor. There was a great gap between two sheets of George's chest armor (which now seemed to be made of oystershells) and Tony struck upwards, in his pain, and drove his blade into George's stomach...

He woke to early daylight and distant sounds of excitement. For a few moments he lay gradually sorting out his dream from George's actual boyhood prank of an undermined stone pillar in the artificial temple ruins of Wyndmont Castle gardens—the trick that had given Tony, at eight years old, the limp he would have for the rest of his life. It would have been easier to forgive Geroge the impishness of his tenth year if he had outgrown it by his twenty-sixth.

The shouts coming up from outside grew louder. They were real, and sounded abnormal. Tony rose, went to the window, opened it, and leaned out. He took some seconds to locate the principal source of commotion, a small crowd beginning to gather in the Fields, almost out of his line of vision. He hailed a bent, rheumatic old fellow who was hobbling away from the crowd as if to fetch help. "Hey! Jerry! What's happened?"

The old man stopped and squinted up at the figure in the upper-story window. "'Is Lordship of Wynd-

mont, it is, stabbed clean through the lights and..."
Jerry's voice died as he seemed to realize who was at the window, then rose again in a wail of apology. "Lor', your Lordship! I'm to Bow Street now—they'll take the bloody murderer, right enough!"

Jerry scurried off, and Tony closed the window, breathing hard. Jerry Catnach would not be mistaken. The former chairman, now turned into a messenger and kind of paid fag for the Inns, had seen the Earl of Wyndmont often enough.

Tony's bloodstained clothes still lay on the floor where he had dropped them last night. He had had some idea of producing them this evening at the Cock and Bull as evidence of his killing a footpad. He had no time to build a fire and burn them now.

To stay would be either to hang by a silken rope or, if his story of supposed self-defense were accepted, to live as the new Earl of Wyndmont, the very title a constant reminder. By the time Jerry had completed his mission to Bow Street, Anthony Beverton was in a Bloomsbury post house waiting for the next mail coach, his hat pulled down over his gray eyes and his portmanteau holding bloodstained garments for disposal at the first fair opportunity. His only other baggage was his flute in her leather case.

Chapter 1

The Country Miss and the Gentleman Farmer

"I really cannot walk another step!" said Miss Sally Merryn of Bolventor House, sitting down on the top step of the stile just before the crossroads.

Miss Parsons sighed. "It is scarcely a fifteen-minute walk from St. Finn to the crossroads, though you've made it the work of half an hour, and it is ten minutes more from the crossroads to the house, if we walked at a reasonable pace. Are you unwell?"

"Oh, don't be stuffy this afternoon! Go on ahead, if you wish. I'll catch you up as soon as I've rested."

The governess stood for a moment, swinging her reticule by the strings and studying her young charge. "You know very well," said Miss Parsons, "that if Mr. Jellicoe had brought his wagon today, we would have solicited him to drive us home. But when he had brought only his tim-whiskey...and, moreover, you have no idea how long he may sit at the Bal Maiden with his acquaintance."

"At least it's quite sure that whenever he does come out, he will still be steady enough to drive!" Sally tossed her head. Her bonnet, looser than she had thought, fell off and hung by its ribbons round her neck. She fetched her comb out of her reticule and began drawing it through her golden ringlets preparatory to settling the bonnet back in place. "Besides, why should you think my whole aim is to wait here for Uncle Robin?"

Miss Parsons smiled. "Oh, Sally, Sally, Sally! Do you think me such an old fogey already? Why, you're as transparent as glass, my dear! But you don't really love him, you know," she went on in a more serious tone. "You've not met nearly enough gentlemen to know your own heart, and you're still too young—"

"If we lived in Town, I should insist upon being brought out this Season!"

"Are you so very eager to leave the schoolroom, my dear? But I think your grandparents would have waited a year or two yet."

"Oh. Grandpapa." Sally shrugged. "If you're going to hide behind Grandpapa and Grandmama again, this conversation will be quite impossible. They think I've all the time in the world—they've so many years themselves, two or three more mean nothing at all to them. And besides, if I don't hurry and provide for myself, I shall make the acquaintance of this new gentleman you talk about when Grandpapa introduces him to me as my intended!"

"I believe if you'll examine what you have just said, you'll find a *non sequitur*. If your good grandparents are so unobservant of the passage of time, they are not likely to precipitate you into an ill-considered engagement."

Sally shrugged again. Her bonnet, its ribbons coming completely untied, started to slip down her back. She caught it just in time to prevent its falling into the fields behind her.

"There, you almost lost your lovely new headpiece in the latest London mode to a sheep who would have thought it merely another bit of straw," Miss Parsons remarked, more as if she were making a joke than a moral. "But to return to our subject. I believe I can safely say, after all these years with your family, that under no circumstances would your grandparents engage you to a gentleman you found objectionable."

"Well, I know Grandpapa could not possibly object to Mr. Jellicoe. He may have been a mere foundling from the Plymouth orphanage ten years ago, but he has certainly brought himself to our own level today—Grandpapa says as much himself. And I'm sure he's quite as handsome as—as that tall, strange young gentleman who came in on the Truro stage this afternoon—the one with the limp, you know, and I had the best of chances to compare them, since they went into the Bal Maiden together."

"By your own showing, the tall, strange young gentleman is quite as handsome as Mr. Jellicoe," replied Miss Parsons. "Though I must confess I did not notice that he limped. You must have observed him far more closely than I, child."

Sally felt a slight blush. "Only because I thought he might have a flute in his long case."

"Ah! And so that's the reason you want to wait here for Mr. Jellicoe, is it? To be after him again to teach you the flute?" Smiling a little, Miss Parsons shook her head and lifted her hands in mock exasperation. "Very well, then. I ought not... but I suppose you'll be safe enough here, so close to home. Especially with Sir Despard still away. But do remember this, Sally," she added in the quiet voice she used for what she considered Important Admonitions, "you cannot know yet whether you may be truly in love or not, and until you can be perfectly sure of your heart, you must be very careful how you try your wings. I would not like to see you turn into a cruel coquette. Particularly not with Mr. Jellicoe. Don't risk spoiling your old friendship, child."

The younger woman sighed. "Well, I won't, if you tell me you want him for yourself. _Do_ you want him for yourself, Miss Parsons?"

"I?" The governess laughed. "Why, I'm seven years his senior, and used to draw up lists of authors for him! And I made up my mind when I was little older than you are now that I should prefer to spend my life educating other people's children, with the opportunity of giving in my notice should they prove too naughty, rather than raising babies of my own."

Sally laughed. "Then it's a wonder you've stayed to see me quite grown, is it not? But do go now, my dear, or he'll be on us before you're around the turn, and then he'll insist on seeing us both home! And since his tim-whiskey only seats two, you know he'll walk and have you drive and me ride."

"Horrors! How should I ever manage old Rosinante? Well, don't wait until sunset, dear." Miss Parsons laughed, blew her charge a kiss, and proceeded down the road.

Sally watched her walk away, aware that she would stop just out of sight beyond the bend and wait there until her charge either chose to rejoin her or was safe in Uncle Robin's little carriage. Miss Parsons always wore lead in the heels of her shoes, even on a peaceful spring day like this when attack by anyone was far from likely along the quiet road.

Dear Miss Parsons! Sally's governess since the girl's seventh year, she seemed very like a mother. If Miss Parsons is seven years older than Mr. Jellicoe, Sally mused, then she must be thirty-three, and that is old enough to have really been my mother, though she would have had to be sixteen— a year younger than I am now—when I was born. I wonder if I truly did give her those half-dozen silver hairs, as she is so fond of saying? No, she must have had them by now in any event, though it is a shame, she's still so pretty otherwise. Of course, I'm very glad to have blue eyes and gold hair myself, rather than brown of both; but hers are such a lovely shade of brown, and the hair so near a match to the eyes! And I wish my eyes were set as wide as hers, under such dark brows, and I wish my skin was so clear, and not inclined to freckle...Well, but my nose turns up at just the right angle, and my cheeks dimple beautifully. And Grandpapa says I have lovely, bow-shaped lips. That all makes up for a good deal.

Sally watched Miss Parsons turn at the crossroads and wave her handkerchief before disappearing behind the high roadside hedge. Then the girl twisted round and looked at the sheep in the field. Several of them were finding nothing better to do than stare at her. She stared back, thinking it might be almost as easy to make her wishes clear to them as to Mr. Jellicoe of Oakapple Farm.

Edith Parsons leaned against the hedge, sighed, and settled herself for a wait of indeterminate length. She began to say Donne's "The Ecstasy" over in her mind, shifting her balance from one foot to the other at the end of every quatrain.

> To our bodies turn we then, that so
> Weak men on love revealed may look;
> Love's mysteries in souls do grow,
> But yet the body is his book.

It was one poem she had never taught Sally. The girl had amorous fancies enough in her head without being encouraged in them. But at her own time of life Edith Parsons felt sufficiently staid to indulge at odd moments in reveries of what might have been, had she not taken the warning of Paul and Violet perhaps too much to heart.

Her brother Paul, a dozen years her senior, had gone to Manchester in his late teens to make his fortune. Instead, he had married within a twelve-month, and within eight years he and his wife had produced five living heirs and precious little to divide amongst them. Edith had lived with the family for a time in order to go to school in town at a minimum of expense. Although as an aunt she had thereafter sent the children as much of her earnings as Paul's pride would permit them to accept, she had taken a post in the south country, as far as possible from Manchester, precisely to escape the duty of frequent visits to that noisy, malodorous, and—yes, though she was a dear relation who thought it—squalid household, seeing her brother and his wife both growing old before their time.

Young ladies like Sally could afford to plot their little flirtations. The Merryns of Bolventor House were a wealthy family, at least in their part of the world, and capable of preventing too gross a mismatch. But as for Edith Parsons, she had been both wise in her choice and fortunate in her position, and she knew very well that, despite any late stirrings to the contrary, her most prudent daydream was to move smoothly from the role of Miss Sally Merryn's governess and companion to the role of governess to Mrs. Sally's children.

Yet it did no harm to muse a little. That tall stranger whom they had seen descend from the stage this afternoon, as they watched from the windows of Goody Pendeen's small, clean pastry shop.... Had he really limped? If she had been too rapt in studying his face and shoulders to notice a limp, then how fortunate that he was visibly too young for Miss Edith Parsons!

It was growing coolish in the shadows, and Edith had made up her mind to go back in five minutes and end Sally's vigil perforce, when at last she heard slow hoofbeats and wheels on the road. She stood away from the hedge and listened until she heard the driver stop his vehicle and exchange greetings with her charge. As soon as the governess recognized Robin Jellicoe's voice (she still found it hard to think of him as "Mr.," after those years of helping guide him in the study of good authors) she began her walk alone to Bolventor House. In another fifty yards she would turn into the footpath through Mr. Treherne's spinney, thus avoiding the chance that the whiskey would overtake her on the road. She misdoubted that Sally could persuade her adoptive uncle this time, either, but she prudently began to think over what arguments she might use with Mr. and Mrs. Merryn, in case.

"Why, Sally!" he said, with the slight tug at the reins that brought his gentle old mare from a walk to a stop.

"Good afternoon, Mr. Jellicoe." She attempted a

coy smile with her bow-shaped lips, accompanied by a fluttering of her eyelashes.

To her frustration, he turned pink at once and shifted his gaze from her to the hedge. "That is to say—I thought you'd have been home an hour ago...and Miss Parsons."

"Oh, Uncle Robin! I wore new shoes today, and they've rubbed such sores on my feet! So Miss Parsons went on ahead to bring back the gig for me."

"Oh, I see." Fixing the reins, he jumped down from the whiskey and walked over to the stile, his nervousness dissipating at her resumption of the old, childhood mock-relationship. "Have we any chance of saving her the drive?"

"Very little, unless she stops for a dish of tea before coming back."

"I greatly doubt Miss Parsons would not leave you any longer unattended than strictly necessary."

"But I'm not unattended any longer, am I?" Sally made room for him.

But he did not seem quite sufficiently recovered yet from the fluttering eyelashes to sit beside her on the narrow stile. "Well, even if we meet her coming back, we'll have saved some few minutes in getting you home."

"But if we meet the gig where the road is narrow, and that's most of the way," Sally pointed out, "we may have the most dreadful time turning the carriages around again."

"That danger must be balanced against the probable impossibility of persuading Rosinante to start again if she stands nibbling the hedge much longer."

Sally giggled. "Poor old Rosinante! Maybe *her* shoes pinch, too. I really don't see how I can walk another step just yet, Uncle Robin. Not even to the whiskey."

"Come, make the effort!" He held out his hand to her.

"I had meant to take off my shoes and walk over

to the gig in my stockings, when Miss Parsons came..."

"Shall I pledge my word not to glance down at your...er...hem?"

Sally judged she had now dallied long enough to give Miss Parsons time to reach the footpath through the spinney, so that they would not risk overtaking her. "I should much rather you carried me, Uncle Robin. As you used to in the old days, you know."

He began to reach out both arms, hesitated, and drew back. "I...er...fear you've grown just a trifle too big to ride pickaback. At least, you'd want a man with broader shoulders. Not that you've grown too...too...But on the other hand—"

"Oh, I didn't mean *quite* as in the old days, of course." She held out one leg a little, pointing her dainty toe. "But surely there's nothing improper if a gentleman carries a lady in his arms for only a few steps, is there? I'm not so very much heavier than I used to be. And my poor feet are so very, very sore!"

He approached bravely, put one arm about her shoulders and the other beneath her knees. Flinging her right arm around his neck, she wiggled free of the stile, laughed, and looked into his brown eyes. He smiled back, but in such a carefully avuncular way that she decided against snuggling close or planting a kiss on his cheek. The transfer from stile to carriage was accomplished with as much propriety as if there had been anyone else besides the uninterested Rosinante to witness it.

"I will still guarantee not to look down," said Uncle Robin, remounting to the driver's place, "if you care to remove those uncomfortable shoes."

"Oh, they only pain me when I try to stand or walk," she said, and immediately regretted losing what might have been a chance to display her ankles. "Did you have good success in the shops, Uncle Robin?" she went on as he shook the reins and chucked to the mare.

"In the shops, not particularly." He shrugged, at

which Rosinante turned her head as if hoping for a countermand to his previous signal. For a few moments, all conversation died save that needed to cajole the old mare into resuming her walk. When they were safely under way, he went on, "Only a copy of the new edition of Mr. Rogers's 'Pleasures of Memory,' and one of 'The Hibernian Muse.' The latter has some melodies that look promising. Still... Well, well, perhaps next winter I'll make an excursion to Plymouth and see what the music-sellers there may have to offer. And your morning?"

"Oh," she laughed, "Mr. Poet Pye's newest volume. Miss Parsons is carrying that, you see. It was really her purchase more than mine. And I found some lovely lace for my new ball gown, and ordered a new bonnet from Mrs. Simmons, that ought to be perfectly charming for this summer. In the very latest London mode, she promised me.... I wish I might go with you to Plymouth, when you go."

"I don't suppose that Plymouth receives the London fashions that much sooner than Bolventor House. Although one cannot deny the Plymouth drapers and haberdashers offer a far greater selection then Messrs. Trevannion." (Trevannion & Son were St. Finn's sole dealers in textiles.) "But your grandparents and Miss Parsons are the ones you must cajole into taking you on that expedition, Sally. Not I."

"Neither Grandpapa nor Miss Parsons could guide me through the music-sellers' stocks."

He shook his head. "You do Miss Parsons a wrong there. She has superb taste—"

"In music for the pianoforte! Oh, *don't* pretend you've misunderstood me again! I will not learn to play the pianoforte. I find it a tedious, boring, jangly, bulky instrument, with no grace nor wit at all, and *everybody* is expected to learn it."

He drove in silence for a moment, as if choosing which of the old arguments to begin with this time. "It hardly seems promising for the development of a love for music in the abstract, to harbor so strong a prejudice towards one instrument in particular. Each has its place—"

"Oh, stuff! Would *you* exchange your flute for any three pianofortes, Uncle Robin?"

He smiled. "Very probably, provided that with the three pianofortes came the option of selling them off again and thus turning a tidy profit. But for one pianoforte and the requirement of learning to play it—no, there you have me. Do you also find the harp a jangly, graceless instrument?"

She made a face. "And every young lady who escapes the pianoforte plays the harp. Besides, when you play the pianoforte or the harp, everyone expects you to sing, too. And you know I have no voice."

"You have a very pretty voice."

"I have not."

"Well. Not, I confess, for singing. At least, it did not use to be, but since you haven't favored me with a song for years..."

"And with very good reason! But if I were to play the flute, you see, no one could expect me to sing to my own accompaniment. And don't tell me I will spoil my face, because I can see very well that you have not spoiled yours, and you don't puff out your cheeks when you play, no matter what Grandmama *will* think in despite of the evidence of her own eyes. And don't tell me what Plato says about flute-playing destroying a female's virtue, because if Grandpapa strictly believed it himself, he ought not even allow me to listen when you play. And young ladies played the flute in Plato's and Socrates' own time, did they not?"

"The young ladies were not..." He hesitated, blushing again. "Those young ladies may have been the reason Socrates banished the flute from his Republic."

"But he allowed the shepherds their pipes in the country, and one cannot be much more in the country than we are here!"

Mr. Jellicoe sighed. "And in his dialogue with Meno, Plato further refers to the folly of trying to learn how to play the flute from one who is no professed teacher."

"Oh, this is too bad! You're worse than Grandpapa and Grandmama. Next you will be telling me it is written somewhere in Sacred Scripture that flutes are not for gentlewomen to play upon! And yet Miss Parsons herself had two schoolfellows in Manchester who did play it. They learned it from their brother. —Uncle Robin," she added cajolingly.

"Even if I were qualified—and we cannot be sure of that—I could hardly offer you furtive instruction behind your grandparents' backs."

"Oh, Miss Parsons has promised to make it all right with Grandpapa and Grandmama. And then, if you will only join your persuasions to hers—"

"Not I!" He shook his head. "Privileged old acquaintance or no, I should be accused of self-interest in trying to bring your good grandparents around to such a scheme. Now if you could reconcile yourself to the pianoforte, you need look no further than Miss Parsons for a first-rate teacher."

"And if you would teach me the flute, I need look no further than Miss Parsons for a first-rate accompanist."

"Well, if she can persuade Mr. Merryn," he offered, "and if you will prove your determination to learn music by practicing a little every day on your Grandmama's pianoforte..."

"Uncle Robin! You are—you are a regular rackmaster! But I'll guarantee to practice every day if you will, too," she bargained.

"Unfair, child! You're a young lady of leisure, and I a farmer."

"And therefore, if you can play so beautifully on the flute, that proves it can be done without practicing every day."

"No, I don't do so badly, for a dilettante. Though there is always room for improvement," he added

21

with unconvincing modesty. "But then, you've never heard any other flutist since old Jem Tremiggan passed on, and that was...six years ago? Seven?"

"Ah, but I may hear another one soon, may I not? That very handsome gentleman from the Truro coach, the one with the limp and the long leather case? That *was* a flute, was it not?"

"Ah, spying, were you? Goody Pendeen's window again?" Mr. Jellicoe shook the reins and snapped the whip once or twice in the air high above Rosinante's head, as if to make her trot. She twitched her ears, sighed, and continued her walk. He then whistled a few bars of "The Red Herring's Head" as he had used to do when Sally plagued him with childish questions and he meant to tease her in return. "You'd be well served if I told you it was an oboe or clarionet, even a dull and unmusical piece of surveying equipment," he said at last. "But, yes, it was a flute."

"Ah-ha! And now you are no longer the sole flutist between Pennyquick and St. Ives! Are you jealous? Will you murder him now, and throw his body into the bay?"

"Don't say such things, Sally! Not even in fun."

"They say it's the sort of thing Sir Despard might do, if he were jealous of someone. Or his uncle the old baronet before him."

"But not the sort of thing that folk like you and I would ever do. Moreover, I am not jealous of your very handsome gentleman with the limp. On the contrary, it will be rather a relief not to carry the entire burden of the flute part anymore."

"Oh. I had thought you must be jealous, or you might have had a second flutist any time these last three years, merely for the teaching, you see. What is his name?"

"Mr. Armstrong. He may not grace our country very long, however. He has come in search of a bucolic retreat wherein to complete a piece of work he's been commissioned."

"Oh. And when it's finished, back he must dash

with it and leave you to struggle on alone with the flute part again, I suppose. You'll introduce me to him, of course."

"Perhaps. When I'm well enough acquainted with him to be sure his character is suitable."

She slapped his shoulder playfully with one small, gloved hand. "You *are* jealous! You won't teach me yourself, and you won't allow me to learn from anyone else, now I may have the chance."

"He's come to write music. He may not wish to spend his time teaching a very headstrong little Niece Sally. But...very well, if Miss Parsons can obtain your grandparents' permission, I'll see what I can do."

Sally threw her arms around him not quite as a true niece would have done, forgetting the fluster into which this would throw him. Rosinante took advantage of the moment to stop and nibble at the hedge until her master had recovered himself sufficiently to coax, urge, and cajole her on.

Driving back alone after delivering Sally to Bolventor House and stopping long enough for a cup of tea and a slab of Mrs. Merryn's famous saffron cake, Robin Jellicoe tried to imagine Sally at the polished pianoforte in her grandparents' drawing room. Except that he could not, even in his mind, make her sit there as quiet and dignified as Miss Parsons, she made a very pretty picture. Next he imagined her learning to play the flute from Mr. Armstrong. They were still in the bright winter parlor of Bolventor House, with Miss Parsons sitting at the pianoforte to help the lesson along with an occasional chord and an ever-watchful eye. But...

Robin sighed. He could laugh and sport with Sally easily enough as long as they remained on the old footing, established when she had been a child of six or seven and he a boy of fifteen. But let her show the least awareness of her budding young womanhood, let her offer the least hint of flirtatiousness, even were it no more than to Mister him formally, and he became a quavering coward before her charms. And he feared they would not be able to maintain the old relationship much longer. It was a rather suspicious circumstance that Miss Parsons had apparently reached Bolventor only a little before his own carriage, and that she had looked startled on seeing her charge in his arms, as if she had forgot both Sally's painful shoes and the need to go back for her with the gig.

Well, Armstrong seemed a decent fellow, and Sally would hardly be allowed in any case to take lessons from him unchaperoned. Besides, where "Uncle" Robin would have been expected to give "Niece" Sally her lessons gratis, Armstrong would naturally receive payment, and the young farmer suspected that a man traveling with no other baggage than his flute and one half empty portmanteau would not find the money unwelcome.

In fact, Robin thought without enthusiasm (for he knew the value of a shilling), possibly he should have been more insistent on paying Armstrong in coin for the music he had commissioned in the taproom of the Bal Maiden a few hours ago. But the composer himself seemed more than willing to take payment in kind: an opera libretto for a flute concerto. If the libretto proved unsatisfactory, then would be the time to speak of monetary reimbursement for the concerto, but to do so meanwhile would smack of rudeness. Come to that, Robin had as yet no evidence that the concerto would prove satisfactory. And he was confident in his own powers of poesy. The libretto would be a masterpiece, well worth two or three compositions for the flute. He occupied his thoughts for the rest of his homeward drive with what he could remember from his own reading and what Armstrong had sketched out to him of the history of *Balin and Balan*.

Chapter 2

The Noble Widow

Two people sat over their port wine in the dining room of the late Lord Wyndmont's town house.

Mr. Artaxerxes Dromgoole did not deserve his name. Of middle height and middle age, he had a cheerful, open countenance, with features that, though unremarkable, were regular and pleasant, and a body that inclined to rotundity. Had he been baptized Thomas, John, or Richard, those of his acquaintance who were married would have been christening their sons after him and soliciting him to stand godfather. But as soon as most folk learned his name, they suddenly discovered sinister aspects in his appearance, and he had not only reconciled himself to this fact through long practice, but had taught himself how to take professional advantage of it. He rarely assumed an incognito.

His hostess was Lady Isabella Wyndmont, widow of the late earl. The dowager countess was a tall, dark woman in the classic mold, who had occasionally been mistaken for a Spaniard or Italian, and once been asked if she numbered the Virginian Princess Pocahontas among her ancestors. Although Lady Isabella despised her wedded surname and title, she would never have said otherwise than that she deserved them.

"You may smoke if you wish, Mr. Dromgoole," she told him now. "It's a vile habit, but I learned to endure it from my late lord."

"I don't smoke, my lady. But I am addicted to snuff. Unfortunately."

"Then I hope you will not mind if I smoke." She rose, went to the sideboard, and selected a small ivory pipe carved into the image of a bearded face. "You see, in order to endure the noxious fumes with which my husband used to fill every room wherein we were together, I was forced at last to take it up myself."

"Madam," said Dromgoole, "if you refrain from smoking, I'll refrain from bringing out my snuffbox."

She raised one fine black eyebrow.

"Because one is born male," he explained, "it don't necessarily follow that one is born with an appreciation for the fumes of smouldering tobacco. I have to suffer them in company with my fellow men, and I've always looked forward to the society of the fair sex because they like to banish those clouds from their presence."

"You drive a hard bargain, sir. It's true I mean to rid myself of the habit, but not this evening." She returned her pipe to the stand, came back to the table, and, having drained her glass of port, replenished it with brandy. "I could, of course, leave you for half an hour and enjoy my pipe alone in the drawing room, but I see no reason to delay my business with you any longer, for the mere sake of custom."

"Being your ladyship's only dinner guest, ma'am— pretty much to my surprise—I confess I'm puzzled why you've left your business this long."

"Oh. So you had thought I might give a full dinner party within a week of my late lord's interment, had you? And perhaps you had fancied yourself included among the guests on the strength of having once stopped Wyndmont from duelling in Hyde Park and so prolonging his life for another three-quarters of a year?"

Mr. Dromgoole inclined his head slightly. "I hadn't expected a full social celebration, no. But with all respect, ma'am, your lack of grief for the departed has been enough noised about town that I'd thought to make one of a small party of, say, six or eight."

"I trust you do not fear becoming involved in a scandal when it comes to be noised about the town that the widow who is anything but crippled with grief has entertained you alone?"

"As it touched myself, that kind of talk would gloss my reputation a bit in my usual circles, my lady."

"Oh?" she said. "I had thought it to your best advantage to be considered above corruption."

"Above certain kinds of corruption. For the rest, we're only men, like any others. But I doubt it wasn't for fleshing out a scandal you brought me to Wyndmont House this evening?"

She nodded. "I am beyond caring what gossips may say of me. But I am now able to begin again at last to care for what is done with my own body." Gazing steadily at what was visible of him above the tabletop, she nodded once more. "I have had a lover, Mr. Dromgoole. Does that shock you, that I confess so easily to the fact?"

"It surprises me, ma'am. You seem to have been extraordinary discreet until now. Though I don't keep completely up with the buzz of your circles."

"Except to know I do not grieve for my husband. But no doubt that's the buzz of all circles. It makes little difference. I have not seen my lover since my husband's death. I may wish him again someday, of course. Or another." She continued to gaze at her guest in the candlelight. "In six months' time, sir, I may undertake to enter upon a course of scandal with you in earnest. Or, again, in six months' time I may decide to turn papist and enter some cloister of nuns in France or Italy. But for the present, I must have at least half a year to my own devices."

"Feeling as you do towards the memory of his late lordship, I wonder you want my professional services, ma'am."

She took a long drink of brandy. "I think you may have an inaccurate understanding of my reason for wishing to engage your services."

27

"I'd assumed the obvious, ma'am. That you was unsatisfied with the apparent explanation of the affair and wanted me to track down Lord Wyndmont's real murderer."

She waved her hand and drank more brandy. "I would rather reward my late husband's killer for that deed than see him brought to what the uninformed call justice. No, Mr. Dromgoole, I wish you to locate the new Lord Wyndmont."

"Your husband's younger brother, you mean? Then may I take it—"

"I am not with child, if that was to have been your next question. Anthony remains his brother's heir."

Dromgoole absentmindedly drew out his small silver-plated snuffbox and opened it, but caught himself before taking a pinch, closed it and returned it to his pocket. "It might be best if you didn't advertise this last fact just yet. In the vulgar mind, the possibility that the late earl may have left a posthumous heir of his own body makes one argument against Mr. Anthony's being involved."

"God knows that Tony would have had sufficient cause against his elder brother without the bait of lands and title, had he been a young man whose thoughts ran to murder."

"Maybe, but the people at large don't know it. And with all due apologies, ma'am, supposing you're wrong. Supposing when I find the new Lord Wyndmont, I also find the old one's murderer?"

"You will not find them in the same person." Lady Wyndmont rose, fetched her pipe, filled and lit it. "You must forgive me, Mr. Dromgoole. Pray take your snuff." Sitting again, she blew several smoke rings, the first few ragged, the last few round and smooth. "Of that I am absolutely certain. Anthony did not kill George, no matter how his sudden disappearance may strike the vulgar imagination. No, we will leave my husband's murder charged to the footpad."

Dromgoole took a pinch of snuff and considered

his next question. "And can you give me anything to help me in the search, descriptive details and suchlike? Including the grounds for your faith in his innocence. If you can see your way to sharing them with me, of course."

Apparently she could not, for she dropped the matter of Mr. Anthony Beverton's innocence. "I met my brother-in-law only once, at my wedding. He was not the sort of young man who would cheerfully have made one of the late Lord Wyndmont's circle. I know Tony chiefly from George's tales of their boyhood and Grand Tour together; I am not sure I would recognize him at once by sight. I believe he shares the Beverton features—tall and dark, with some superficial resemblance to his brother. He has a limp, which he owes to an old prank of George's, but I do not remember if it is in his right leg or his left. He is fortunate to carry no further obvious scars."

"Fortunate for him, but not so much for me. If your ladyship would have difficulty knowing your brother-in-law by sight, I'd have been hard pressed to pick out your husband's face from a crowd. Beyond knowing that his late lordship was called uncommon handsome, the Beverton features mean very little to me, ma'am."

"Tony also plays the flute," said Lady Wyndmont. "He used to send us invitations from time to time to hear him play with one of his musical societies. George naturally refused either to go himself or to permit my going, since he saw I would have enjoyed it."

"So do a great many young gentlemen in our island play the flute, if they don't play some other instrument," observed Dromgoole. "Far from a distinguishing mark, it can be a good means of disguise. If he was to play virtuoso, or even in a concert quartet, the audience might mark his face, but if he's clever enough to disappear into some opera or ballroom orchestra, he'll go as good as invisible. You

29

don't recall the names of these musical societies of his?"

"I do not. All such names sound very much alike to me, and my husband burned each invitation within minutes of my glimpsing it. But as a Bow Street runner, I assume you have resources for finding out such things?"

Dromgoole smiled. "I may not be our best man, but that makes these little extra commissions all the more welcome. Lady Wyndmont, I will seek to justify your confidence in my ingenuity."

"I put all the more reliance in your ingenuity, Mr. Dromgoole, in that you may be sure, if you can show me no evidence of progress within three months, I will use your fee to hire another in your place."

"Not all my fee, I hope? If Mr. Beverton—I beg his pardon, the new Lord Wyndmont—has left the city, I'll need something on account for traveling expenses."

Lady Wyndmont smiled. "Very well. One-third now, to be yours whether you succeed or fail. The other two-thirds when you bring back the new Lord Wyndmont to claim his title and free me from responsibility for the Wyndmont estates. We will seal the bargain in my late husband's study within the half hour." She blew another series of smoke rings, drank more brandy, and leaned back in her chair. "Are you musically inclined yourself, Mr. Dromgoole?"

"No. Not especially."

"Inconvenient, since a good part of your time within the next few months is likely to be taken up with scrutinizing members of orchestras. As for me, I should greatly have enjoyed hearing Tony and his musical confreres." Another swallow of brandy. "Are you acquainted with the old song of Lady Isabelle and the Elfin Knight, Mr. Dromgoole?"

He shook his head. "It don't touch any familiar chord, ma'am."

She was not obviously mellow, but he began to

suspect she had drunk more that day, both before and since his arrival, than was consistent with absolute prudence. Leaning forward a little, she sang in a low, clear contralto:

"Lady Isabelle sits in her bower sewing,
Aye as the woodlands grow gay,
And she hears the horn of the Elfin Knight blowing,
On this the first morning in May.

"If I had yon horn that I hear a-blowing,
Aye as the woodlands grow gay,
And yon elfin earl to sleep in my bosom,
On this the first morning in May.

"The Elfin Knight charms Isabelle from her bower by means of his musical talent and the beauty of his person," Lady Wyndmont went on in a speaking voice. "He rides with her to a grove in the greenwood, and there he reveals that he is about to murder her." She sang again:

"O sit for awhile, lay your head on my knee,
Aye as the woodlands grow gay,
For I'd pleasure my elf-lord before that I die,
On this the first morning in May.

She stroked him so soft, in her lap he did creep,
Aye as the woodlands grow gay,
With her own little charms then she lulled him to sleep,
On this the first morning in May.

With his own sword-belt fast there she bound him,
Aye as the woodlands grow gay,
With his own dagger there then she slew him,
On this the first morning in May."

As Lady Wyndmont appeared to have finished her song, Dromgoole remarked, "I think I have heard something like it, but the false knight—I hadn't remembered he was of faery origin—brought the lady to a high cliff and promised to push her off into the sea. As I remember, she made him turn his back while she disrobed, and then she pushed him over instead. I'd thought at the time it was rather a nice point that a deceiver, robber, murderer and general scoundrel should still have enough delicacy to turn his back whilst his victim took off her gown."

"I believe they sing these tales differently in different parts of the island. I prefer my greenwoods version." Lady Wyndmont began to clean the half smoked tobacco from her pipe. "But the false knight was indeed elfin. How else could he have charmed the lady? And I find it of singular interest that my own Christian name should be Isabella."

"Of interest as concerning your late husband, or as concerning your lover?...I ask out of pure professional interest."

"Perhaps as concerning them both." Lady Wyndmont replenished her glass. "Or perhaps as concerning neither. Since neither my husband nor my lover was a musician, after all, the only possible application of the elfin horn would be as a reference to Tony's flute, and that makes nonsense of the analogy. Well, Mr. Dromgoole, shall we repair to his late lordship's study and conclude our agreement?"

Chapter 3

The First Music Lesson Begun

Mr. Anthony Armstrong sat in Mr. Robert Jellicoe's comfortable parlor, holding up his own flute on one knee and his host's on the other. Jellicoe's instrument, like Tony's, was of boxwood, with a light varnish that enhanced the natural color of the grain, but it had only the one key, the D sharp, near the foot. "I could wish," Tony remarked, "that you had a four-keyed flute also."

Jellicoe sighed. "I fear Miss Merryn may find it difficult enough to produce a good tone on the hard notes, even with the best of instruments."

"The need for superior power in the bellows has perhaps been exaggerated," said Tony. "Nor, I fancy, did the old Greeks recruit all their flute girls from the ranks of the Amazons. It's true that the few fair flutists I have heard in drawing room Society were dames of ample bosom, but I suspect that the power resident in even the daintiest female breast has been underestimated. I've heard small sopranos bring forth notes of remarkable resonance." He winked. "And among the less musical but more complaisant class of ladies I personally have experienced—"

"And I personally have vouched for your honor," said Jellicoe with a slight flush. "I trust you do not confuse Miss Merryn with the ladies of that class simply because of her choice of instrument."

"Not at all, not at all." Smiling a little at Jellicoe's almost womanish delicacy, Tony laid both flutes side by side across his lap. "But it may prove awkward for the tutor to play on one style of flute and the pupil on another."

"Lend the young lady your instrument, then."

Tony shook his head and passed a caressing hand over his flute. "I never allow any other lips to touch my Cynthia. A peculiarity of mine."

Jellicoe smiled and shrugged. "Come to that," he said indulgently, "I'm rather amazed that such a musician as yourself should still prefer an instrument cluttered with keys. Has it not been established beyond any reasonable doubt that the more keys, the worse the tone and intonation?"

"Here!" Tony tossed the single-keyed flute back to his host, who caught it neatly. "I challenge you on the spot, your instrument and your lips against Cynthia and my lips."

The roads and fields being wet from a recent rain, Sally and her governess had taken the gig from Bolventor House to Oakapple Farm that morning. Meeting old Gideon, Mr. Jellicoe's servant, below the garden, they had entrusted him with their equipage and Brown Bess the carriage horse, and were now climbing the gravel walk to the house.

"Oh, listen!" Sally exclaimed half under her breath, clasping her hands as the twin threads of music started to issue from the house. "They're playing a duet!"

Miss Parsons listened a moment and wrinkled her nose very slightly. "An impromptu invention, I'd say, both of them improvising, and neither one knowing what the other is about to do next. And they don't sound at all in tune."

"They sound glorious to me. Which do you think is Uncle Robin?"

The governess laughed. "If they were singing, I might be able to tell you."

"If they were singing, I shouldn't need to ask. Well, I thought you might know, since you've so fine an ear that you can hear the least little fault in their tuning."

"Don't pout, Sally," said Miss Parsons with a touch of impatience. "I am helping you to deceive and disobey your grandfather and Mr. Jellicoe as well. You know Uncle Robin would never have agreed to this if he knew Mr. Merryn had withheld his consent. Heaven knows how long we can continue hoodwinking them both; but for the present, now you have your wish, pray do not show your appreciation for my pains by beginning your first lesson with a pout."

"Then do not *you* begin by insulting their beautiful music!" But in the next moment Sally flung her arms round her governess in a burst of contrition. "Oh, dear, dear Miss Parsons, you know how thankful and grateful I am! Say you forgive me?"

Miss Parsons forced another laugh and kissed Sally's cheek. "Well, no doubt it's my fault for indulging you too much in everything and bringing you up a spoiled, forward, self-willed child—"

"Spoiled!" Sally protested. "Child!"

"But do at least try to pretend you are a lady before Mr. Armstrong, and we'll see what comes of it. There, I believe they've stopped. Let's hurry and reach the house before they start again."

Tony was the first to desist, though only by a few notes. "You've heard Cherubini's *bon mot* apropos of flutes and flutists?" he cried, laughing.

"Cherubini, the composer of *Armida* and *La Prisonnière*? No, I don't believe I have heard it."

"Why, it seems that a fellow musician, trying to gather a decent orchestra, sighs to Cherubini, 'What can be worse than only a single flute?' To which Cherubini replies, 'Two flutes!'"

Jellicoe chuckled. "He must have had in mind two dissimilar flutes improvising at cross-purpose." Beginning to search through the short pile of music on the table before him, he went on, "I think I have a duet by Quantz or Boccherini."

"Do you really want a second trial? Why not bring out your favorite solo, and we'll each have a go at it in turn. Cynthia and I will still produce the better tone."

"Oh, you thought your tone was the better just now?" Crestfallen for a moment, Jellicoe soon recovered. "Of course, any man who devotes himself to a single interest will naturally become more proficient at it than one with a number of demands on his time. Besides, it can hardly be called a fair contest until we try exchanging instruments."

"My dear fellow, I've already surpassed you on the style of flute you claim to be inferior. What could you hope to gain by an exchange?"

"The style may be inferior in general, and yet one individual specimen superior, through craftsmanship or perfection of materials. That unusual length of Cynthia's headjoint above the blowhole, for instance, may have something to do with the tone. Or you may simply have accustomed yourself to your instrument's peculiarities to a degree that allows you to rise above its defects." Jellicoe smiled and held out his flute to his guest. "If you can produce a better tone than I on a strange instrument, I'll own myself vanquished utterly. But at the same time, if you should produce a better tone on my instrument than on your own, the greater perfection of the single-keyed flute is proved."

Tony shook his head. "Whoever heard of gentlemen exchanging their pistols for a second shot after one had already wounded the other on the field of honor?"

Jellicoe withdrew his flute and sat back, regarding the other. "You're quite serious about it, then? You really are as jealous of that flute as—"

"As if she were a woman." Once again Tony ran his hand lightly over his instrument. "Why do you think I call her by a woman's name?"

"Have a care, or folk will suppose she's plated with gold inside and has diamonds concealed in that long screw." Jellicoe laughed and held out his flute again. "Here, have a go on mine, anyhow. You'll want to accustom yourself to it, if you propose to use it for teaching."

At this moment the expected knock came at the door. Since Jellicoe's was a strictly bachelor household, and his servant had waited outside in case the ladies should ride or drive, the host himself went to let them in, leaving Tony alone in the parlor.

The young man drew a deep breath and glanced anxiously into Cynthia's blowhole. So far, no one had ever noticed the thin, oiled blade inside; but as a rule he and his fellows had played in dimly-lighted chambers, with candles set up to illuminate primarily the music, and only incidentally the players and their instruments.

Perhaps he had been foolhardy to bring Cynthia with him, but it was true that he felt almost a lover's passion for her, even now. Perhaps especially now, when she shared his guilt. He might be wise to remove the blade and make an innocent turning-screw of cork and wood for the upper end of the flute, but that would be to eviscerate her, to remove the spark that made her seem more than a mere inanimate piece of craftsmanship. Moreover, the hidden weapon that might constitute his greatest danger also provided his only sense of protection. As other men felt secure with pistols tucked about their persons, so Anthony Beverton felt secure with the dagger concealed in his flute.

Besides, even in the comparatively bright light of Jellicoe's somewhat pretentious country parlor, the blade seemed almost invisible, aligned parallel as it was with the blowhole and coated with the darkest oil Tony could procure. And musicians themselves rarely peered into an instrument's mouthpiece unless something sounded amiss.

His scrutiny of Cynthia had taken less time than

his host's progress to the front door. He laid her down beside him on the sofa, lifted Jellicoe's flute to his lips, and essayed a scale in A major. He had tried both single-keyed and multi-keyed instruments before choosing Cynthia's design, but had played only with the four keys since, so that regaining his touch on a single-keyed flute absorbed him and he hardly heard the interchange of greetings in the entrance.

He had completed two scales of increasing tempi and begun a third ascent when the ladies appeared in the parlor doorway. He lowered the flute at once and rose to meet them.

"Oh, don't stop!" cried the shorter and younger, clasping her gloved hands. "It sounds so unfinished—as if it will hover in the air forever, waiting for the rest of the notes. Do hurry and finish it, sir!"

He lifted the flute again and finished the scale, at a rather uneven tempo. He had expected a plain country child, hoydenish, flatchested, and freckled, accompanied by an aging and angular, or perhaps aging and fat, governess in black homespun. Instead, he saw a golden-haired young maiden in her first bloom, her high-waisted frock of pale blue muslin accenting a dainty but developing bosom and small but delightfully rounded hips, and a governess who was neither angular, fat, nor aging, and wore an ivory-colored shawl over a gown of cotton calico with a rich brown print that matched her long hair in its neat lace cap. Though they could hardly have been mistaken for creatures of the *ton,* they would not have disgraced one of his late mother's dinners at Wyndmont Castle.

The scale mounted and descended to completion, he lowered the flute once more and bowed.

"Ladies," said Jellicoe, who had followed them into the room, "may I present Mr. Armstrong."

For a moment Tony felt confusion at the surname, before remembering his own incognito. The ladies' appearance must have engrossed him indeed.

"Mr. Armstrong," his host was continuing, "may I present Miss Parsons and Miss Merryn."

Tony bowed again and stepped forward to take the small hand that Miss Merryn of the golden ringlets was holding out to him. He made a conscious effort to minimize his limp.

"Goodness, how very formal we've become, Uncle Robin!" said Miss Merryn, with a little laugh, shaking Tony's hand. "Cannot he be my Uncle Armstrong?"

"That, I think, might be a trifle premature on first meeting," said the governess. "Perhaps, by the time you've learned to play a scale as nearly perfect as the one we've just heard, we shall consider the adoption of uncles." Her words to her young charge were a little stern, but her smile, as she turned to the musician, was gracious. "You'll forgive us, Mr. Armstrong, if we refrain from burdening you with a niece and a pupil both in the same hour?"

"I should be honored to stand in whatever relationship you choose to the young lady." Miss Merryn's eyes were blue. Now he could see her complexion more closely, he did indeed discern a few freckles; but somehow they added to the sweetness of her face, rather than detracting from it.

"Yes," said Miss Parsons, "but as her uncle you might be in danger of spoiling her as shamelessly as Mr. Jellicoe has done in that role. No, Mr. Armstrong, if she is to learn anything from you, I really believe you must remain simple tutor and pupil."

He turned to shake Miss Parsons' hand in turn—a courtesy, he suddenly realized, that he had delayed unconscionably long. He noticed a few silver strands in her brown hair. So his preconception of an aging governess had been partially correct, like his preconception of a freckled country child. In both cases, the partial accuracy of his former notion served only to make the truth more charming.

He had supposed that the country child would accept whatever instruction he gave her and never guess it was less than expert. Now for the first time his total lack of experience as music-master worried him. "I do not like to sail under false colors," he said. "Mesdames, I have never taught before. Miss Merryn, if she accepts me, will be my first pupil."

"Oh, I don't suppose that signifies a bit," said Miss Merryn. "Miss Parsons had never taught anyone anything before she came to teach me, either."

"It signifies more than you might think, Sally." The governess took her seat on the sofa. "You were simply too young when I began to remember all the mistakes I made at first. But if Mr. Armstrong can play the flute as well as advertised, that's the chiefest thing. Better to learn from an inexperienced master who knows his subject than from an experienced one who has no idea of the matter in hand."

With a bow, Anthony put the single-keyed flute into Miss Sally Merryn's hands, took up Cynthia, and played the allegro from K.P.E. Bach's concerto in A major; he had most of it by heart, and where he had forgot the written notes, he practiced the old-fashioned art of improvisation so deftly that an uninitiated listener would not be able to tell the difference. As he ended, Jellicoe breathed an envious sigh and Miss Parsons nodded calmly, while Miss Merryn, whose opinion was the dearest to him, gazed at him enraptured.

"Oh, Mr. Armstrong!" cried Miss Merryn. "Oh, Mr. Armstrong, that was—that was the Music of the Spheres!"

"Yes," said Miss Parsons, "I think Mr. Armstrong may do. At least, it sounded well enough to me. But then, I can call myself a judge only of the harpsichord, the pianoforte, and the voice. Robin?"

"The execution was superior," Jellicoe concurred. "I had heard him play well, or I should not have recommended him. But I had not heard him play *this* well before."

"Well?" said Miss Merryn, as if the compliment were so inadequate as to be contemptible. "It was

Apollo's lyre! If Apollo had played a flute and not a lyre."

Jumping up from the armchair into which she had sunk while listening to the allegro, Miss Merryn put Jellicoe's flute to her own pretty lips and made an obvious attempt to echo what she had just heard. All that resulted was a thin, breathy sound like a weak wind in a sooty flue, and a tangled tapping of fingertips bouncing up and down frenetically, with no idea of how to work together.

The governess laughed. Flushing as she lowered the instrument, Miss Merryn shot a timid glance at Tony and another at Jellicoe.

"Never mind—" Jellicoe began, but at the same moment Tony smiled and said, "Nobly attempted, Miss Merryn! That same spirit will, when trained and disciplined, conquer the intricacies of Quantz, the Bachs, and Boccherini without hesitation. Frederick the Great himself could not have been more intrepid in his first attack upon his beloved flute."

"Oh, do you really think so?" Miss Merryn asked, returning his smile with a grateful radiance.

"I had been about to say," Jellicoe put in, "that I did no better on my own first attempt."

"The Emperor Frederick, Mr. Robert Jellicoe, and now Miss Sally Merryn!" said Miss Parsons. "Here we see how the great and the humble alike are all put upon a level, not only before the mysteries of the grave, but also before the mysteries of the flute. Well, Robin, will you come sit with me and help me chaperon the music lesson?"

"No, with your leave, I think I shall go and put the kettle on the fire for tea. Or would you prefer chocolate?" He directed the question to Miss Merryn and her music-master, who were still gazing at one another over their flutes.

"Oh, tea, by all means," said Tony. "I find that drinking chocolate while playing puts a sweetness in the breath that causes the pads of the keys to stick slightly."

"Another disadvantage to the many-keyed instrument." Jellicoe retired, leaving his fellow flutist morally alone before the awful moment of beginning to teach.

Chapter 4

The Music Lesson Concluded

Tony cleared his throat. "Well, Miss Merryn, if you will raise the instrument to your lips again, so..." He lifted his own flute once more. Like an awkward mirror image, she lifted hers.

"No...no...Not quite right," he said over his mouthpiece. "Let the end drop a little lower—no, not quite that low...I believe you are holding your fingers a little too stiffly. Do you think you can relax them somewhat? No—not that much, we must not let the instrument slide from our hands."

She looked up, flushing and blinking as if to hold back a tear. "I think I must have done better a moment ago, the first time I tried it?"

He flinched before the thought that tears were about to spill down upon her cheeks. "You're not nervous, Miss Merryn? You've no cause to be nervous...Perhaps your form was a trifle better that first time, but it was only because you were not nervous, you lacked self-consciousness. If we can regain that lack of self-consciousness...once you have the correct form, that is..."

"Perhaps if she were to take off her gloves and give her hands more freedom of movement," Miss Parsons suggested. "Yes, Sally, under the circumstances I think you may unglove without impropriety. And possibly you had best move a little closer, Mr. Armstrong. I fail to see how you can effectively demonstrate the correct form with half the length of the room between you. Go on! Music-masters, like dancing-masters, have some special license, do they not?"

Hardly knowing whether Miss Parsons' presence made the task easier or more difficult, he took a step forward with his good leg. Miss Merryn did not take a corresponding step, but she did draw off her fingerless net gloves and drop them to the armchair as she waited for him to close the distance. He continued towards her, limping as little as he could, and stopped at last within arm's reach.

"Are my fingers right?" She held the instrument up almost vertically to show him how her dainty fingertips were covering the holes.

"One moment, let me look...Yes, yes, you have them on exactly the right holes." Indeed, it would have been difficult for her to have them on the wrong ones, there being only six holes.

"But what am I to do with my left little finger? The right little finger, I suppose, is for the key, but..."

"On a single-key instrument, you must just let the left little finger rest. Or you may arch it up, if you prefer. Whatever seems to allow your other fingers more freedom and ease of movement." He longed to take the tiny digit and arch it tenderly between his own brown fingers, like a sculptor shaping a fine statue. "Someday I hope you'll have a keyed flute like mine, and then we'll have a use for the left little finger. But meanwhile it may be best for you to learn on the simpler instrument. If you cound turn it a little more; to let me see the placement of your thumbs?"

She obeyed. Balancing his own flute in the crook of his right elbow, he ventured to move her thumbs more exactly into place, not without a glance at Miss Parsons, who sat smiling and sharp-eyed on the sofa. Perhaps Anthony's fingers touched Miss Merryn's for a second or two longer than absolutely necessary, but not for long enough to inspire a reproof from the governess.

"Will my thumbs have something more to do, also, when I have a flute with keys, like yours?"

"The left thumb, yes." Having positioned her hands to his satisfaction, he held his flute and showed her how his thumb operated the B flat key on the underside of the instrument. "The right thumb has only to balance the flute, but that in itself is a very important task, you see, when the other fingers are raised to play a B or a C sharp."

"Oh," she said. "The fingers are raised to play a B or a..."

"I think I should wait to show her the various fingerings, Mr. Armstrong," said the governess, "until she has learned to produce a tone."

"Oh, Miss Parsons!" cried the younger woman. "Mr. Armstrong knows how to play the flute, and you do not!"

Miss Parsons raised her hands, palms outward. "I am silenced. Forgive me, Mr. Armstrong."

"Not at all, not at all. I am grateful for your suggestions, ma'am, being no experienced instructor myself. Miss Merryn, perhaps it would be best if you were to try blowing it again."

"But how shall I hold my fingers?"

"I think...hold down only the left forefinger and the right little finger—on the key, so—and that will give us the B. An easy note—comparatively—both to balance and to blow. Now?"

"B," she repeated. "B." She put the blowhole to her lips and blew. He could not help thinking that it would have been a delicious, soft, teasing breath if blown directly into a man's ear, but all it coaxed from the flute was a dull, toneless whisper.

"Can you draw back the corners of your mouth, Miss Merryn?" he suggested, trying to remember his own earliest lessons. "And cluck your tongue a little when you begin to blow, as if you were about to pronounce the letter T."

She stretched her pink lips into a tight grin and tried to pronounce a T into the hole. The resultant sound was a soprano voice saying "Tea," coupled with a soft explosion of air in the body of the flute. Miss Merryn looked up at her musicmaster, and a tear spilled down onto her rosy cheek at last.

"I do think I heard a sort of whistle that time," said Miss Parsons. "Though it was short-lived at best."

"Perhaps if you were to try for a while with the headjoint alone, Sally?" said Jellicoe, who had returned to stand in the doorway.

"Do you mean...to take it apart?" Miss Merryn held the flute up helplessly. "How?"

Tony laid his own flute on the nearest chair, took Jellicoe's from his pupil, and twisted the headjoint from the body with a few unforced turns. Putting the rest of the instrument on the chair beside Cynthia, he blew three or four tones on the disembodied mouthpiece to demonstrate, then wiped it with his clean though mended silk handkerchief and passed it over to Miss Merryn.

Using both hands to hold it to her lips, she commenced a series of soughings, sputterings, plosions, and half whistles, striving desperately to adopt his suggestions and merely going from one unflutelike sound to another. "Oh, I shall never find the trick of it!" she cried after a score of attempts.

"But you've scarce begun, Miss Merryn," Tony protested, aware it might be questionable comfort but finding nothing else to say. "With persistence—"

"Persistence! How am I to persist with everyone staring at me?"

"We are here in all sympathy, Sally," said Miss Parsons. "Here, I'll wager that if I try it with you, you'll have a tone before me. How odd!"

Tony turned and saw that the governess had taken Cynthia from the chair and was examining her curiously. "The joint seems to be *above* the mouth-hole on yours, Mr. Armstrong," she said. *"Is* it a joint at all, or merely decoration? Yes, it turns..."

"Miss Parsons!" In two quick steps—careless of his limp—he reached the sofa and half snatched the instrument from her hands.

"Mr. Armstrong!" she exclaimed.

"Forgive him," said Jellicoe, coming forward into the room. "He won't allow even me to touch his flute. A little eccentricity not uncommon among musicians. Both Mr. Killian of St. Finn and old Tremiggan of Pennyquick are almost equally jealous of their violin and oboe respectively."

"But what is the use of—" she began.

"Tuning, ma'am," Tony explained. "You see?" He gave the joint a slight turn and twisted it back tight again at once. "Mr. Jellicoe's instrument can be tuned by adjusting either the screw at the upper end or the joint below the blowhole, mine only at this joint. The design is quite satisfactory, but it's a delicate piece of craftsmanship—very delicate. That's the reason I don't like anyone to handle my flute but myself. As a matter of general principle, you understand. I...I do hope you'll forgive me, Miss Parsons, for my seeming rudeness just now."

The governess sighed. "I do not entirely understand your eccentricity, sir, but in view of the beautiful sounds you brought forth for our benefit earlier, I suppose I must accept it. Very well, henceforth I shall not make so bold as to touch your instrument with so much as a feather. Sally, perhaps if you were to be seated, you might come along a little better with Uncle Robin's flute."

Looking awed by the unexpected storm, Miss Merryn sat on one of the straight-backed chairs and resumed her efforts. By the end of another quarter-hour she had managed half a dozen sounds that were almost tones, and Jellicoe had brought in the tea tray.

"This was a very sad showing, I fear," Miss Merryn apologized, turning her teacup round and round in its saucer. "Is there any hope for me at all, Mr. Armstrong?"

"As much hope as for anyone in the land." He had his private fears, but he could not bring himself to damp her spirits. And it was still too early to say anything for sure either way. He had no idea of her ear for intonation or sense of rhythm, but her enjoyment of his playing augured well. (He would not permit himself to think she might have appreciated his impromptu concert as much for his person as for his musicianship; the incident of Miss Parsons handling Cynthia had reminded him of the folly of seeking an attachment of the heart.) "If you can practice every day..."

"But she can hardly do that, I fear," said Miss Parsons, "since she lacks a flute of her own."

Jellicoe tasted his tea, added another dab of milk, and glanced at Tony. "You're welcome to borrow my instrument, Sally," he said, "if you'll promise to return it on Thursdays."

Tony thought he saw the young lady and her governess exchange a puzzled and puzzling glance.

"We're greatly obliged," said the governess, "but if Sally robs you of your flute all the rest of the week, I fear you may pipe a rather poor tune yourself on Thursday evenings with the Penwith Musical Society."

"But here's what," said Miss Merryn, "I'll come here every day to practice! Perhaps Mr. Armstrong will give me a lesson every day?"

"I should be honored—" Tony was beginning, but Miss Parsons cut in:

"And when would Mr. Armstrong find the time to compose his music, or Uncle Robin to see to his farm?"

"I'm sure old Gideon can oversee the laborers very well," Miss Merryn replied with the suggestion of a pout. "And besides, dear Miss Parsons, you'd be here to watch us, even if Uncle Robin couldn't be. And even if Mr. Armstrong could not come up every day, at least I could sit in the parlor and practice. You'd trust us with your things, wouldn't you, Uncle Robin?"

"My parlor is at your disposal," said Jellicoe.

"But my time is not," said Miss Parsons. "Nor is her own, for that matter. And when do you propose to study any of your other lessons, Sally, or sew or do anything else at all, if we are to be spending all our mornings coming here? No, I'm afraid you must be content with twice a week."

Tony held back a sigh. Would *he* be content with twice a week? "I might come directly to you at Bolventor House," he suggested.

"And thereby more than triple your own distance to travel," said Jellicoe. "But if we were to have the lessons on Tuesdays and Fridays, Sally could take my flute home with her each Friday and return it to me the following Tuesday, giving each of us half a week with it."

Again Miss Merryn glanced at her governess.

Miss Parsons said, toying with her teaspoon, "Thank you for your offer, Mr. Armstrong. It is more than generous, but it would too often prove a complete waste of your time. Mrs. Merryn, Sally's grandmother, suffers unpredictable health. Many days she keeps to her bed with a wretched headache until dinnertime. I dare not play the pianoforte, and a flute sending its tones through the house would hardly conduce to her comfort. Especially if the flute were in the hands of such a beginner as Sally."

"I could go into the fields and practice," said Miss Merryn.

"You shall not risk borrowing Uncle Robin's flute," said Miss Parsons in a tone of final authority. "You'll have one of your own as soon as we can manage it, but meanwhile we will not have you frightening any sheep and cows."

"I'm very sorry to learn of Mrs. Merryn's poor health," said Jellicoe. "Have you consulted Mr. Killian yet?"

"Oh, it's a recurrence of an old indisposition she suffered some years ago," the governess replied. "Not dangerous, simply bothersome. And you know she has had no faith in any doctor or apothecary since Mr. Etheridge passed on, but she does still have the receipt for the powders he prescribed. If she gets no better within a few months, of course we'll insist on calling in Mr. Killian. Perhaps Sally could practice producing a tone by blowing across the mouth of a bottle?"

"A bottle?" said the new music-master.

"Yes. My brother taught me the trick when I was no more than five. We used to gather as many bottles as we could find, fill them with varying levels of water, and blow across the tops. I know the shape of a bottle is very different from that of a flute, but as nearly as I could observe today, the role of the human mouth is much the same in both operations."

"Of course, a bottle." When Tony's older brother had shown him the trick, it was only so that George could break the half filled bottle in Tony's hands by hurling a stone at it whilst Tony was engrossed in blowing. But Miss Merryn would have nothing of that sort to fear. "I'm sure you can find bottles aplenty, and at this stage, Miss Merryn, the chiefest thing is to develop your *embouchure*—your technique of blowing out a tone. When you have that, we can put it together with the fingerings and other points at our regular lessons."

How much more eagerly he would now anticipate the twice-weekly lessons he could guess by the heedless way in which he had offered to come to her at Bolventor House.

From the first it had seemed a very accommodating gesture that the gently-bred young lady should come to her music-master at the house of a mutual acquaintance rather than insist the music-master make the journey to her own home from the lodgings Jellicoe had helped him find in the little fishing hamlet of Pennyquick. Perhaps, too tender of his limp and too observant of his straitened circumstances, they had chosen this arrangement in order to spare him the necessity of hiring a horse; and, after a private struggle with his pride, he had decided to accept it for the sake of avoiding, as far as possible, acquaintance with the local gentry. He ought to be safe enough from recognition here in the far west, but...he would not have agreed to give Miss Merryn these lessons at all, had his purse been thicker.

Now Miss Parsons' story of Mrs. Merryn's delicate health struck him as an invention. Had not Jellicoe not expressed some surprise that the good old couple, after long opposing their granddaughter's desire, should have extended their permission at last? For a moment Tony wondered if they really had, or if the young lady and her governess were not making himself and Jellicoe parties to a deception. But he dismissed the thought as unworthy. Because he was hiding a secret, must he imagine that everybody else about him was doing so as well? Nor would he now have been willing to cut short his acquaintance with his fair pupil, neither for honor nor for prudence.

Chapter 5

Sir Despard Rudgwerye

Jerry Catnach, the rheumatic chairman turned errand boy who had been among the first to find Lord Wyndmont's corpse, swore he had paused on his way to Bow Street and shouted the news up to young Mr. Beverton. But Artaxerxes Dromgoole preferred a cautious approach to the unsubstantiated tale of a garrulous gossip like Jerry. The old fellow might have mistook some other head poking out of an upper-story window for Beverton's, or he might simply have added a dramatic embellishment to the morning's events, and come to believe it himself. Apart from Jerry Catnach, Dromgoole had found no one who could swear with unreserved certitude to having seen Beverton later than the evening before the murder was discovered, nor closer to the inns than the Cock and Bull Tavern, some streets away.

Dromgoole gained admittance to Beverton's rooms. Had it not been for Lord Wyndmont's murder, and those individuals who had come up to inform the younger brother of it, would Beverton's disappearance have been discovered yet? Dromgoole liked to think it would have been, for Beverton seemed to have been reasonably sociable; but would his acquaintance have been the sort to come round to his rooms and inquire about his long absence from their circles? As Dromgoole glanced round, comparing Beverton's apartment with his own modest but tidy boardinghouse accommodations, he could not help misdoubt that these were rooms in which a young man of gentle birth and personal pride would choose to entertain his friends. It was obvious that Lord Wyndmont's generosity had done little or nothing to help ease his younger brother's path through life.

There were brown stains on the threadbare carpet, but there were also black stains, blue stains, green stains, and yellow stains, the residue of years of overturned inkpots, drinking bouts, and makeshift culinary experiments. It was a secondhand carpet, and had obviously been worn by many pairs of feet. If the brown stains were blood, they might have been put there by a shaving accident or carelessness with inadequately-wrapped butcher's meat.

Unacquainted with Beverton's habits, the Bow Street man was unsure how much of the apartment's disarray was the usual untidiness of a young bachelor's lodgings and how much might be due to a hasty departure. Possessing no inventory of Beverton's belongings, he could not be sure how much luggage Beverton had taken; he thought it could not be a great deal, but it might have been none at all. A dented silver candlestick marked with the family crest remained as the one item of possible value, and this suggested that Beverton had left his rooms on ordinary business or pleasure, with no thought of peril and no plans of taking flight.

The one item Dromgoole could be sure was missing was Beverton's flute. But this the young fellow had had with him at the Cock and Bull. Its absence was therefore no evidence that he had come home at all on the fatal night. Dromgoole mused with a certain not quite professional melancholy that the younger brother's mutilated and decomposing corpse might yet be found in some dark alley or dragged from the river.

Dromgoole sought out and interviewed all those members of the Gentlemen's Concert and Operatic Society who had given their small concert that evening in the upper room of the Cock and Bull. No one recalled that Beverton had complained of any unusual trouble with creditors, nor mentioned any immediate designs of dropping from sight. On the contrary, he had looked forward with all his customary enthusiasm to the next rehearsal, and spread hints that he was planning to compose an opera. The members of the Gentlemen's Concert and Operatic Society could, at least, direct Dromgoole to other musical fraternities with whom his quarry was associated. Not only was there considerable overlap in the memberships of all these bodies, but certain members of the Confraternity of Musical Amateurs and the Sons of Handel directed him back in all goodwill to the Gentlemen's Concert and Operatic Society.

Dromgoole learned that Beverton's opera was to be based on some subject drawn from Britain's mythic history and that he had still at latest report been seeking a librettist. More to the point, Dromgoole learned that most of Beverton's acquaintances had been aware of the strained relations existing between him and his elder brother, to the degree that some of them preferred certain broadside ballad versions of the murder to the more probable explanation accepted by Bow Street. Dromgoole nodded, privately musing that some words of Beverton's, now recounted in retrospect as an ominous threat against Lord Wyndmont, would have been remembered as a mere tipsy jest had it not been for the manner of Wyndmont's subsequent death.

One young solicitor-violinist said that Beverton used to speak fondly of the Lakes, another amateur musician remarked that he had always talked of Italy in the most enthusiastic tones (it appeared the fourth Earl of Wyndmont had seen to it that both his sons made the Grand Tour together), and a third acquaintance believed he had distant but well regarded cousins in Carmarthen or Cardigan. Aside from this, no one could offer any convincing suggestion of where he might have fled. Dromgoole struck off the Lake District and Wales on grounds that if Beverton wished to vanish from sight, he would hardly go to any place in Britain that he had been known to favor. Italy seemed less unlikely, as being a foreign land and attractive for its music—the artistic temperament was something of a mystery to Dromgoole, and he toyed now and then with the idea that Beverton might simply have indulged a sudden whim to travel as far as his means might allow and complete this opera of his. But Dromgoole knew no Italian, and Italy was some distance away. If he had to search for a needle in a haystack, he preferred to search the English haystack first.

When reason and research led Mr. Dromgoole into a blind alley, he not infrequently turned to impulse and fate. So one morning he packed a small portmanteau, took a hackney to the Cock and Bull, and began to walk from there to the inns, trying to reconstruct some possible chain of events, keeping his mind keen for any clue in the scenes and buildings around him as to what direction his search might take.

In Took's Old Lane, he came upon a gentleman in the act of buying a halfpenny ballad from a ragged street urchin. The purchaser was tall, darkish, and thin beneath his black Jean de Bry coat. A portmanteau even smaller than Dromgoole's rested beside him on the pavement. He seemed to be sneering as he riffled through the ballad sheets, and the wretched seller, who did not come quite up to his gold brocade waistcoat, shifted from one foot to the other before him, as if fearful not only of losing a sale but of gaining a box on the ear.

As Dromgoole neared them, however, he saw the thin gentleman make his selection and pay for it with a golden guinea, thrust into the boy's hands along with the sheaf of rejected broadsides. Dromgoole paused to observe the outcome of this transaction.

The urchin stared at the guinea. "Lor', sir, I ha'n't enough small change by half to—"

The gentleman waved his hand. "Did I ask you to

restore the difference? Count your blessings and go. I will stand for no haggling."

With one glance up at his customer's face, the boy clutched the coin to his breast, folded his other arm over to enclose his prize in the bundle of ballads, and scuttled down the street and out of sight.

"If you'll pardon the observation, sir," Dromgoole remarked, "I fear you ha'n't done that boy any great favor."

"Oh?" The thin gentleman turned to him.

"Questions will be asked how the poor little beggar came into possession of a whole guinea. It will probably be assumed he picked someone's pocket."

The thin man's lips curved into an ironic smile. "Then he must needs exercise his native wit, must he not? I have helped to further his education in this hard world; I remain his benefactor. But how would you have gone about it, friend? Or are you one of those who consider it virtuous never to do a good turn to the deserving poor?"

"Why, I'd have gave the boy a round handful of shillings and pence."

The thin gentleman shook his head. "No, sir, you must be happily unacquainted with the lower elements of human civilization if you suppose that lad will be unable to find a certain type of shopkeeper ready enough to accept his guinea with no questions asked. Besides—" he slapped his pocket, "I lack any desire to weight my person with an excess of small coinage. But I see by your portmanteau that you're another wayfarer, like myself. Have you the time of day? I believe my watch was lifted yesterday by one of the less deserving but equally enterprising poor of this metropolis."

Dromgoole drew out his silver watch. "It wants twenty minutes of the hour."

"Good. Time enough for a pint or two of British champagne. Have you the leisure to join me, sir, and discuss ways and means of assisting the worthy indigent?" He waved his rolled-up ballad towards a nearby public house.

"Delighted. Dromgoole is the name, sir. Artaxerxes Dromgoole."

The other laughed aloud. "Nature smiles on me today, Mr. Artaxerxes Dromgoole. At last I have met a fellow creature with a name almost as unique as my own. Rudgwerye, sir. Sir Despard Rudgwerye, Bart."

"Rudgwerye?" repeated Dromgoole, trying to imitate Sir Despard's pronunciation.

"Rudgwerye," the baronet repeated slowly as they set off for the public house. "From the ancient Cornish. Since in that dying tongue the adjective generally follows the noun, the kindlier and likelier derivation of the name is from *rid gweres:* the guarded ford. The more commonly preferred theory, however, is to interpret *rud,* despite its position before the noun, as a shortening of the adjectival form of *rudh* or *ruth*—the color red—and *gwerye* as deriving either from *gwrah,* witches, or from *gwrgi,* a cannibal or a man-dog, possibly a werewolf."

Dromgoole smiled. "It ain't everyone who can give the roots of his own name so scholarly. Afraid I couldn't do it. You fire me to dig into the subject, though."

"And risk finding yourself such another etymological beast as a red man-dog?"

They entered the public house, called for their pints, and sat, the baronet dropping his ballad on the tabletop, careless of unwiped crumbs and circles of liquid.

"A sheet worth a guinea—I'd think you'd treat it with more care." Dromgoole retrieved the broadside from a puddle of spilt ale and wiped it with his handkerchief, taking the opportunity to unroll it and cast his eye over the contents. In a score or so of crude four-line stanzas beneath a woodcut, the ballad retold one street version of Lord Wyndmont's death: the younger brother had hired a rogue to help him

57

murder the earl and then, when the deed was done, paid his hireling with sharp steel in place of round coin, to prevent his blabbing.

"Pure balderdash, of course," said Sir Despard with a shrug. "But I've made something of a hobbyhorse of the affair. I believe I've succeeded in collecting most of the popular tales extant to date, and have instructed my solicitor to be on the watch for any new versions that may appear during my absence from London."

"Ah!" said Dromgoole. "And do you have a favorite theory?"

"Of the extravagantly horrid species, or of the plausible? For the extravagant, I favor a little version which, so far as I know, is my own: the younger brother seizes upon the hapless footpad and offers him as a sacrificial victim to Beelzebub, in return for which dark rites the fiend obligingly dispatches the elder brother but then cheats the younger of his expected earthly wealth and honors by flying off with him at once to the pit. Not a very logical hypothesis, perhaps, but you'll notice it accounts for all the parties involved, and I fancy I could make a very pretty novel out of it. For the plausible, I confess a taste for the same bland theory Bow Street is reported to prefer: that Lord Wyndmont and the low toby man mortally wounded each other, and the younger Beverton's disappearance at the same time was pure coincidence, probably motivated by debt."

"The highly imaginative and the highly prosaic," Dromgoole commented.

"Brandy and water. The Guarded Ford in me prefers the plausible, the Red Werewolf the extravagant. It's a strange mixture, friend, and not entirely comfortable. Well, shall I write my novel, or spare the world?"

"Oh, I'd write it, and let the world look for itself; if it ain't practiced in taking these books at their worth by now, it deserves a few more."

The barmaid brought their pints. Sir Despard

chucked her under the chin, and Dromgoole thought her pleasure seemed genuine, even before the baronet tucked another guinea into her low-cut bodice. Had Dromgoole attempted the same, she would doubtless have merely pretended pleasure at his fingers beneath her chin, and intercepted the coin with her own hand before his could reach her bosom. The runner became aware that his chance companion was not only interesting, but handsome. Perhaps, to the fair sex, disarmingly handsome. For some reason, Lady Wyndmont's adjective came into his head: elfin.

Turning his gaze to the broadside's single illustration, Dromgoole went on, "But getting back to the plausible, if the younger Beverton simply disappeared for debt, why ain't he come forward since?"

Sir Despard shrugged. "I conceive it may be one thing to trust an official explanation as printed in the papers when you are not involved, and another thing to trust that you will continue not to be suspected under circumstances such as these when you actually step forward to claim your inheritance."

"Suppose someone aimed to settle both brothers?"

"That would hardly account for the dead robber."

"Unless he'd done for the younger one first. Or unless there were more of 'em in it."

The baronet chuckled. "I prefer the eccentricities of my peculiar demon. Had Lady Wyndmont a son, now, I could see that she might consider it well worth the expense to be rid of her lord. But unless she's enceinte, or means to become so within a few weeks by some fortunate surrogate earl..."

"I understand that Lady Wyndmont has a comfortable fortune in her own right and don't depend on her late husband's riches. But no doubt there's cousins to claim it, if Mr. Anthony Beverton fails to appear."

Sir Despard shrugged again. "Oh, aye, collateral heirs. We do not allow our titles to die out easily, do we? But if you're proposing the next heir as the murderer, I can only call him damned foolish in his procedure. Having so gone about his work as to create a nine-days'-wonder and encompass the disappearance of his second victim, he must now wait to come forward until Mr. Anthony's demise can also be brought to light or until he can be declared legally dead."

"Murders are done for other reasons, too," said Dromgoole. "Anger, revenge, honor..."

Sir Despard waved his hand. "The brothers moved in different circles. They'd have had difficulty inspiring any one common enemy's anger against both of them at the same time." He lifted the pint to his lips for a long draught.

"You explained your surname in the ancient Cornish language, just now," said Dromgoole. "Bred up in that part of our island?"

Sir Despard dabbed his lips with a silk handkerchief. "In a region near the Land's End itself. I am returning there today."

"Extraordinary coincidence! My own destination."

The Bow Street runner was not a superstitious man, but when he had nothing more tangible to go upon, the chance meeting with a stranger who took a keen interest in Lord Wyndmont's death and spoke with an almost wistful ease of the virtue of Lord Wyndmont's widow was sufficient omen on which to base a decision.

"Extraordinary coincidence indeed," said the baronet, "considering that country. Might I inquire what business could take you from the city on such a tour at this Season?"

"The social Season means nothing to a cuff like me, sir. I'm an author out looking for antiquities and curiosities, relics of the past, and I find this a good time of year for the quest." In his earlier days, Dromgoole had sometimes, under similar circumstances, claimed art as a profession, for he was in fact an amateur artist. But he had soon found that the daubish quality of his charcoal drawings and watercolors was apparent to all but the most uncritical observers, so he fell back on literature for a blind. As an author, he had only to carry about a small memorandum book and pencil. Whereas everybody was eager to glance over an artist's shoulder, almost nobody ever asked to read a writer's notebook, and the curious few who did were soon put off with the advice to wait for the printed page. Moreover, a literary student in search of local curiosities had more freedom than an artist to ask questions without rousing suspicion.

"A writer, Dromgoole?"

"I publish under a *nom de plume,* of course."

"Not 'Silverquill' or 'A Lady'? Or, bless us, the infamous R.A.D.? Oh, Lud, and I've just gave you my plot," the baronet said calmly.

"Be at your ease. If I wrote novels about fiends and such, would I hesitate to have a name like Dromgoole on the title page? No, my work's the scholarly kind, more in the line of Carew and Bishop Percy."

Sir Despard drained off his pint. "Well, if you've no other place to put up, I can offer you curious antiquities and perhaps a few family ghosts in my own ancestral pile."

"You'd take in a stranger as guest?"

"If you'd take a stranger as host."

Dromgoole was tempted to accept the invitation, but some sense of honor held him back. Chance-founded and unformed as his suspicions might be of the baronet, he preferred not to enjoy a man's hospitality until he could be sure of never having to help put that man in the dock. "Thank you, sir, but mingling's easier with the common folk, to pose them my questions and all, if I put up at an inn, at least for the beginning of my stay."

"I've not had the pleasure of stopping at any hostelry in my own neighborhood," replied the baronet. "The Bal Maiden in St. Finn is said to be clean, and the fare is wholesome, if plain. But I doubt you'll find it or any other establishment west or north of Penzance to match the comfort of even a second-rate house in, say, Bath or Plymouth. Well, whenever you may tire of lumpy porridge and coarse, possibly flea-infested bedding, there will be a room for you in Rudgwerye Castle." Taking back the broadside ballad, he rolled it again and tapped it with his thumb as he rose. "And there will be two armchairs before the fire, where we can sit and discuss Lord Wyndmont's murder. If we will not have already discussed it to our mutual ennui aboard the stage."

Dromgoole stood and took up his portmanteau. "You travel by the public stage, Sir Despard?"

"From time to time. I, too, like to mingle occasionally with my common fellow man." Portmanteau in hand, he led the way out of the public house.

Chapter 6
Doubtful Propriety

Sally had slipped away from Bolventor House when she ought to have been in the library reading John Locke's *Essay Concerning Human Understanding*. It was hardly the first time over the years that the child had taken advantage of a fine morning to quit her indoor occupations, and Edith Parsons was not unduly alarmed. Her first thought was that her charge might be reading the day's allotted chapters in one of her favorite outdoor nooks. But no, the first volume of Locke's great work lay on the window seat, and the governess could only hope she had already read enough to make an intelligent discussion about the philosopher's thoughts on innate principles with Mr. Merryn at supper.

Her second thought was that Sally was perusing some lighter book or blowing at a bottle. Accordingly, she searched the hillock, the ancient stone cairn in the east meadow, and the summerhouse beside the pond. She did not, however, climb to the hayloft, because on reaching the stables she discovered that the best sidesaddle was missing.

Edith sighed and summoned Thomas, the stableboy. He said he had not seen the young mistress this morning, but had been working one of the colts for an hour and she might have slipped in and out of the stables then. It was not the first time Sally had secretly saddled her own mount, either; Edith guessed that a check of the pasture would reveal that the little chestnut mare Friskey was likewise missing.

She sighed again and instructed Thomas to harness Brown Bess to the gig.

Riding would have lent Edith more freedom than driving to scour the neighborhood, but she had never been able to make a good horsewoman of herself, and the situation appeared more bothersome than desperate. Mr. and Mrs. Merryn had gone to spend the morning and dine with Mr. Botallack of Carnsew, who was trying to interest his neighbors in shares in another tin mine. At least, thought the governess, though I may have spoiled the child, I have taught her some sense in choosing when to make these junkets of hers.

The governess drove first to St. Finn. It was not Sally's likeliest destination, but it was the nearest. Probably the girl had gone to bedevil Uncle Robin again, but if so it would seem a pity to cut her excursion too short, and if she had merely gone to pay a morning call on one of her friends in town, or to seek a new novel at the lending library or a yard of ribbon at the draper's, it would seem an irony to drive the distance to Oakapple Farm whilst the quarry had been in St. Finn all along.

On reaching town, she found that Friskey was not in evidence, nor had Mr. Kenidjack of the lending library, Messrs. Trevannion the drapers, Mr. and Miss Jameson the booksellers, nor Biddy Pendeen of the pastry shop seen Miss Merryn that day. Nevertheless, as long as she was here, Edith completed a round of all the shops, finishing with the Bal Maiden, from whence she intended to proceed a little beyond the town square to the homes of the Vivyans, the Strattons, and the Trengwaintons.

But when Edith emerged from the Bal Maiden, she saw the Truro mail coach pulling into the innyard; and as she naturally paused on the threshold, she saw Sir Despard Rudgwerye descend from the coach's interior.

The doorway of the inn was no place to take refuge when the mail coach had just arrived, so Edith shrank back into the shadow of the wall and continued watching. A stranger followed Sir Despard out of the coach: a conservatively-dressed gentleman of comfortable shape and middle height.

"Well, Dromgoole," said Sir Despard, "behold the chief and proudest metropolis between Penzance and lost Lyonesse, and behold her choicest hostelry." He waved his right arm first at the town square and then at the Bal Maiden, and, though he seemed to use no more than a normal conversational tone, his deep voice carried clearly to where the governess stood. "Now that you see them, you're sure you would not prefer to take advantage of my hospitality?"

The stranger smiled and shook his head. "If I find the fleas fighting tonight for possession of the bedding, I'll present myself at your door first thing tomorrow. But if this place is reasonably clean, you know my professional reasons for stopping here." His voice was a little lighter than the baronet's, but Edith thought she could be sure of all his words.

Sir Despard shrugged and clapped him on the shoulder. "Well, at least you will come and dine with me some evening. I can show you the contents of a very good cellar, I promise you that. But for now I'd best be about my own business. With your leave."

Half turning, he caught sight of the governess and tipped his hat before striding away toward the stables. He might, of course, have gone on in the mail coach to Pennyquick; but he might also have some business to settle in the neighborhood of St. Finn before completing his journey to the castle, and even if not, the Bal Maiden had better mounts for hire than any Pennyquick could boast.

Breathing deeply, Edith studied the strange gentleman. His face seemed open and guileless. There was a boyish quality in his eyes, despite the touch of silver at his temples. He roused in her the instinct, not of self-defense, but of protectiveness.

Following Sir Despard's glance, the stranger had likewise tipped his hat to the lady, but made no further move towards her, lingering in the yard as if delicately awaiting her departure so that he would not need to pass too near her while entering the inn. Edith made her decision in a moment. It was a bold and brazen thing when they had not been introduced—she risked his mistaking her for what she was not, and she risked even greater dangers if she had misjudged the innocence of his association with Sir Despard. Nevertheless...

"Mr. Dromgoole?" she said, approaching him and extending her hand.

"Ma'am?" He shook hands, albeit in obvious puzzlement. "I fear you've the advantage of me."

"I could not help but overhear your name when Sir Despard spoke it just now. Under the circumstances, I must seize on that as an introduction, however unconscious." She thought of the apparently easy way in which Robin Jellicoe had struck up an acquaintance with Mr. Armstrong on his arrival, and wished she were a man. Or did she? "Mr. Dromgoole, you will find the Bal Maiden a clean, respectable house, as free as anyplace of fleas. You're very wise to stop here and not at Rudgwerye Castle. And you would be equally wise not to accept Sir Despard's dinner invitation unless there are to be several other guests."

Mr. Dromgoole brought out a silver snuffbox, glanced at it as if surprised to find it in his hand, and returned it unopened to his pocket. "No doubt Sir Despard's wine and brandy are smuggled, but I'd took it that was so common as to be counted almost virtuous in these parts. You don't mean to say he's also a local Borgia?"

Edith shrugged, half wishing she had not begun. "That might perhaps depend upon one's understanding of the word 'local.' Where his own neighbors and tenants are concerned..." Ought she to mention Jan Coombe or Hob Trego? Or the lost elder brother? She decided not—no unsavory conjecture about them had ever risen above the level of gossip. "Amongst his

own people, he seems well disposed, even benefi-
cent." Towards the men, that was; but Mr. Dromgoole could not be affected by the care families took
of their daughters, and husbands of their wives,
when Sir Despard was at home. "Indeed, his tenants
swear to his kindliness. He came into his property
not quite a year ago, and one of his first acts was to
lower the rents. But there are tales..."

"Ah?" said Mr. Dromgoole. "Tales that when he
is abroad, then let 'em beware amongst whom he
travels, those folk who are not his neighbors and
tenants? Tales concerning disappearances of strangers
like m'self who come to this pleasant corner of our
island?"

Edith tried to laugh. "You must think it rather
dramatic of me to come at you like the village crone
or gypsy soothsayer and utter dire warnings in your
ear on the strength of country tales."

"On the contrary, ma'am, country tales are my
chief passion, and—I hope you'll pardon the words
from an unconsciously introduced stranger—if the
village beldams and gypsy soothsayers who come
round with their dire prophecies in the first act or
the third chapter all looked like you, then the her-
oines, ma'am, would be out of employment."

"You may flatter me, sir, but I assure you that to
young heroes twenty years your juniors, I would not
appear so very far from an aged beldam. And if you
will make light of a kindly meant caution, why, no
doubt I insulted your courage by offering it." She
turned and began to walk away, hardly knowing how
she had intended her words to sound. Had she scolded
or bantered? God alone—and Mr. Dromgoole—knew
what Mr. Dromgoole had thought of her retort.

But she had only a moment to ponder, for he
caught her up almost at once. "An excellent thought,
ma'am, to move farther away from the door, and not
risk blocking the passengers. But where shall we go
to carry on our conversation?"

Lord, thought the governess, he does think me a

light woman. A score of withering set-downs that she ought to have made to his compliment flitted through her head. And yet she was not completely sorry she had not made them. She stopped and faced him. "Mr. Dromgoole, understand me at once. My concern for you is entirely of the sort a sister might feel for her brother."

"And appreciated as such, madam." Was there just a hint of disappointment in his voice? "Maybe I'd best be your long-unseen brother, come at last for a visit after years abroad? In order not to make ourselves the center of another country tale, y'know. Or, better, a cousin you hadn't seen in years. People don't tend to mention their cousins so often as their brothers."

She smiled. "A cousin would undoubtedly be best, Mr. Dromgoole. As a brother, you might expect accommodations in your sister's house, and that would scarcely be possible when your sister is a governess in her employers' household. As a cousin, you may of course fend for yourself."

"At the Bal Maiden, but not at Rudgwerye Castle. You see, ma'am, I'm honored to take your advice. But won't it look odd if I've forgot my cousin's name?"

"Miss Parsons, sir. . . . Well, as a cousin, I suppose you'll want my Christian name. Edith."

He bowed. "Artaxerxes."

"I shall call you Archie, then. Or would you prefer Arthur? It's not a pet name, but I suppose it can be made to serve as one."

"Archie will do capital. Name of one of our monarch's favorite fools, as I recall."

"Archie Armstrong, jester to the first James. Yes, as a governess I do have some knowledge of history."

"And some of country tales. Which I hope you'll share with me, now we can sit together somewhere as cousins with no harm thought of it. You know the neighborhood better than I do, so I'll follow your lead."

She shook her head. "Not so much better. I've only

lived here thirteen years; I am still counted a stranger myself. But I really cannot stay and chat any longer."

This time his disappointment, though faint, was definitely detectable. "But won't it look deuced odd if a pair of cousins reunited after long years don't sit down at once and bring each other current?"

"Not under the circumstances. Mr. Dromgoole—Archie—my scholar has chose today to go wandering. She is seventeen, and..." Edith stopped speaking. Mr. Dromgoole was a stranger, and he had come in the same coach and apparently on the best of terms with Sir Despard. Ought she not mistrust the instinct that urged her to trust him so very far?

"She's seventeen, and Sir Despard's home again, is that it?" said Dromgoole. When the governess made no immediate reply, he gave a single low whistle, but did not appear surprised. "Shall I help you find her, Cousin Edith?"

"That's hardly needful, Cousin Archie. Little as the advantage may be by native logic, I still have thirteen years' more experience than you with the countryside, and can cover it as fast or faster alone." Unwilling to say that reason told her not to trust him to make his own, separate search for the girl, she added, "My employers' grandchild cannot be even an adoptive relation to you, and of course you've never met her and could not know her by sight, so you'd really do just as well to settle yourself. Ask for one of the north rooms. They have the best view and are farthest from the stables and courtyard."

"But I will see you again, Coz? To learn the young lady's safe, and to hear some of your country tales?"

"Are you so very interested in hearing evil gossip about a gentleman whose local repute may be worse than he deserves? Can you not accept a simple warning and be content?"

He shook his head. "Not that at all. Mine's a general interest in the popular romances and relics—superstitions, if you will—of country folk. Of course, your warning's gave me a particular interest in Sir Despard, but my collecting don't stop with him by a considerable sight. Maybe I could pay you a call at your employers' house this afternoon? Tomorrow?"

She was tempted to accept that afternoon. She restrained the impulse. "Tomorrow morning will be best, I think. I can then present you to Mr. and Mrs. Merryn, and give you letters of introduction to some of the local people who may be able to help you in your studies. Anyone can direct you to Bolventor House; it's a mere half hour if you should choose to walk. Oh, Mrs. Lanhoose!" she cried to the innkeeper's wife, who had appeared in the doorway and was watching them. "This is my cousin, Mr. Dromgoole." Hooking his arm over hers, she walked back with him to the threshold, completed the introduction, and then, having done her part to establish their relationship, made her excuses and took her departure.

She regained the gig and drove away in some little shock with herself. Because the man looked like anybody's godfather, had that been any reason to take it upon herself to warn him? Because he spoke genially, had that been any reason to stand and chat with him so long when her duty was to find her charge? And to have adopted an utter stranger as a cousin in that casual way! If the truth should come out, it might be as much as to cost even her well established position. And yet she did not regret it.

Am I so desperate to have an adventure before I settle down into a middle age as staid as my youth? she thought. Never having indulged in dreams of romance as a giddy girl, have I taken to that habit now in the last, fading twilight of my young womanhood? And then she laughed at herself, for by no one's estimation could Mr. Artaxerxes Dromgoole be made to resemble the figure of a romantic hero. It's a comfortable browny of a gentleman, she thought, and in that lies the best safeguard of my reputation. If he were some dashing officer of romance with a Grecian nose and a chest three times the girth of his hips, I should be in serious danger of suspicion, but as he is what he is, people will accept him as my cousin and never think to whisper of intrigue. But to have adopted him so! And after refusing to let Sally make an uncle of Mr. Armstrong. Well, I hope I am old enough to look out for myself.

Her thoughts returned to Sally. The girl would be safe enough if she were calling on one of the good families in the immediate neighborhood of St. Finn, but she must be found as soon as possible if she were roaming the fields and seacliffs between the town and Sir Despard's castle. Edith began the drive to Oakapple Farm at once, keeping a sharp watch for her errant pupil in every field along the way.

"Young Missis Paarsons' coosin, be ye, sir?" said Mrs. Lanhoose of the Bal Maiden, looking Mr. Dromgoole up and down. "Iss, I wondered how long ye stood there and talked, what with her going all through the town to ask for Miss Sally and where she might be got to today. Young folk!" The landlady shook her head. "Iss, iss, 'tis a new century and all, they do say. There's mutton today, and a good, fine fresh pollock. Jaacob caught 'un this morning—my oldest boy. Or plaice if y'd prefer."

"Any fish brought fresh from the sea, ma'am," said Dromgoole, following her into the building. He trusted she had lengthened Edith Parsons' title in the respectful, old-fashioned way, as applying to any lady of quality, accomplishment, and a measure of authority, whether wed or unwed. Had not his new cousin distinctly introduced herself as Miss? He wondered at his concern with the question, but then, he wondered at almost every detail of his behavior since the forthright young woman had approached him.

Lord bless us, he thought, I hain't talked so much like a gallant since Jenny Tupper chose Harry Brown instead of me fifteen years ago. Or was it sixteen?

Chapter 7

Tea with Uncle Robin

Three little girls sat with Mr. Jellicoe in his sunny parlor. They had climbed up from Pennyquick that morning to run him down in the sheep pasture where he was looking at the spring lambs and talking to Will Shepherd; and he had brought them inside for tea before sending them home to the village.

Zorrie, who behaved very much like a grown lady because she was ten years old and could make her feet touch the floor when she sat on the edge of a full-sized chair, was still sipping her third dish of tea, but the younger children had finished as much tea and saffron cake as they could hold, and their host had folded two of the napkins into dolls for them. Nancy, who was six and a half and (not necessarily for that reason) easily entertained, seized her napkin doll and began trying to make it dance as soon as she had finished clapping her hands to see Uncle Robin hold it up.

But eight-year-old Rose looked doubtful. "It's right to put out napkins, Uncle Robin," she said, "so that the guests don't need to use the tablecloth or their clothes to wipe their fingers on. But I'm not sure whether it's good manners to play with the napkins afterwards."

"Oh, Rosie!" said the ten-year-old from her armchair.

The doll in Uncle Robin's fingers put its arms up to its head and approached the doubtful child with as much heaviness of spirit as possible for a little being to manifest while walking on air. Reaching her, it knelt on her arm and bowed its head lower in its arms. This was too much for any eight-year-old to resist. Forgetting her doubts, Rose snatched the napkin doll from the man's fingers and began fondling it.

At that moment the front door knocker sounded.

"Let's don't answer it!" cried Nancy.

"Nonsense!" said Zorrie. "Of course he must answer it."

"The genteel thing would be for a servant to go to the door and receive the caller's card and bring it in to us, would it not?" said Rose.

"But Gideon is out, so I shall be the servant!" Zorrie set down her teacup and left the room at something between a stately pace and a skip.

"But I don't want to go home yet," said Nancy.

"If we don't like whoever sends in a card, we pretend we are not at home," Rose explained, causing Uncle Robin to smile.

"Yes, that will serve the purpose admirably," he said, "provided that whoever is at the door can also pretend that Zorrie is old Gideon."

"Let's listen hard," said Nancy, hugging her doll.

But they had already missed hearing Zorrie's initial exchange with the caller at the door. The pretended servant tripped back into the drawing room suppressing a smile and waving a card.

"It ought to be carried in and presented on a tray," said Rose.

"Oh, Rosie!" The oldest child handed the card to Uncle Robin. "I think she wants it back. She only had a few with her."

"We are in," he began, glancing at the card and handing it back.

Nancy interrupted him by jumping up with a squeal and running to the parlor door. "Miss Parsons! Miss Parsons!"

Unable to wait in the hall, even for the sake of the game, Miss Parsons had appeared in the doorway. As great a favorite as Uncle Robin, the Bolventor House governess was at the same time considerably less accessible to the children of Pennyquick, living as she did at a farther distance; and even Rose, after a brief struggle, gave up the game and ran after Nancy to dance at Miss Parsons' skirts.

"Tell us a story!" the youngest girl was shouting. "Robin Hood! Robin Hood!"

"Horatio at the Bridge," said Zorrie.

"The Babes in the Wood," said Rose.

"Robin Hood!"

"Hush, children, hush. Two moments, if you please." Trying to quiet them by gathering them into her skirts, the governess peered about the room. "Is not Sally here, then? Have you not seen her this morning?"

Abetted by the children's chorus, he denied it. "But I was out looking at the sheep until an hour ago..."

"Uncle Robin let us pat the lambkin's head," said Nancy.

"...she may have stopped round at the house at that time and found no one home."

"And borrowed your flute without asking? No, I see it there on the sofa. Besides, she would have sat here and tried to play it while waiting for you." The governess sighed and looked down at the little girls. "She was simpler to keep track of when she was their age."

"Uncle Robin is going to play for us after tea," said Rose.

"We'll have a concert!" Zorrie clapped her hands. "You can play the pianoforte and Uncle Robin can play the flute. And I shall sing!"

"Is Sally lost?" said Nancy.

"No, not lost, I hope," Miss Parsons replied. "But gone away like a very naughty child without leaving word where she was going." The three children looked a little guilty, but Miss Parsons did not pursue the matter except to add, "Never fear, she shall take her punishment this evening." The children looked a little apprehensive as well as a little guilty, and while they stood silent at last for a moment the governess went on, after a short hesitation as if deciding whether or not to speak of it in their presence, "Sir Despard is come home. I saw him arrive in St. Finn this morning."

"Sir Despard!" said Rose.

"Ooo," said Nancy.

"Then we must find Sally at once, must we not?" said Zorrie.

"Miss Parsons and I must," Uncle Robin told them, "but first we must get you safely home."

"I want to help search," said Zorrie. "I'm ten years old, you know."

"Will you drive us home in your tim-whiskey?" asked Rose.

"I've my gig all ready," said Miss Parsons. "Perhaps it would be best if I drove the children back to Pennyquick. She may have gone to the Pilchard's Head."

Nancy was willing to ride in anybody's carriage, but Rose looked disappointed.

"If she's not in Pennyquick," the governess went on, "I can search the roads with the gig while you mount and search cross-country. I suspect she's riding the little chestnut mare, Friskey."

"I'll saddle Bayard at once. I can begin by scouring the fields to the south and west while you take the roads to the north and east."

"I can ride," said Zorrie. "And I'm not afraid of Sir Despard."

"And you're probably wanted at home to help your mother get dinner," said Miss Parsons.

"Can I keep my doll?" said Nancy.

"What a very rude thing to ask," Rose told her. "Of course we must give them back. What will Uncle Robin do for napkins?"

"But I want to keep my doll!" the youngest repeated, clutching it more tightly to her chest.

In the interests of saving time, Uncle Robin

agreed to let her keep it for the present, provided she bring it back on her next visit. This point settled, Rose dropped the question of propriety and quietly kept her own napkin doll as Miss Parsons shepherded them out to her gig.

Somewhere in a dresser in Bolventor House, Sally still kept a similar doll, made several years ago from a handkerchief, which had never been unknotted nor returned.

Chapter 8

Miss Merryn and Mr. Armstrong

Sally had come first to Mr. Jellicoe's house that morning, but found no one in. She might have searched round the fields for him, as—unknown to her—the three little girls from the village were doing, but another scheme took her fancy. She left Oakapple Farm (missing the tea party by a quarter of an hour) and rode down to Pennyquick.

She knew that Mr. Armstrong had taken lodgings in the village, but she had never been told where. So she went first to the Pilchard's Head, the larger of Pennyquick's two public houses, and the only one with rooms for paying guests.

Old Mr. Tremiggan glanced up at her as she rode into the small courtyard, then returned his attention to his newspaper whilst she tied Friskey to one of the posts. He sat outdoors whenever the day was sunny and warm. When it was bad or chilly he sat indoors by the fire in the common room, smoking his pipe, building ships in bottles, playing his oboe, reading newspapers and tracts, enjoying an occasional game of draughts or dominoes with his wife or somebody else. He met waggon, stage, and mail coach when they came, always in hopes that someone would descend to stop in one of his rooms and almost always disappointed since the only people to get off in Pennyquick were local folk who could walk the rest of the way home from the hamlet; everybody else had generally alighted in Penzance or St. Finn where they had better accommodations and horses for hire. He also helped Mrs. Tremiggan with the trade when the fishermen, the farm laborers, and the few miners whose cottages were nearer Penny-quick than another place gathered in the taproom. But otherwise he let his wife see to the business of their establishment while he digested all the news that found him out from his own neighborhood and the world beyond. He was more ears than mouth, however: he repeated his hearsay only when questioned, and, young as she was, Sally could already appreciate that this was a genial trait.

He folded his newspaper and laid it in his lap as she came up. He volunteered no comment on what he had been reading, but she saw it was a London paper with the earliest report of Lord Wyndmont's murder. She had already perused that, and later accounts as well, at Bolventor House, for her grandfather was one of the gentlemen who received the London papers first, read them and passed them on to his neighbors; indeed, the sheet in Mr. Tremiggan's lap might be the very copy that Mr. Merryn and his family had finished with a fortnight ago.

Sally had a more important matter on her mind today than stale news from London. "Oh, Mr. Tremiggan, is Mr. Armstrong stopping here with you?"

Tremiggan puffed at his pipe with his famous lack of expression. "Naw, naw, he be lodging above Jan Taylor's shop yonder."

"Oh? Why?"

The innkeeper shrugged. "To have the more rooms for the less money, might be. Takes his meals here by times, though, he do, and stops in for his pint of afternoons, and a game of draughts."

Sally recognized this, in Mr. Tremiggan's mouth, as a hint that he was disposed for a game now, and on another morning she would have acted upon it. But she had no wish to be found by her governess playing draughts with an old man before she could carry out her plans for a stolen interview with a young one. "Thank you so very, very much, Mr. Tremiggan," she said, giving him a threepence from her reticule. "Stable Friskey for half an hour, won't you?" Bobbing him the hint of a courtesy, she turned and set out in the direction of Jan Taylor's shop at the other end of what passed for Pennyquick's principal thoroughfare.

Tremiggan let her get to the edge of the courtyard before he called her back. "Young Maester Aarmstrong's not to home this mornin'."

"Not at home?" she repeated, turning round again.

"Naw. Unless he do come back when I weren't watching."

"Oh. Where did he go, then?"

Mr. Tremiggan puffed at his pipe and turned the small silver coin over in his hand. "Southwards, I do think. Up along the cliffs, belike."

That was even better. She would much rather be out-of-doors than indoors today, and Miss Parsons would not be able to find her so quickly up on the cliffs and meadows above the sea as down here in Pennyquick. "Thank you so much, Mr. Tremiggan! Keep the threepence," she called, crossing to untie Friskey and lead her to the mounting block.

Glancing back, she saw the leathered innkeeper put the coin in his pocket, puff his pipe, and shake his head. She could imagine him saying to himself, "Young folk!" as he watched her ride away, and the thought all but made her giggle aloud.

The few clouds this morning were high, white, clear in their outlines, and slow to change. She saw one that was shaped like a turtle as she and Friskey started up the slope; and when they reached the top of the hill overlooking the village, the turtle had lost only its tail and part of one leg. Its head, though seeming to look in a different direction, was still recognizable. Sally hummed an improvised tune and put Friskey into a canter along the path between the slope of furze on one side and the field of unmown grass on the other. Even if she did not find Mr. Armstrong today, she would have spent a happy morning.

So she told herself, but when, as she was passing

by the great headland, she heard the notes of a flute, her heart beat faster than could be accounted for by the exercise of riding. So he had brought out his instrument and was piping along the sea cliffs, like Pan of old, setting free a stream of gold and silver notes to float on the zephyrs of heaven. And, more to the point, to guide her to him. It might have been a signal, if only they'd arranged it in advance.

She followed the melody. From time to time it stopped for a few moments, then started again, sometimes slightly altered. But it seemed a simple tune. She could not imagine such a virtuoso as Mr. Armstrong having difficulty playing or remembering it, and she began to wonder if it was not Mr. Armstrong after all, but Uncle Robin. That would be all right, too. This was rather far afield for Uncle Robin to have brought his flute, but there were no other flutists in the vicinity. Not yet. Within a few months Sally would be another. For one moment she teased herself with the notion that by some faery magic in the air today, she was hearing her own future notes.

At last she came in sight of him, and the mystery was explained. In a hollow dotted by rocks and boulders on all sides, Mr. Armstrong sat amid the thick grasses, with a commonplace book resting on a rock before him, propped open and its pages held down with smaller rocks. He would play for a while, bend over and write down the notes in his book with a pencil, and then play again.

She watched him a few moments. So intent was he on his work that he did not notice her until Friskey snorted and stamped a forehoof. At that he gave a violent start and looked up.

"I'm sorry," she said. "I would not have broke in on your work for the world. You're composing, are you not? But Friskey is a woefully ignorant mare, I'm afraid, and does not understand art a bit."

"Perhaps you underestimate your horse. She may be a more astute critic than any of us." Smiling, he got to his feet. "But I think you're rather far from home this morning, Miss Merryn?"

"I must take my exercise, you know. Half an hour's stroll around the garden may do for some ladies, but not for me." She patted the mare's neck. "Friskey wants plenty of exercise, too."

"I see. And Miss Parsons? Or have you raced her and left her behind?"

"No, but I should have if she had come with me. Miss Parsons can't ride, you see."

"And you've come out alone?"

"Oh, yes, quite alone. Except for Friskey, of course. Well, Mr. Armstrong, will you hand me down?" she said, although she could have dismounted perfectly well by herself.

He glanced around. She tried to follow his gaze, wondering what he was looking for.

"We are quite alone, Mr. Armstrong," she repeated. "There are no Piskies nor Spriggans peeking out at us from behind the boulders."

"It's not that, Miss Merryn...If you'll forgive the delay..."

Perhaps he was looking for his flute case. She saw it on the far side of the rock he had been using as a writing-desk, but she said nothing, interested in what he would do next. He took off his coat, spread it on the grass, and laid his instrument on it before coming to help her down from the saddle.

"Now," she teased him, "you'd best tie Friskey fast, or she may wander over and step on poor Cynthia. That is what you name your flute, is it not? Here's the tether."

While he tethered the mare and loosened her girth, Sally strolled over to his coat and walked round it, gazing at the flute. "I'm rather jealous of Cynthia, you know. Would you have spread your coat so readily for me to sit upon?"

"I would spread my coat as eagerly for you, Miss Merryn, as Sir Walter Raleigh spread his cloak for his sovereign Queen, should the circumstances call for it. But—"

"But the grass is dry and not a bit dirty today," she supplied. "I'm sure Cynthia would have been perfectly safe, and if she did get a little dusty, you could simply wipe her clean again in a moment, whereas dresses must be washed."

"She might have slipped down between the tussocks and been lost from sight. But if you'll accept it..." he said, finishing with the horse and turning to Sally.

"And are you so sure I won't slip down and be lost from sight?" The young woman sat beside the coat, scrunching down and ducking her head. The long grasses had bent and matted to form a cushiony pallet perhaps two feet thick, as they did every year until and unless mown, and when she was a little child she had indeed been able sometimes to wiggle out a hollow for herself and very nearly vanish, provided any onlooker was at the right distance and angle.

"I was going to offer you my handkerchief to sit upon." He crossed the field and sat on the other side of his coat.

"Pooh! If you won't spread your coat for me, sir, I scorn your handkerchief. Besides, this is a very old frock, and a few smudges and stains won't signify."

"I trust not, since the damage, if damage there is, must already have been done."

This was not what she had wanted him to say. "And our Betty is a very good laundress," she went on, giving him another chance. "Although this frock has been washed so often it is quite faded, and nothing can help that, you know."

"You show very good sense in wearing it when you ride out, then."

To be complimented on her good sense mollified her, but she was not ready to give up on coaxing a commendation of her appearance from him. "I did not ride out to show myself off and be gazed at, you see. That's what the fine ladies do in Town, is it not? But I hardly expected to meet anybody of consequence."

"Miss Merryn..." he began. For a moment she thought he was at last going to praise her appearance, perphaps even compare her with the Town ladies to their disadvantage. But instead, after a slight hesitation, he continued, "In Town, people have little else of the picturesque to see except the fine ladies."

"Oh." She sat up and looked everywhere about her but at him. "And in the country, I suppose, we have so many picturesque sights that a fine lady or even a passably pretty lady must go unnoticed? Pray point one out to me, sir."

"A pretty lady can go unnoticed nowhere, Miss Merryn. But in Town, more of the fine ladies than not have little true beauty to recommend them save what has been lent them by their dressmakers and milliners."

That, she thought, was a little better. It was not quite what she had hoped to draw from him, but with a bit of imagination she could believe he would have gone further except that he was making valiant efforts to behave with a shade too much respect.

"As for the sights, has long acquaintance really so accustomed you to your countryside that you can fail to appreciate the gothic splendor of these rocks and cliffs about us? That formation, for instance," he said, indicating it with his arm, "that islet of crags and boulders in the sea."

She rose and took a few steps forward so as to see it better. "Oh. You mean the Knight."

"The Knight?" Having politely got to his feet when she did so, he came to stand beside her.

"Oh, it hardly looks like an armed and mounted knight now, of course. They say it used to, but the knight fell off into the sea when King Charles the Martyr was beheaded." She leaned her elbows on a waist-high boulder and turned her gaze from the sea back to him. "Would you have been a Cavalier or a

84

Roundhead, Mr. Armstrong? If we had lived in Civil War days?"

"I like to think that I would have been loyal to my King then, as now."

"Ah, a Cavalier." She turned and leaned back against the boulder. "And we Merryns should most likely have been Puritans, I think. Oh, not that Grandfather is not the most loyal man alive now, you know, but he is so very strict, and the Cavaliers were so very dashing. And then, I heard him say once that at least the Americans need no longer fear such terrible things as happened in France when the people rose up against their King. So I think I should have been a Roundhead lady. And you a Cavalier. Suppose you had besieged our manor and won it and had me at your mercy. What would you have done?"

"I would have treated you with the utmost respect, Miss Merryn. Then, as now."

"And if you had not, who would have avenged me? Grandfather would have had to be grievously wounded before you could take Bolventor House at all. Which side would Uncle Robin have took, I wonder?"

"Having a taste for music, I suppose he would have been another loyalist, like myself. Though as for a fighting Cavalier..." Mr. Armstrong smiled and shook his head slightly. "Well, they also served their fellow countrymen who stayed and tilled their land during those hard times," he went on, leaning one hand on the rock beside her. "And whether or not of the same political mind as your family, I have little doubt that your personal safety would have been at his heart."

Sally giggled. "I am trying to see him fighting you for my honor. You must have won, I'm sure."

"But I assure you, that particular quarrel could never have arisen between us." He moved his hand closer to her waist, then snatched it away and stood a little back.

She made a grimace. "But how, precisely, is it different to be treated with honor by your enemy and treated with dishonor? No one will ever tell me, not exactly, not even Miss Parsons."

"And I pray that you will never learn, Miss Merryn."

"But why not? Why will no one ever tell me?"

Mr. Armstrong looked away from her, stared out at the Knight again, and changed the subject. "They say this was King Arthur's land. All Britain was that, of course, but Cornwall peculiarly so."

"Oh, yes, I suppose so. There's a rock in Goody Crean's field by the Mawney crossroads that they call King Arthur's Table. Shall I take you to see it?"

"The Mawney crossroads? That's some little distance, I believe."

"It's nothing at all," she replied. "To call *that* 'some little distance,' when you've come here from Pennyquick this morning, and I've come all the way from Bolventor House."

"Exactly. Because you've already come so far, I cannot ask you to prolong your absence." He took her elbow as if to guide her back to her horse. "I shall look forward to inspecting King Arthur's Table at another time."

"But it will be directly in our way, and it may be another week before I can ride out again so far. And one can never be sure of the weather. We'd much better take advantage of today."

He smiled. "Had I a mount, ma'am, you might tempt me."

"Oh, I am sorry, Mr. Armstrong!" she cried, appalled at the realization that she must have hurt his pride by forcing him to comment on the disparity in their modes of transportation. She thought of assuring him that she very often walked abroad herself, of offering to ride double with him, of leading the horse as they walked side by side...but some instinct told her it might be best to say nothing, lest she only repeat the offense. At the same time, she did not want to leave him yet, especially not with such an unfortunate parting exchange, so she seized her turn to change the subject. "What were you composing just now?" she asked, sitting on her knees before his commonplace book to examine the pages. Every right-hand page was lined off into musical staves, some of them partially filled with notes, whilst the left-hand pages had lines of poetry and poetic dialogue, like a play in verse. "Is this an opera you're writing? Is it the piece you've been commissioned and come here to finish in solitude?"

He knelt facing her in the grass. "It is. But who told you of it?"

"Oh, Uncle Robin, of course."

"I see. And did he also tell you he has undertaken to provide the libretto?"

"No, has he really?" Sally clapped her hands. "We would have acted some of the plays he used to write, only Grandfather frowns on amateur theatricals. Is it a splendid story?"

Mr. Armstrong smiled indulgently. "The story I believe to be one of power and irony to match any production of the old Greeks. The treatment..." He shrugged. "Well, the work is barely begun. I'm not sure whether he has told you so little out of a sense of discretion towards his part or towards mine."

"Indeed, he's only said that you were at work upon a commissioned piece, and he only mentioned that once, at the very beginning, but anyone could see it. Why else should a musician leave Town and come here? Is it a secret?"

"Not a secret, precisely. But neither would I wish too much made of it, lest the excitement defeat my very purpose in leaving the bustle of Town for the tranquility of the countryside, you understand."

"I understand, Mr. Armstrong, and you shall be proud of my discretion." Despite his disavowal, she had the sense of being let into a great secret, and she was aware that her eyes must be shining. "But what is it about? Surely you can tell me all about it, I know so much already."

He stood and took a few steps seaward, gazing out

at the Knight. "It is drawn from our island's mythic history, from the *Morte d'Arthur* of Sir Thomas Malory. It is the tale of two tragic knights, Balin and Balan, brothers, who fought one another unaware each of the other's identity and died in each other's arms of the wounds each gave the other in that fatal combat."

"Oh. How very sad." She rose and joined him again at the waist-high boulder. "But I thought operas had happy endings."

"Most of them have had, in past years. It is not an absolute law of the musical stage, as witness the work of Metastasio. Indeed, I believe that to contrive a happy ending for a tragic plot, as has so often been done, is to destroy much of the effect."

"And is that why you came here? Because of your plot?"

"Yes...yes, I suppose it is. Here to the land of Tintagil where Arthur was conceived, where Lancelot slew his giants and Tristram worshiped his lady. Those very rocks you call the Knight may form a last visible evidence of Sir Tristram's sunken land of Lyonesse." He nodded and looked around. "Yes, it may well have been in just such a place as this that Balin and Balan fought their last battle."

"Well, yes, but there was Sir Despard's brother, too."

Mr. Armstrong looked at her questioningly.

"Had you not heard of it, then?" she went on, delighted to have a sort of discretionary half-secret to share with him. "It happened years and years ago, when I was only a little child. Sir Despard's brother fell from those cliffs, there..." She pointed to the headland. "And all they ever found of him was one of his shoes on the ledge and his torn coat in the water. Some people say it would have been like Sir Despard—only he wasn't 'Sir' then, of course—to have pushed his brother off. But maybe it happened just as with Balin and Balan. Maybe they were wrestling without recognizing one another. It would have had to be at night, I suppose."

As if suddenly aware that he had been staring at her, he turned his head with a shake. "This sounds very close to gossip, Miss Merryn."

"Well, it is not *my* gossip, sir! And now you sound very much like my grandfather. I thought you would like to hear it, if you hadn't already, it seems so very close to the story of your opera, and I suppose you must have chose that theme yourself if you decided to come here because of it."

"I came here for Balin and Balan and Arthur, not for Sir Despard Rudgwerye's unfortunate brother, of whom I had never heard. I've no wish to disparage your local baronet, Miss Merryn, but notable as he may be in Penwith, there are many other gentlemen in England more notable than he, and many higher titles than his. Had I wished to model my opera on some modern family tragedy, I could have found one more recent and closer home."

She thought he shuddered as he said this, and the fear crossed her mind that Sir Despard's reputation might drive Mr. Armstrong away before she had got the chance to become as well acquainted with him as she wished. "Oh, I daresay Sir Despard is not one-tenth so wicked as some people say," she hurried to explain, "and if he did push his brother off the cliffs, it must have been by accident. And other people say he is showing himself the very best of all his family, you know. Besides, you cannot possibly leave us, now, until you've taught me to play the flute. I know I haven't done so very well up till now, but I have been practicing with wine bottles every moment I've had the chance and I really think I've caught the trick of it at last. Listen!"

In two skips and a pirouette, she was back at his coat, from which she snatched the flute. She put it to her lips, puckered them, closed her eyes, and blew. The sound was still breathy and tended to snuff itself out if she did not keep her lips just so, and it seemed strangely echoey, but to her ears it was a definite note. She blew again, trying to attack with a clear "tu" as he had instructed her, but only succeeding in edging into the tone with a waver. What note was it? Hitherto she had used Uncle Robin's flute, with its single key. Now she held Mr. Armstrong's flute...her right little finger was pressing down the D-sharp key at the end, but she was not covering any of the fingerholes nor touching any of the other keys, and what note did that make? She blew a third time and opened her eyes.

She was startled to find herself looking up into his face—he had come quite near, almost near enough to kiss. But she conquered her surprise and, still blowing, smiled at him in the pride of accomplishment. Unfortunately, as she smiled, the tone whiffed out again.

"There!" she cried, lowering the instrument a few inches. "But you *did* hear it, did you not? I *can* do it now when I put my mind to it, you see! What note was it?"

"Miss Merryn," he began, lifting his right hand to touch hers.

"Oh!" She glanced down at their fingers, resting on the flute. "Oh, I'm sorry, I quite forgot—you don't wish anyone to touch Cynthia but yourself, and I've..."

He shook his head. "No, keep her a moment longer, Miss Merryn. I believe we can suffer it this once. Will you try blowing for me again?"

She nodded, a little nervous under his close gaze, lifted the flute, and after a moment found the right pucker to produce the tone.

"Now try drawing back the corners of your mouth ...Once more, please...a little further, if you can..."

For what seemed an age, he directed her how to move her lips, until she could have stamped. At least half the time what he told her to do was the very thing she had already discovered for herself made the tone poor or snuffed it completely. And whilst he instructed her to do this and do that, he was peering at her uncomfortably close, from all angles, even lowering his body to stare up at her face from below.

At last, shaking his head, he put out his hand again and reclaimed his flute, gently drawing it from her grasp. "It is as I feared. Miss Merryn, I hardly know how to tell you this..."

"As you feared, sir?"

"Will you sit, ma'am?" Taking her hand, he half guided her to a seat in the cushiony grass. "Yes, I've feared this almost from the first, but..."

"But what have you feared? And why have you not spoke sooner? Mr. Armstrong, what is it?"

"Miss Merryn...The gods have so fashioned us that some of us cannot play the flute. You, I fear, are one."

"What?" she cried. "I don't believe you! Why not?"

"Your upper lip," he said, tracing a wavy line in the air. "Its shape—"

"My mouth is deformed?"

He shook his head. "Not deformed, Miss Merryn! No, hardly that, never that! Your mouth is charming, beautiful, a small, perfect bow. Too perfect, you see." Again he traced his line in the air, then plucked a blade of grass and began bending it as if by so doing he could demonstrate more clearly. "Your upper lip is shaped like Cupid's bow. It is a type of beauty, Miss Merryn—a cause for vanity, never for shame. But this very downward curve in the middle, this curve of grace and loveliness, even while lending your features a peculiar charm, must always, unfortunately, interfere with your direction of the airstream across the instrument's blowhole."

"But I have begun to be able to play! I *can* make the notes—you heard them! With practice..."

"With long and diligent practice you can hope, at best, for a tolerable control. Never for brilliancy nor easy fluency. I misdoubt you could ever produce a much better tone than you have done this morning."

She blinked back her tears. "And why did you not tell us so at once?"

"I could not make sure of the fact. I hesitated to look closely enough before, lest your governess think me wanting in respect, or to—"

"You wished to go on giving me lessons until I should make a fool of myself!"

"Miss Merryn! Had that been my purpose—or even the money—would I have told you this now?"

She jumped to her feet. "You are diddling me out of nasty revenge because I dared to touch your precious Cynthia."

"Miss Merryn! Dear Miss Merryn!" He was on his feet now, too, holding out one hand to her. But she noticed he was also still holding his flute, in the other hand, a little out of harm's way.

"And you needn't come to give me any more lessons," she said, "since you would only be wasting your time and making a mock of us all, so good day to you, Mr. Armstrong, and I wish you well!" She ran to Friskey and began fumbling with the tether.

"Miss Merryn."

She glanced round and saw that he was approaching her. Could he not even allow her the parting words she had just uttered? Tossing her head, afraid that if she did not get away soon he would have the satisfaction of seeing her cry, she looked down at the tether again before his limp could catch her sympathy.

"Do you think I have not often wished that I could join in the dancing?" he said. "Whereas you have the great gift of natural grace; your very walk is a dance. Believe me, if it were not for this old injury of mine, I would study with the best masters of London until I made myself fit to stand up with you in the set."

There! She had her horse untethered, and just in time. Quickly, before he could offer to help her, she pulled the girth tight, used the stones for a mounting block and gained the saddle. "Then how convenient it all comes out," she said, looking on him from her new height: "I cannot play and you cannot dance, so by great good fortune we shall always find the barrier of the orchestra between us." Without wishing him a second good day, she turned Friskey's head and put her into a canter almost at once, leaving Mr. Armstrong to limp his way back to Pennyquick alone, or to sit in the grass forever and play his own music if he chose.

Tony stood looking after her until she was out of sight, then limped to the nearest rocks and sat, facing out to sea but resting his forehead on one hand. Reason said it was as well. Had he been free to approach her as her family's social equal—come to that, as more than their social equal; if these simple country folk near venerated their local baronet and cherished their gossip of Sir Despard's dissipation, what honor might they not do an earl stained with his brother's blood? Even as they summoned the constables and bound him over to be hanged with a silken halter...But by disguising himself as a mere professional musician, he had indeed put the barrier of the orchestra between them, even if the barrier of his crime had not already been there. And emotion said he should have kept silent about the shape of her upper lip and retained at least the happiness of continuing as her musical instructor on Tuesday and Friday mornings.

Chapter 9

Miss Merryn and Sir Despard

Sally was not wearing a spur, but she kicked her horse mightily with the heel of her boot, and the little mare responded by bounding into a gait that was nearer a gallop than a canter. They sped the length of a field or two, covered a quarter-mile or so along the footpath, followed a short cut to nowhere in particular over a stretch of furze, and so on, jumping hedges, low boulders, and other obstacles as they appeared. The young woman lost what vague conception of distance and direction she had begun with, and the horse, while not actually running away, took her own head and progressed at errant will towards home.

All at once Friskey caught herself up short into a trot. Even whilst finding her balance again, Sally looked around for whatever had caused the mare to break pace. She expected to see that they had been about to run over a cliff or smash into a boulder too high to jump. Instead, she saw a mounted man at the top of the field.

The sun was overhead and slightly behind him, casting his face in shadow beneath his high beaver hat, but he seemed to be regarding her. She pulled Friskey back to a walk.

The man put his bay into a slow trot and rode down as if to intercept her, reining to a walk when he was within easy speaking distance. "Bravo, madam," he hailed her, bowing from the waist. "My hopes of saving you from a runaway and thus winning your eternal gratitude are baffled by your own horsemanship."

"I was never in danger, sir. Friskey was no runaway." Sally tried to ride away from the stranger at a trot, but he soon brought his horse round to the other side, not heading her off, precisely, but riding abreast of her and ever so subtly influencing her direction.

"If your mount was not the runaway," he said, "then I assume you must have been. From what dangers were you flying?"

"I was not flying, sir. I should have needed another Pegasus to fly. And there were no dangers whatsoever. I was merely taking my exercise."

"Were you? And that is not a tear I perceive running down your left cheek?"

She wiped the drop away. "My eyes often water like this. It's the exercise and the rush of the air that does it."

"Or perhaps a particle of dust? I have been called exquisitely adept at removing particles of dust from ladies' eyes with the tip of my handkerchief."

"No, it is not dust, and you are very rude to press me so. I ought not even to be talking with you."

"Nay, you must not deny me even the rough and ready introduction that my rescue of you from your runaway steed would have constituted perforce."

"That was all in your fancy, sir." Her heart beat very hard and a pressure of anticipation filled her organs. "It was only hypothetical and as my horse has *not* run away and you have *not* rescued me, it don't count. Besides, I think I've already guessed who you are, and you ought to be able to arrange a formal introduction very easily."

"Oh?" Leaning forward in his saddle, he took Friskey's rein near the bit and gazed into Sally's face. "I am Sir Despard Rudgwerye. Is that who you had guessed me to be?"

She tried to suppress a shiver. "It is, sir."

"But I cannot guess who you may be, ma'am. And

how am I to find you again in all this countryside in order to solicit your family for an introduction?"

"La, Sir Despard! You ought to mix with your neighbors more. I'm sure you'll be able to ask about if you really want to meet me again."

"And how shall I ask? 'By the by, Mr. Trepolpen, not long ago I had the happiness to glimpse a sylph-like vision—age, I should say, between eighteen and twenty, golden ringlets, blue eyes, alabaster skin, cunningly uptilted nose, willowy form encased in rather faded but becoming muslin. Say, do you know who such a creature may have been? Or was she, despite the testimony of several fetching freckles on said uptilted nose and alabaster cheeks, a nymph indeed, an unattainable sprite or pisky of the woods and fields?' And when Mr. Trepolpen presses me for particulars of how and where I had my vision, what am I to say that will approximate the truth and yet spare your reputation?"

"If you will kindly let go my horse, Sir Despard! I don't care what you say. If it makes me sound unrespectable, I'll deny it. Now be so good as to let me go!"

"You'll deny with a sober face that you've been out riding alone this morning? Nay, then, you're a more artful creature than I should have took you for."

"I am *not* alone," she lied. "Why should you think I'm alone?"

"Because no companion has yet appeared, and this despite the fact that your horse was not running away with you, but was all the while firmly under your control. Now, my dear, will you not give me your name?"

"If you would mix with your neighbors more, and not always be with your tenants and the laborers whenever you are not away in Town..."

"Is it I who disdain to mix with my fellow gentry of Penwith, or they who shy from receiving me into their circles?" He shook his dark head. "But I'll strike a bargain with you, Lady Pisky—for by such a cognomen it seems I must call you—I will keep your reputation safe in return for the chance to remove that particle of dust from your eye."

"There is no dust, sir, and my reputation is safe enough without your keeping."

"Don't be too sure of that," he said, and immediately made it unclear which of her two statements she ought to be unsure of by adding, "Even the fairest blue eyes are liable to redden if dust and cinders are left in them unattended."

"It does not signify. I'm going nowhere but home and I'll have all the rest of the day before I need see anyone else but—anyone else of consequence."

"By which I take it you mean any handsome young gentleman?"

"I don't suppose I'll even go out of the house again for the rest of the week. So you needn't worry about my eyes."

"In fact, a red and bloodshot eye may earn you such pity from your family as to bring about some mitigation of the punishment you've no doubt earned by riding out wantonly alone. Is that it?" Again he shook his head. "No, Lady Pisky, as a lover of justice—after my fashion—I can no more allow you such a ruse than as a lover of beauty I can allow you to let your countenance be marred by a red eye for half a week amongst your own family circle, even though you may not count mere relations to be anyone of consequence. Not even a servant should have his pleasure lessened in stealing his glances at your face."

She jerked her horse to a standstill. She was trembling too much to handle the reins gently, and the mare snorted and tossed her head in protest. I'll turn her sharp to the right and put her into a gallop all in the same moment, Sally thought, and so I'll be able to get away. She lifted her heel a few more inches from Friskey's side so as to drive it in harder when the moment came. But would not Sir Despard be able to overtake her? "If you do not let me pass, sir, I will scream."

He smiled. "But if a man shall come upon a maid in the open fields, then the man alone shall be held guilty, for though the maid may have cried out, there was no one to hear and come to her assistance. As it says in one of the middle chapters of Deuteronomy, I believe. At least let me know which church or chapel you will attend when you emerge on Sunday from your half-week's cloistration at home."

"How do you know there is no one to hear me?" How far had she come? Was Mr. Armstrong still within the sound of her scream?

"And how do you know what the limits of my desperation may be? Scream, and I shall wait here to see who may come and whether I cannot defeat him or them. Ride away from me in disdain, and I shall follow and learn your abode. Come, Lady Pisky, would it not be simpler to give me your name and half a minute at your eye with my handkerchief?"

"And you don't mean...you won't hurt me?"

"Yesterday I robbed an innkeeper and this morning I cheated a stableman. I am sated with wrongdoing for the moment, my dear. I mean you only good."

Mr. Armstrong had not a horse, and Sally did not know whether he could fight. Besides, she remembered that she was very angry with him. And Sir Despard would not dare hurt her, because she was one of his neighboring gentry. But perhaps she had best make that clear to him with no more delay. "Very well, sir. You asked me who I am. I am Miss Merryn of Bolventor House, near St. Finn, and my grandfather is Mr. Merryn. And we attend St. Finn Church every Sunday morning, and the chapel of St. Weneppa in Centry for vespers, since it's so much closer. Now will you let me pass?"

"Not without having had my chance to examine your eye for that speck of dust." He dismounted. "You see, Miss Merryn? As earnest of the fact that I mean you no harm today, I am dismounting first, leaving you the opportunity to take a fair start of me if you so choose."

He led his horse a few yards off, left it cropping grass, and returned to her. Perplexed at her own feelings, she had not taken the opportunity to gallop away. If Sir Despard had not offered her any injury so far, it seemed unlikely he would do so now. His expression, she thought, was much more sad than wicked, and there were as many stories of his generosity as there were rumors of his wickedness. She allowed him to help her down.

"Is your mount any more apt to run away without a rider than with one, Miss Merryn?"

Sally shook her head. "If she does, it will be back to Bolventor."

"And that will be more to my taste than otherwise, furnishing me the pretext for taking you up on my own mount, if only for the purpose of returning you to your home." Leaving Friskey to graze beside the bay horse, he took off his coat and spread it on the grass for Sally to sit upon. "Now, Miss Merryn, if you'll make yourself comfortable, you'll find the operation quick and painless."

"And really unnecessary, I assure you." Nevertheless, she sat, pressing her hands tightly together in her lap to help hold herself steady.

Kneeling, he seemed still to loom over her. He had to bend down further. "Now then, if you'll tilt back your lovely head a little."

Shutting her eyes, she tilted her head. Her bonnet seemed beginning to slip, and she reached round to hold it on.

He put one hand on her forehead. "Which eye was it?"

"Neither, so I have quite forgot, sir."

"Then I must needs examine both." He drew apart the lids of her left eye. "Look up."

She had a glimpse of the tip of his white handkerchief hovering at the periphery of her vision, and, beyond it, his dark, long, handsome face. His eyes were brown, like Miss Parsons' and Uncle Robin's, and that helped her to trust him. His fingers were surprisingly gentle. She happened to think of her conversation with Mr. Armstrong half an hour ago. "Sir Despard, if you had lived during the Civil War, would you have been a Cavalier or a Roundhead?"

"I have never given the matter much thought. Let me see." He bent closer and studied her eye. "My ancestor of those days, Sir Jasper, was a devoted Royalist. But he met his death fairly early in the war years, and his successor was an equally devoted Parliamentarian, who thus held our property undisturbed during the Commonwealth. So I should have precedent for taking either side. And it must have been your other eye."

Releasing her left eyelids, he moved his fingers to her right. In the pictures that flashed through her fancy, of them all living in the middle years of the seventeenth century, she saw Mr. Armstrong fighting back his fellow Cavaliers to defend the honor of his Puritan captive, whilst Sir Despard hovered in the background, committed to no cause but his own, waiting to take his chance when the others had disposed of each other. Then she scolded herself. Sir Despard's touch was much too gentle, his generosity too unquestioned for her to think such thoughts of him.

"Ah!" said Sir Despard, and she wondered if by staring into her eye he had seen her thoughts. Then his handkerchief came at her, blotting out all else and becoming itself a blur. She cried "Oh!" and tried to shut her eye as the cloth touched it, but he held her lids open.

"There," he went on, releasing her. "Not dust or a cinder after all, but a troublesome eyelash, weary of its exile on the fringe of so fair an orb, attempting to nestle closer."

He showed her the eyelash on the tip of his handkerchief. She blinked and rubbed the corner of her eye. She had not been aware of it, but an eyelash could behave that way when it got into the eye, sometimes more annoying than anything and sometimes hardly felt at all. And she had been very troubled.

"Now if I were your true romantic," he went on, twirling the lash between thumb and forefinger, "I would have this set in a ring and wear it always. But as there's a limit to my excesses..." He snapped his fingers and the eyelash disappeared.

"Sir," she said, "while you were busy about my eyes, did you...did you notice my lips?"

"I noticed your every feature, ma'am. Had I the skill, I could paint your portrait from memory." He put his hand beneath her chin and began to tilt back her head once more, seemingly to scrutinize her lips.

She shook free and got to her feet, holding tight to her bonnet. "And did it look deformed to you? My upper lip?"

"Premature, Miss Merryn," he said, rising. "You should allow the gentleman to stand first, so as to help you to your feet. Your upper lip deformed?"

"Mr. Armstrong says it is shaped like a Cupid's bow and I can never play the flute because of it!"

"You inspire me with a certain degree of jealousy towards this Mr. Armstrong, whoever he may be, who has obviously been allowed the time to study your lips at leisure."

"Well, you need hardly be jealous of Mr. Armstrong, sir! He is only my music-master—I mean he was, but he has already decided it's not worth his while to teach me."

"Foolish fellow! Still, I have known ladies who made shift somehow to continue in existence without being able to play on the flute." Somehow, when Sir Despard said it, it did not sound quite the unwanted bit of advice it always sounded when anyone else said it. "And so we have a flutist living in our midst?" he went on. "I had not been aware of it."

"Two flutists, Sir Despard. Mr. Armstrong and

dear Mr. Jellicoe. Mr. Armstrong is only here for a little while, thank heaven!"

"*Two* flutists! Bless my soul. I was aware that Mr. Killian played the violin, and I believe there's an oboist in Pennyquick, and a trombonist in St. Finn or Mawney. How many other musicians have we tucked about West Penwith?"

"There is a whole club of them, sir. Ten or a dozen at least. They call themselves the Penwith Musical Society, and they meet in St. Finn on Thursday evenings, and they played for Mr. Botallack's ball last Christmas, as you would know if—"

"As I would know if I mingled more with my neighbors, as a gentleman ought. Well, well, a whole society of Penwith musicians, and my own man FitzNeil apparently no more aware of it than his master."

Sally looked around for Neil, wondering if the servant had fallen behind and would shortly come into sight. But Sir Despard waved his hand. "Oh, I left Neil behind in London for a few days to see to the shipping of a number of purchases I made there. You see, I've rode out this morning as unchaperoned as you. But amongst his other talents, Neil plays the violin, if not with the skill of a David to soothe a Saul, at least well enough to soothe a Rudgwerye of an evening. He'll be most interested in learning of this Penwith Musical Society. Assuming, of course, that they prove willing to accept my valet into their circle."

"I don't see why they shouldn't. They accepted Mr. Armstrong readily enough." Sally considered how to get to her horse, whether to walk around the baronet, who stood in her way, or to ask him to help her remount.

"A dozen musicians at hand, and a gentleman who has just been as good as ordered by one of the prettiest mouths in the West country to mingle with his neighbors. You have inspired me, Miss Merryn. Why should not I give a ball this year, say at Midsummer?

I suppose the Penwith Musical Society would accept my payment as well as that of the good Mr. Botallack for their evening's services."

Sally clapped her hands and abandoned her plans for immediate escape. Surely no gentleman who proposed giving a ball could harbor evil intentions. "Oh, Sir Despard, it would be lovely! But you wouldn't need to pay them, you know. They don't want money, they play for the love of music."

The baronet smiled. "And if I choose to pay them for the love of spreading my wealth about, I fancy I'll manage to persuade them to accept. But that's a mere detail that I can best settle with the musicians themselves. As for the ball...you've a better formed opinion than I concerning such entertainments, I don't doubt. What would you say to an open-air ball, under pavilions set up on the cliffs so that the revellers could stroll out and see the Midsummer bonfires on the strand below?"

"Oh, sir! It would be...it would be Vauxhall brought to Cornwall, would it not? But how can I have a better formed opinion than you? I've not even been properly brought out yet."

"No, I did not think you had. But I assumed that as a young lady of obvious taste you would have read much and dreamed more of such fêtes, whereas a mere jaded and dissipated male like myself had wasted his hours chiefly at the gaming tables. I trust that not having been brought out will not prevent you from dancing?"

"No, no, of course not. I stood up in all the dances but two at Mr. Botallack's little ball." There was a danger that her grandfather would not permit her to go to a ball given by Sir Despard, but she tried to dismiss that doubt as soon as it came. After all, if everyone else were there, and Uncle Robin among the musicians, it could not but be respectable.

"Excellent. And masks, I believe." He nodded. "Yes, masks should be quite appropriate to the occasion. You in a white gown, of course, with a rose-colored satin domino, or perhaps a blue one. Of those details you will hardly attempt to deny a more perfect knowledge than I can hope to boast. And you will not break your heart to be amongst the dancers rather than amongst the musicians?"

"Oh," she said, "I never expected to play at a ball. Only to play in the drawing room, instead of singing like other young ladies."

"I am at once reassured and grieved. Reassured in that I may hope to stand up with you in the set, grieved in that I may not, as it seems, hope to hear you someday in the drawing room. And the cause, you said, lies in the shape of your upper lip?"

"That is what Mr. Armstrong says. But I do not believe him, I think he was only jealous."

"Jealous?"

"Or tired of teaching me, then."

"Jealous of his precious time." Sir Despard shook his head. "A jealousy I find incomprehensible."

"I can see you do, sir, or you would have let me go before now," she replied out of a sense of recollected duty, though in fact she no longer felt any need to escape from him.

Provokingly, now that she would not have minded lingering, he acted upon her hint and offered her his arm to escort her to her horse. "And so you've been put to the expense of purchasing an instrument for nothing? But stay—I think you said there was a second flutist in these our parts. A 'dear Mr. Jellicoe'? Of course you will not despair until after receiving his opinion as well."

"Of course I will not! But I had not yet bought a flute of my own, you see," she confessed. "I was practicing on bottles, and I have learnt to produce a tone, so that's why I am persuaded that Mr. Armstrong is only telling me a taradiddle."

"What, the fellow's dared pronounce so fatal a judgment on the unsupported evidence of tones produced from bottles? Intolerable!"

Sally realized that this was not quite just to Mr.

Armstrong, but she was still in a pet with him and so, instead of attempting to undeceive Sir Despard, she silently allowed him to boost her into the saddle.

"But with an instrument of your own," he went on, holding Friskey's head, "you could more perfectly prove the truth or falsehood of this Mr. Armstrong's theories concerning your ability. Now, I think I know where I can lay hands on a flute of more than usual beauty, one that would well befit the fingers of the fairest drawing-room performer. If I might offer—"

"Oh, no!" she cut in before she had time to weaken. "Oh, no, Sir Despard, I couldn't accept a present from you."

"In that case I'll demand payment: an invitation to hear you play it. For I assure you that I would far rather listen to the music of a flute than that of a series of bottles."

"Oh, of course you shall hear me play, Sir Despard, if ever I can learn." And if ever we can persuade Grandfather that it is quite as respectable for me as the pianoforte, she thought. "Only that might be a very long time yet, you know."

"This is a unique scene, madam, that the buyer should haggle with the seller to *raise* his price. But if I must do so to satisfy your scruples, I shall also demand that you meet me alone to complete the transaction."

To conceal her emotions, Sally began to pat Friskey's neck in short, circular strokes. She ought to go on refusing the flute; but she did want it so, and improper as it would be to meet Sir Despard alone, how else could she arrange to let him give it to her? with her Grandfather still disapproving her ambition and unaware that she had actually begun taking lessons. "May I not bring one friend, at least?" she said, thinking that she could surely find a willing companion from amongst the friends of her own age and sex, perhaps Diana Vyvyan.

But he shook his head. "No. In memory of this our first meeting, during which I think I have offered you neither harm nor disrespect, you must return here alone. That is the price, you see: a proof of your trust in me."

"Oh. And...And when shall I meet you, then?"

"Though I know where the instrument is, I'll want some time to fetch it. Shall we appoint a fortnight from today, at this same hour? Let me see." He brought out a golden watch and consulted it. "To round off the extra minutes, we'll say noon."

"Oh, dear, is it so late already?" She became acutely aware that she wanted luncheon. "Suppose it rains?"

"Then we will meet on the next ensuing day that it does not rain." He smiled.

"So it's settled, then. And thank you for getting the eyelash out of my eye." She held down her hand to him.

He shook it firmly. "One more thing, Miss Merryn," he added before relinquishing her fingers. "Think well before you decide whether or not you will trust me, even for the sake of a very pretty flute."

Taken aback for a moment, she soon realized he must have meant it for a joke, or perhaps a compliment, and laughed accordingly. "Then do not you follow me home," she said, "and don't tell anyone of our meeting. *Au revoir,* Sir Despard!" Slipping her hand from his, she turned Friskey and, as soon as they had left the baronet a few yards behind, put her into a trot.

Sally looked back two or three times, and each time Sir Despard raised his hand and waved to her. She waved back, holding both reins in her left hand, her right hand still tingling a little with the warmth of his clasp. She felt as if they had concluded a gentleman's agreement to meet again, and it made her rather proud.

"*Au revoir,* child," murmured Sir Despard, gazing after her and chuckling at her schoolroom pronunciation of the French. "Until our next meeting. For I very much fear the little fool will not take even my own warning now. Well, she will be wiser by and by." He sighed. "No, Miss Merryn, the last thing you need fear is that I should breathe an unseasonable word of this affair."

He seemed about to sigh again, but smiled instead. She was almost out of sight now. He remounted the bay gelding from the Bal Maiden stables and continued his way southward.

He passed by Mr. Armstrong at a distance of two fields without either of them being aware of it, for Tony had not yet regained sufficient spirit to return to his playing and composing, and nothing in the hoofbeats of the baronet's mount suggested that the rider came fresh from an interview with Miss Sally Merryn.

Chapter 10

Miss Merryn and Uncle Robin

Mr. Armstrong was rude beyond belief—he *would* intrude upon Sally's very thoughts, to the extent of driving out for moments at a stretch even such matters as the flute and ball Sir Despard had promised her. And whenever she did succeed in banishing her erstwhile instructor from her mind, some obstacle to be jumped or gone around, or some break in Friskey's gait, would call her attention to her riding, and when the way was smooth once more for reverie at a canter, there would be Mr. Armstrong back again!

She had begun to doubt whether she had not been unjust in her parting words to him, whether she might not have actually hurt him. At length she pulled her horse to a standstill so that she could mull the problem over once for all. She was trying to persuade herself it was only because Sir Despard had turned out not to deserve the bad side of *his* reputation that her conscience was now treating Mr. Armstrong with a tenderness he did not deserve.

But she had not time to follow this idea properly through before she heard her name called and looked up to see Uncle Robin, on his dapple-gray Bayard, at the far side of the field.

She must have come half a dozen fields at the least since leaving Sir Despard, so there was no fear of that encounter being suspected. With good courage in lieu of good conscience, she cried "Uncle Robin!" and turned Friskey to meet him.

"It's past midday, I believe," he said as they met

and stopped their horses. "Have you lunched, or will you take a bite at the farm?"

"Oh, I should love luncheon at the farm! I haven't had a bite since breakfast, except for a few biscuits that I brought out to eat on my way."

"A picnic more handy than sustaining," he agreed, turning Bayard back towards the farm.

Dear, dear Uncle Robin! Of course Sally guessed he had been out searching for her, but not a word of reproach, not so much as a "Where-have-you-been?" No, he would leave all the scolding to her governess. "Shall we race?" she asked, and put Friskey into a gallop before he could refuse.

Bayard, she was sure, was the faster horse; but Uncle Robin was the more cautious rider, so it evened out. They would have arrived at the stables at almost the same moment, if he had not paused as they skirted one of his cultivated fields and called a laborer to come along, riding double with him the rest of the way, and serve as temporary stableman for their horses. When Sally saw this, she realized that old Gideon must be away from the farm, too.

On entering the parlor, she found fresh evidence of the haste with which Uncle Robin had come out searching for her. There had been a little morning tea party and the things were not yet put away, despite his usual tidiness. "Oh!" she said. "Who has been here?"

"Only a few little girls from the village."

For a moment Sally envied the little girl that she herself had been not so very many years ago, to enjoy tea at Oakapple Farm with no gentlemen jostling each other for prominence in the background of her thoughts and no more serious guilt about slipping away alone than the childish naughtiness of it. "And is Gaffer Gideon out looking for me, too?" she asked apologetically.

"As a matter of fact, Gideon took the boat out to fish this morning." He turned the apology from her account to his by adding, "I regret I dare not offer you an egg boiled to the Gaffer's famous perfection."

"I'm not worried in the least. I have never gone hungry here," she replied, as if she had ever gone hungry (except for punishment or out of a quirk of taste) at Bolventor House. "I'll just clear up these things for you."

He thanked her and proceeded to the kitchen. By the time she followed, with all the used tea things balanced on the tray, he had a new tray already partially set with a cold pasty and some olives.

"Oh, you needn't," said Sally, putting one of the olives in her mouth. "We can eat very nicely in the kitchen today, can we not?"

"But, you see, I'm afraid I'll not be able to join you." He began cutting slices of boiled tongue. "And won't you find the drawing room pleasanter for lunching alone in? Or the dining room if—"

"Not join me for luncheon? But why not? Oh," she answered herself as she realized how he must have learned of her excursion. "Because Miss Parsons is out looking for me, too, and you want to let her know as soon as you can that I am found."

"And the longer she drives about the countryside on a futile chase, the less inclined she may be to temper her justice, don't you think?" He made it more of a joke than a threat, and since Sally had known when she slipped out for her ride what Miss Parsons' justice would be, her appetite suffered not the least check at the reminder. She took another olive. "Poor Miss Parsons! But it's such a lovely day, I'm sure she cannot mind the drive, and if you have a bite with me now, then we can go out afterwards and find her together."

"I think it may be best for me to go at once. And, Sally, I want one promise from you."

"Of course. I'll promise to be good for a whole fortnight, but if I'm not to eat here with you, let me have a little picnic in the garden."

He paused in the act of adding a dish of jelly to

the tray, seemed to consider, and shook his head. "No, I would rather you stayed inside." He had grown very serious. "And promise me you will stay inside until we return."

"Well..." She glanced at what was visible of the back garden through the kitchen window, but shook her head resolutely. "Yes, of course I promise. After all, when I was prepared to be good for a fortnight, I can surely obey for an hour or two."

He smiled and began cutting thick slices of saffron cake. "You see, Sir Despard is home again. Miss Parsons saw him descend from the mail coach in St. Finn."

"Oh." That explained why Miss Parsons would be so worried. She could not know that her charge had nothing to fear from the baronet. Sally thought of revealing that she had actually met Sir Despard and found him an utter gentleman; but after enjoining silence on him, she could hardly break the confidence herself. Besides, she feared there were limits to Miss Parsons' trust.

"Milk or tea?" said Uncle Robin.

"Both. But I can make the tea myself, if you'd rather not wait for the kettle to boil." Sally would have liked to ask for spirits, but she knew he kept none except some sherry, principally for guests, and brandy for occasions when a restorative was needed. She did not quite like to make the suggestion herself that he offer her the sherry, and if she requested the brandy he would be sure to suppose her faint or ill.

He went to the buttery, taking the uncut tongue and the rest of the jelly, while she ate another olive and thought of pouring a little sherry into her tea when he was gone after Miss Parsons. When he returned, bringing milk and a bowl of strawberries with clotted cream, she said, "And is Sir Despard really so very bad, Uncle Robin? I don't think I've ever heard you speak a word against him before, no matter what other people say."

He took a moment to reply. "Sir Despard might,

perhaps, be compared to fire, capable of doing great good or causing great harm. And one would be very foolish to go too near a fire over which one had no personal control."

"I see. . . . I think." Sally gazed at the strawberries, but decided she would resist temptation for now so as to enjoy them the more later. "Well, I promise you solemnly I shall stay snug and safe inside until you bring back Miss Parsons. So there's nothing at all to worry about. I don't suppose Sir Despard means to come and set Oakapple Farm ablaze today? I daresay he's back in his castle by now. If he was setting out from St. Finn when Miss Parsons saw him, I mean," she added hastily, as Uncle Robin looked at her. "But I *did* meet Mr. Armstrong out on the cliffs. You don't think he will be in any danger, do you?"

"We'll hope not." He picked up the tray. "Much depends on the circumstances. But Mr. Armstrong seems an able enough fellow, fit to look to himself. Though I'll try to seek him out after I've found Miss Parsons. Now, then: drawing room or dining room?"

"Oh, the drawing room, of course." Sally rose and took the lead. "And I'm not in the least concerned about Mr. Armstrong, in any event. He was very cruel to me this morning."

Behind her, the crockery clinked on the tray, suggesting that Uncle Robin had jumped at her words. "Cruel to you! How? In what way?"

"He told me I could not ever learn to play the flute." Having gained the parlor, she sat in the nearest chair and looked up at her old friend, a tear starting to her eye all over again. "He said my upper lip is the wrong shape, and I cannot blow properly because of it."

"Oh! And that's all?"

"It's enough, isn't it? It was beastly of him—the very most heartless thing he could have done! And all because I touched his wretched flute."

"But otherwise he offered you no . . . no sort of disrespect?" Uncle Robin seemed determined to receive her explanation with relief rather than due outrage. "Well, no doubt it was heartless of him, though I'm not sure that 'heartless' is a term which admits of comparatives and superlatives."

"Oh, bother grammar! Uncle Robin, it's not true, is it? You don't think it's true?"

He shook his head and shrugged. "I'd never heard of such a thing until now..."

"Look at my mouth." She tilted her face up to him. "Come, look, do! He called my upper lip a—a Cupid's bow."

"What? A 'Cupid's bow'?" Uncle Robin knelt and began to study her face.

She wondered what he would do if she suddenly fell forward and threw her arms around his neck. At that thought, she closed her eyes and imagined him, against probabilities, returning her hug. That might be the very best, after all—to forget the maddening Mr. Armstrong and the fascinating Sir Despard and simply hold fast to the dear old friend of her childhood, forever and ever. She felt as if she were swaying forward a little, half tempted and half afraid to let it happen.

"I think I see what he was speaking of," said Mr. Jellicoe, "though I would have found another name for it. And you're really sure you have no other complaint against him?"

She opened her eyes. Mr. Jellicoe was Uncle Robin again—he had finished scrutinizing her face and moved back to a safe distance. "Well, he did not offer to kiss me or any such thing," she said, "if that is what you mean. He even assured me that if I had been a Puritan prisoner and he a Cavalier, he should have defended my honor with his life against his fellow Cavaliers. Uncle Robin... *you* don't think it will keep me from ever playing the flute, do you?"

"Why, as to that...since Mr. Armstrong is a professional musician and I a dilettante, I fear we must assume that he knows the more about it." But, with another glance at her face, he added, "Nevertheless, I've heard instances of courageous individuals overcoming, by dint of determination and perseverance, even more formidable handicaps than this. Demosthenes, for example, could train himself to orate to the sea with his cheeks full of pebbles..."

She tittered. "I shall *not* fill my cheeks with pebbles before playing, thank you! And if Mr. Armstrong will not teach me any longer, you will, will you not?"

"I...believe we may as well see what we can do towards persuading Mr. Armstrong to continue your lessons, before we despair. But I also think, Sally, that it may be best to continue your lessons only when Miss Parsons or other friends are about, and not to go out seeking Mr. Armstrong alone."

She made a face. "I met him quite by accident today, and if ever I see him alone again I shall give him a very wide berth, never fear. But I think perhaps you had better go and find Miss Parsons, if you're worried about her, because if you tarry here much longer, you'd really just as well have lunched with me."

Although Gideon had indeed gone fishing that day, he had gone very early and returned by midmorning, to occupy himself with mending mousetraps and rat-traps in the barn. Hence, he too had been sent in search of the errant young lady, scouring east and inland while his employer and the governess spread north and south along the coast. Robin wondered if he ought to have told Sally this, and driven it home what a to-do she had created, rather than leading her to believe that the old servant was still out in the boat. He was not sure, at times, how far she was given to simple mischief, and how far she might have been spoilt, by himself as well as others.

Naturally, he would go after Miss Parsons first. But when he had located her and put her fears to rest, should he return with her at once to the house, or let her return alone whilst he went directly to

Armstrong and old Gideon? If he chose the latter course, Miss Parsons and Sally might well be gone by the time he came home again, and he would not see Sally again that day, possibly not for several days to come.

He sighed. No doubt any jealousy of Tony Armstrong was equally unchristian (even dog-in-the-mangerish), premature, and unfounded; and no doubt, in her mischievous innocence, Sally had teased him into a very difficult corner this morning, from which he had extricated himself as respectfully as even Robin could wish. Nevertheless, it had not escaped the young farmer's observation that, whereas before Armstrong's coming Sally had from time to time begun addressing him as "Mr. Jellicoe," he had been returned to the apparently permanent status of "Uncle Robin" since the day of her introduction to the musician. And the avuncular relationship, which had been so pleasant when he was sixteen and she eight, no longer seemed quite so satisfying now that he was twenty-six, with a comfortable freehold property, and she approaching eighteen.

Chapter 11

The Curiosity Shop

Sir Despard had made Miss Merryn's acquaintance on a Wednesday in May. On the following Monday (still in May) he entered a small curiosity shop in Bond Street, London.

It would cause gossip that, after a prolonged absence, he had spent scarcely more than hours at home before departing again, this time on horseback. But so did most of his movements, of whatever degree of guilt or innocence, cause gossip. West Penwith was accustomed to his disappearances, and many of his Cornish neighbors must certainly prefer him elsewhere. It might be called queer that he had left home again while his principal manservant was still en route from London with that load of fine Sheraton furniture and hand-painted Chinese wallpaper. But not even Neil FitzNeil would know for sure that it was to London his master had gone again so soon. Sir Despard's note contained only two instructions: Neil should learn what he could of the Penwith Musical Society, joining same if possible; and he should remember that those servants were happy whom their master, at whatever hour he returned, found watching. (Not that Neil would attend to the last injunction. Though a man of many talents, and serviceable when paid, Neil was a rogue and would more likely await his master's coming in his cups than alert. But the gesture of authority had been made, and as for the furniture, Mrs. Bosweega would see to arranging it, as she saw to the rest of Rudgewerye Castle, quietly and capably, not entirely approving everything she saw or heard, but questioning nothing, out of gratitude to the new baronet's generosity towards her son. Not every landlord would have taken George Bosweega back as a tenant after the last baronet, Despard's uncle, had turned him off for several seasons' nonpayment of rent.)

The curiosity shop, unlike many of its kind in less desirable locations, was bright and well dusted. Sir Despard preferred to give his honest custom to the industrious shopkeepers. Not that he often had occasion to shop for Roman oil-lamps or monstrous Oriental dragons in enameled clay. He was not a collector. But he had come to this particular shop twice or thrice before, in company with one of his longest-lasting amours. He remembered he had once bought her a necklace—had the thing been amber or white jade?—and another time, a small ivory pipe, its bowl carved in the likeness of an old man's head that might almost have been a portrait of the shop's proprietor. The china sparrow in its dainty cage, however, had been purchased new in Pall Mall.

At Sir Despard's entrance, the shopkeeper looked up from a bit of pewter he was polishing as carefully as if it had been silver. "Alone today, sir?"

"Aye, alone. And not to squander my time, neither. You had a porcelain flute, of Dresden manufacture I believe it may have been. White, besprinkled with small flowerets in rose and blue, as I recall."

The shopkeeper nodded. "Aye, sir, I had it. 'Twas sold the other day."

"To whom?"

The old man shrugged. "A gentleman."

Sir Despard strode across the shop, seized the shopkeeper by his neckerchief, and drew him close. "I do not consider 'a gentleman' sufficient identification."

The shopman had never before seen this customer in a violent mood. "I don't ask their names, sir!" he

117

stammered. "I don't ask your name, sir, I never asked his!"

"Describe him."

"Youngish—middling—Lor', sir, I can't—"

Sir Despard pulled the neckerchief tighter. "You would know him again if he returned to your establishment?"

"I—I don't—"

"You recognize me. You would recognize him?"

"I—suppose so, sir."

"Then you can describe him. Quickly, now!"

"Let the poor man go," said a new voice, low-pitched but feminine.

Sir Despard looked around. Lady Isabella Wyndmont stood near the door, holding an old, flange-headed mace she must have appropriated from a suit of armor.

"Ah, my crimson man-dog?" she went on. "I thought as much from your back and your voice. Let go of Mr. Boddles now, there's a good dog. I came to make a purchase from a whole shopman, not to have my day disrupted by the hue and cry attendant upon the discovery of one in pieces."

Sir Despard released Mr. Boddles and gestured at the mace in Isabella's hand. "And it is to your recognition of my voice and shoulders I owe the fact that that weapon is not already buried in my head?"

"In part. Also to the fact that whoever's the body, it would have caused a tedious turmoil, besides most likely breaking some of the wares in its fall." She hefted the medieval weapon. "Short a time as I've held it, I've already grown very fond of its feel in my hand. Yes, I think this shall be my purchase for today. The price, Mr. Boddles?"

"Seven...seven and six, my lady," said the shopkeeper, still panting and readjusting his neckerchief.

Balancing the mace in the crook of her arm, she drew her coinpurse from her reticule. "I may nevermore venture out for a quiet morning's shopping without it. Had it not been here ready to my hand, I might have been forced to summon help."

"I misdoubt it," said Sir Despard, "so long as you had your two hands to slip round a miscreant's neck from behind. As I recall, your grip is not of the weakest, Lady Wyndmont."

"Those who must develop strength, develop it." She put the seven and six into Mr. Boddles' hands. He retreated to deposit it in his till, keeping a wary eye on Sir Despard the while. "Now then," Isabella went on, "had you any reason in particular for bedevilling the poor man? Or is it simply that you cannot behave yourself of a morning without a leash and a companion to hold it for you?"

"You recall the Dresden porcelain flute that caught your eye for a moment when last we visited Boddles' shop? Coming here of purpose to buy it today, I am informed it is sold."

"That's the generally desired fate of items displayed in shops. I trust you did not suspect Mr. Boddles of swallowing the flute in order to lie to you about having sold it. Or do you make a man's pursuit of his own business as good a pretext as any for throttling him?"

"I was soliciting him for the name or description of the purchaser," Sir Despard replied unapologetically. "I do not relish the task of herding every gentleman in London into Boddles' shop for his identification."

Isabella tsked. "Poor, poor Sir Despard! Did it never occur to you that an easier task might be to search every shop in London for a similar flute? As it happens, I saw one much like it only last Friday in Mrs. Gaskins' shop in Cleveland Place."

"Better, might be," Boddles put in, still keeping a safe distance from Sir Despard. "The flute you saw here had a little chip out of it, sir. In the bottom edge."

"I do not recall such a chip," said Sir Despard.

"You hardly glanced at the item," said Isabella.

"None but a mystic seer could have guessed that within two months you would be demanding to purchase it."

"Well." The baronet slapped down a pound note on the Elizabethan oak table that served as Boddles' counter. "If that same youngish, middling gentleman should return, Boddles, you will be well advised to make sure of his name, description, and direction. It might save you considerable grief should the twin of the Dresden flute not prove available at this other shop."

Isabella had moved to the door, where she stood watching the final exchange. Sir Despard turned and followed her out of the shop, joining her in the street as she was sending her footman to find a hack.

So she had had a servant within call the whole time, and had not only refrained from summoning his help to check the assault on a harmless shopkeeper, but had managed the affair so quietly that the footman had apparently remained unaware of the trouble. Her behavior was hardly conventional, nor even prudent, but Sir Despard knew something of how she had had to learn reliance upon nobody but herself while she lived surrounded by domestics of her husband's choosing, and even though her first act as a widow had been to dismiss the entire staff of Wyndmont's town house and replace them with servants of her choosing, traces of the old caution might well remain.

"You did not stop to have Boddles wrap up your weapon in brown paper," Sir Despard observed. "I believe that service is comprehended in the price of purchase."

She smiled and hefted the mace again, gently tapping its head against her left palm. "It is not porcelain, nor even chintz, to want the protection of brown paper. I think I shall call it Masher."

"The paladins of old gave names to their swords, but I do not remember that they extended the custom to their lesser weapons."

"Lesser weapons?" She tapped the mace a bit more firmly. "I conceive that maces must have had their baptisms of blood, as surely as swords. And you of all men ought to be aware of my penchant for naming my possessions."

"True. I trust Philip and Samivel are in good health."

"You've forgot that one of my late husband's last acts in life was to fling my poor china sparrow against my dressing table mirror."

"Poor Philip! No, I think you never told me of his sad demise."

"Oh? Well, perhaps not. It happened on the same evening of Wyndmont's death. As for Samivel, he continues to hold his burning tobacco as well as ever."

"I rejoice to hear it. Meanwhile, you will at least allow me to carry Masher for my lady."

She glanced at him, smiled, and shook her head. "Not while you're still in your violent morning mood, my Despard, as I perceive you to be by your behavior to Mr. Boddles."

"It is in your power to dispel my violent morning mood at once, and ensure the safety of this Mrs.— Baskin?—by an hour's enjoyment either in your town house or mine before we proceed to her shop."

Isabella shook her head. "Not yet. In another fortnight or two, perhaps...but not yet. Although you may dine with me today. Meanwhile, I shall ensure Mrs. Gaskin's safety by visiting her shop alone and leaving you to your own devices until three."

Her servant reappeared, bringing, not a hackney carriage, but a sedan chair with its carriers. So Isabella had intended from the first to visit Mrs. Gaskin's shop alone. Sir Despard appropriated the honor of handing her into the chair. "Until three, then," he said with a bow.

"And see that you arrive in your genial evening mood, my dear." Resting the mace in her lap, she gave him a brief handshake through the chair window before directing the chairmen to Cleveland Place.

Whether she found it in Mrs. Gaskin's or some other shop, she had the porcelain flute awaiting him, displayed in a nest of green satin on the drawing-room pianoforte, when he arrived later that day for dinner. "It cost a full guinea," she remarked. "More than twice what I paid for Masher. And yet how easily Masher could destroy it in a second."

He nodded. "With the objects of man's skill, as with men themselves, the more fragile and useless, the higher their price, whilst the simple and sturdy laborers must needs toil for a pittance."

"If you class the musician and his instrument as being of less use in the world than the farm laborer and his hoe, I am of your thinking. But if you also class the musician and his instrument below the warrior and his mace, my dear, I beg leave to disagree."

"But then you belie your own contention by retaining the mace and giving up the flute."

She shook her head. "I have tried blowing into this length of hollow porcelain. I give it up out of respect for music; I retain the mace because even I can hope to handle such a rude tool with some effect. Thus I refute your argument." She ran her fingers along the glazed white flute with its sprigs of painted flowers. "But I would christen it Meadowsong if I kept it."

"I will christen it nothing," said he, "but I'll have a zebra-wood or calamander box made for it to keep it safe."

"I gather you are not keeping it for yourself?" She laid her right hand, palm up, on the pianoforte beside the flute. "In that case, I demand reimbursement."

He put a pound note into her hand.

She fluttered it with her fingers, but did not close them around it. "I am not a tradesperson, to profit from your famous generosity. Nevertheless, if I have bought this thing on your behalf in order that you may bestow it as a gift upon someone else, I require to be fully repaid."

He added the requisite shilling. "Though green satin is not brown paper, it is included in the price of purchase?"

"The price for the satin, sir, is the name of the person for whom this flute is intended."

After rubbing a corner of the cloth between thumb and forefinger, he added another five shillings to the money in her hand. "Be content, my sweet."

"Well." She closed her fist round the money. "It seems all mortals must have their little secrets from one another, must they not?"

"To guard one's little secrets," he replied, "is, I believe, one of the great unrecognized needs of mortal existence, and all tales of the difficulty of keeping the same are fables designed to disguise the fact."

Chapter 12

Of Cows and the Ether

Gentle Dolly might have been the prize cow of Oak-apple Farm, but, although seemingly in good health, she never gave as much milk as promised by the size of her udder. This May Monday the young cowherd Luke Clemmow claimed to have found the answer to the riddle, and Mr. Jellicoe and Gaffer Gideon stood with him 'round Dolly in the meadow, listening to his explanation.

"So I da s'arch out a clover weth four leaves to 'un, Maester, and so soon as ever I da put 'un in my hat, there they be, plain as eggs, all they little Small Folk and Piskies, a-dancin' and a-playin' 'round about her, and a-drinkin' o' her milk the whiles she da let it rain down like they four rivers o' Paaradise Passon da tell on, and a-catchin' it in foxgloves and buttercups, and she as proud and happy-like as the Queen o' the May."

"Well." Robin pondered the matter for a moment, stroking Dolly's head. "So it seems we've been sharing your milk with the fairies, eh?"

"None of that tribe could never abide the smell of fish nor brine," Gideon suggested, inspecting the cow's hindquarters. "If we was to smear her teats with fish-brine, now..."

Whether or not she understood the men's talk, Dolly emitted a low moo that, to the young farmer's ears, had a plaintive note. Somewhat regretfully (for the idea of twice as much of Dolly's rich milk was tempting) he shook his head. "Even Pisky-ridden, she gives her share, and their company seems to agree with her. Besides, if the Small Folk wouldn't relish a fishy flavor to their milk, no more would I."

Gideon shook his gray head. "May be a bad business, this giving them a share in our cow and a place in the farm."

"It may be a worse business to anger them." Robin rubbed Dolly's ears. "No, I think as long as she stays fat and healthy, we'll leave well alone."

Glancing up, he caught sight through the gate of the Bolventor House gig tied up at the stile on the road below. Luke's story, the lowing of the cows in pasture, the rustling of the meadow grasses in the breeze, and the distance to the road must have conspired to mask the sound of its approach. His heart quickening, he moved his gaze along the direction of the footpath. But when he saw Miss Parsons coming up on the other side of the hedge, her companion was not Sally. Robin tried to let no disappointment show as he waved and hailed the governess. She waved back and stopped at the gate, her arm linked with that of her portly companion, who must be the cousin she had asked if she might bring round and introduce.

Robin added a last injunction to Gideon: "And take care you don't besmear poor Dolly with brine behind my back." Then he gave the cow a final pat and went to meet his visitors.

Introductions were soon made. The stranger was indeed Miss Parsons' cousin Dromgoole, who had arrived unexpectedly last week. After exchanging handshakes, the lady and two gentlemen consigned the gig to the old servant while they three strolled down to the house.

"What was that we heard about smearing Dolly with brine?" Miss Parsons inquired.

Robin repeated Luke's account of seeing the faeries by means of a four-leaved clover in his hat, and Gideon's proposed remedy.

"Wonderful!" said the governess. "Just the sort of popular romance Cousin Arthur has come in quest of. Is it not, Cousin Arthur?" Robin thought she nudged Dromgoole's elbow, though he could not be sure since she was walking between the two men.

"Quite," said Dromgoole. "Remind me to make my notes when next we're stationary, Cousin Edith. Difficult job to write and walk at the same time, y'know," he explained to Robin. "Makes for an unreadable scribble. Not that mine is overlegible to anyone else but myself at the best of times."

"You may wish to attempt producing a more universally decipherable script at my writing desk while we await the boiling of the kettle. You will stay for tea, of course?"

"Never refuse it when offered," said Dromgoole with a wink and a pat on his waistcoat. "But my knee serves well enough for my writing desk."

"Which may be one reason your script is illegible to everyone except yourself," Miss Parsons suggested.

"Quite possible. Still, it's always a comfort to find I can still reach my knee across the rest of my lap. Well, Mr. Jellicoe, you don't propose to try this remedy of brine?"

"No. I've heard one tale too many of the Piskies' vengefulness when angered."

The governess sighed. "I fear, Cousin, that our host has contrived to acquire an impressive store of philosophy, both natural and abstract, without its shaking in the least his belief in faeries."

"The skeptic and the believer," Robin agreed. "We've each been trying to convert the other for several years now, without success. She refuses to so much as hang her charm-stick in her chimney to guard against nightmares."

"Charm-stick?" said Dromgoole.

"A cane of green Bristol glass," the farmer explained. "The little demons who come down the flue at night cannot resist sitting on the charm-stick to count the cracks and air bubbles. This occupation keeps them busy and out of mischief until morning, when they can be wiped off with a rag."

"The rag is then burned," said the governess. "It sounds rather cruel, but I suppose it only sends them back to whencever they came. Wiping the cane also coincidentally polishes it of the night's soot which it would never have acquired had it not been hung in the chimney. The wonderful phenomenon is that I have so far escaped nightmares and mischief as well without a charm-stick to my chimney as Mr. Jellicoe has done with one."

"I doubt it's not the small devils who can flit down your chimney-flue that you need fear of a night, Coz," said Dromgoole, so gravely that one could almost scold oneself for imagining a hint of roguishness in the remark. "And so, Mr. Jellicoe, between the testimony of a man of science and a cowherd with a four-leaved clover in his hat, you would prefer the latter?"

Robin smiled. "Why, as to that, I fail to understand why I should accept the testimony of men of science, whom I have never personally met, concerning the existence of such substances as atoms and the ether, which the men of science themselves confess never to have seen, but rather to have discovered by theory and postulation; and why at the same time I should reject the testimony of a youth whom I have employed these past three years and whose honesty and truthfulness I have never had cause to question, when he tells me of seeing the Small Folk with his own eyes."

"If you don't take care, Cousin," said Miss Parsons, "he will convert you. Persuasive, is he not?"

"I merely record," said Dromgoole. "The truth or superstition of my antiquities I leave for other heads to decide."

"Perhaps you'd prefer to hear young Clemmow's story from his own lips for your volume of popular romance?" said Robin.

"Not a bad suggestion," said Dromgoole without

breaking his forward stride. "But that can wait half an hour, I think. Pity to go back now when we're within call of the house, if I don't mistake."

Gideon, driving round by the road, had arrived before them, with time to put up the horse and gig and gain the kitchen. Robin settled with his guests in the drawing room, where, true to his promise, Dromgoole brought a pencil and memorandum book from his coat pocket and employed his knee, which he could still reach well enough, as a writing desk. "By the way, Mr. Jellicoe, if I haven't mentioned it, I leave my informants anonymous. Unless they request the obscure immortality of having their names recorded in my pages."

"Leave me anonymous, then," said the farmer with a little laugh. "Immortality is a will-o'-the-wisp I prefer to pursue by my own efforts, rather than at secondhand."

Miss Parsons fetched the charm-stick and put it in Dromgoole's lap. "Pretty, is it not? One can see why it would attract and delight the little demons. My charge and I do have one apiece, you know. Mr. Jellicoe gave them us...the Christmas she was ten, I believe. She used to hang hers in the fireplace, but now she follows my example and leaves it permanently at her window, to catch the sunlight by day and more substantial intruders by night, should any make the attempt."

Robin took the opportunity to ask a question he had wished to ask since their arrival. "And how is Sally getting on? She's not still being punished for last Wednesday's escapade, is she?"

"Oh, no!" said the governess. "She was on Thursday, of course, by being kept in all day."

"Mr. and Mrs. Merryn were kind enough to have me stay for dinner on Thursday, too," said Dromgoole. "I don't guess it lightened poor Miss Merryn's penance, having to help entertain an old fogy like me in the evening."

"Nonsense. I've never heard her laugh more at the card table than with you across it from her. But I suppose one could argue that her punishment continued on Friday, for I insisted she visit no one but the Trengwaintons and the Strattons, and have me with her. She was in two minds about whether or not to come here Saturday on the chance Mr. Armstrong had forgiven her sufficiently to offer another lesson, but the weather decided it. I hope Mr. Armstrong did not make a fruitless trip in the wet and dirt?"

"He was here, yes. But we did not lose our time. He's composing a flute concerto for me, you know, and in my turn I'm writing the libretto for his opera." Robin shook his head. "I'm not entirely pleased with the theme he wishes to use for the second movement of the concerto, but since he claims some dissatisfaction with the second act of the libretto, I suppose it evens out." He did not mention what had appeared very acute disappointment on Armstrong's part when Sally did not come.

"So he can be persuaded to continue her lessons in spite of her unfortunately-shaped mouth?" said Miss Parsons.

"He guaranteed to come again at the appointed time tomorrow, unless we learned in the interim that she meant certainly to give it up. Indeed, I had some thoughts of paying you a visit at Bolventor House this afternoon," Robin understated.

Miss Parsons smiled. "If the instructor is to be on hand, I think I can promise that so will be the pupil and her duenna."

"And her duenna's cousin by way of escort to the ladies," said Dromgoole. "If you and they will have me."

"I thought you meant to call on Mr. Trengwainton again tomorrow," said his cousin. "Had he not promised to go through his ancestors' papers and search out more histories for you?"

Dromgoole shrugged. "Any time this week, but

not necessarily tomorrow. And I wouldn't mind meeting your Mr. Armstrong."

Having watched his guests for some minutes now, Robin needed only a second to foresee the probable situation if Dromgoole accompanied the ladies tomorrow morning: the two comfortably distant cousins together in a corner of the drawing room or even strolling about in the garden, Armstrong tutoring Sally with the utmost gentleness in an effort to make up for Wednesday's contretemps, and Robin left a fifth party, more or less *de trop* as far as either couple was concerned, but forced to the lonely and bitter task of keeping his eye on the younger of the two women. "If your interest's in our Cornish antiquities, Mr. Dromgoole," he said, "I don't see that Mr. Armstrong could help you, being a stranger here himself."

"There's where you may be surprised, sir," Dromgoole replied. "Chances are good that something attracted him to this country. There's quite often some reason or other behind even the most random choices, if you can get at it. Since you don't have much else in this country besides legends and picturesque views, the attraction may be pretty much the same for him as for me, and he's had the start of me in exploring the area."

"I'm not sure I'd call it exploring," Robin argued. "Except for ourselves, and the Musical society, he seems to have kept rather close, as one might expect of a man who came here to work in solitude."

"Yes, his opera, that you're doing the libretto for. What's his subject there, if I might make bold to ask? Cousin Edith says she don't know."

"I'm not aware that it's meant to be any secret," said Robin, who, not quite satisfied with Armstrong's musical settings, had begun to dream of the day when his libretto, like those of Metastasio and Rousseau, might find more than one composer. "It's the tale of Sirs Balin and Balan, drawn from the *Morte d'Arthur*."

"Balin and Balan." Dromgoole furrowed his brow. "The noble brothers who killed each other by mischance, doing battle anonymously."

"Ah, yes! *That* Balin and Balan," said Dromgoole. "An opera drawn from Britain's mythic history, eh? Your choice of subject, or his?"

"His, though quite congenial to my own small talent."

"Well, there you have it," said Dromgoole. "The proof of my point. Mr. Armstrong's taste is for antiquities, and you'd perhaps be surprised how often an interested visitor knows more than any one given native about a neighborhood's antiquities. Yes, I'll be very eager to meet him."

"By your argument, Coz, you'd best not lose a moment's opportunity to question me," said Miss Parsons, "since I'm a stranger here myself, if you remember. Nor Mr. Jellicoe, neither," she added (as a sop to propriety?) "He's only been here a mere eleven years, making him even more of a stranger than I am."

"And a more sympathetic one to the unseen world than you are, Cousin Edith," said Dromgoole with a smile and the suggestion of a wink.

"I fear, however, that my interest is more practical and utilitarian than it is romantic," said Robin.

At about this time, Gideon brought in the tea tray at last, like a small, castellated bastion to preserve order in the world.

It was not that the young farmer begrudged the governess her obvious flirtation, though he had been amazed at this hitherto unseen and unsuspected side of her character. But he was rather envious of her and of Dromgoole. Everyone except himself, it seemed, knew how and when to be bold. There was, however, this much consolation: if Dromgoole were really intent upon interviewing Tony Armstrong, Robin might also have his chance on the morrow for converse with the ladies.

Chapter 13

The Middle Music Lesson

As she rode beside Miss Parsons to her next encounter with Mr. Armstrong, Sally felt none of the hopes and joys that had marked the earlier occasions. She wondered whether, if that fateful last meeting with her instructor had taken place regularly, in Uncle Robin's house as it ought to have done, would she not have been much happier today? No doubt that would only have been to postpone hearing his pronouncement about her lip, and in a way she did not regret having the revelation behind her; she felt as though it had projected her from the unconscious innocence of childhood to the sad but calm dignity of womanhood, but she did not entirely mourn the loss of what now seemed her foolishness. On the other hand, it might have been better if she had heard the judgment when Miss Parsons or Uncle Robin had been present. They would have helped her check the excesses of her reaction. But then, had she not gone out riding last Wednesday, she would not have met Sir Despard.

Thinking of the Midsummer Ball (which she had inspired and which, so far as she knew, had not yet been announced to anyone else) helped her through the awkwardness of exchanging polite civilities with Mr. Armstrong and taking up Uncle Robin's flute to begin the lesson. All this accomplished, she must turn her entire attention to what she had learned till now, for she meant to play a complete scale. Alas, for all her determination, she could remember only half the notes, and now that she wanted so very much to blow clear tones, they blurred more than ever!

From between the pages of his opera manuscript, Mr. Armstrong extracted a sheet of paper covered with neat diagrams in ink. "Here, Miss Merryn. I have drawn up a chart of the various fingerings for you. Until you can obtain your own flute, you might practice them upon any suitable length of cane or rod, perhaps marked with circles to represent the holes. The darkened circles on the chart, you see, show the holes to be covered for each note. When the last circle is darkened, you are *not* to press the key, since pressing down on the key uncovers the hole."

"Thank you, Mr. Armstrong," she said very formally, accepting his chart. "But you hardly needed to remind me of that last point, you know. And I have engaged the brother of a dear friend to procure me an instrument of my own. Meanwhile," she went on, "I have a cane that will do quite nicely, a beautiful one of Bristol glass that Uncle Robin gave me years ago, but I think I shall not need to spoil it with painted circles, thank you. I fancy I shall not need such a childish trick as that to help me move my fingers up and down."

"It was a mere suggestion, Miss Merryn. I thought it might help...Well, never mind."

His hesitancy softened her, but only a little. "I am glad that at least you do consider me capable of learning to finger the notes, Mr. Armstrong. Even though the shape of my mouth must prevent my ever producing a decent tone."

"I spoke in haste that day, miss. I advised you as I would have advised a young man hoping to make music his livelihood. Having had ample time to reconsider, I have come to see that for your own pleasure—"

"Oh, for my own pleasure I may hope someday to play well enough to bore my friends of an evening, is that what you were about to say? Thank you very much, but if I cannot learn to play as well as a true musician, I shall give it up entirely. But, however, I have had time to reconsider, too, and I think you may not be so very old and wise even if you are my senior by a few years, and I am your first pupil by your own confession, and so I'm not sure by half that you know what you're talking about when you blame my lip!" More successful than the scale, the latter part of this speech tripped from her tongue almost word for word as she had rehearsed it, and the first part, though more impromptu, also turned out very well. Or so she thought at first, until she looked up at his face and almost wished she had contented herself with the simple threat to give it up if she could not learn to play well.

"If you would rather find a more experienced teacher, Miss Merryn," he said, "I shall bow myself out, more in regret for the loss of your society than in wanhope for your eventual success."

"Oh, no, Mr. Armstrong, I didn't quite mean that! And—and at any rate, who else could I find to teach me?"

Hardly had she uttered the words when they both glanced at Uncle Robin, who turned a page, seemed to frown slightly, and flipped back as if to verify some earlier point in his reading.

"You might, of course, persuade your grandparents to bring you to Town for a while. There's no dearth of music-masters in London, but you might find a superior one as near to hand as Plymouth or Exeter. Or Mr. Merryn might be able to persuade some struggling musician to remove to St. Finn even for a single pupil. But if you are serious in your wish to play well or not at all, beware of a teacher so sympathetic he will toad-eat you rather than try to speak the honest truth."

"I...see. And perhaps you could find out such a struggling musician for me, whenever you return to Town."

He shook his head. "If you wait for me to return

to London, I fear your resolution may be put to a severe test."

"Oh. You don't mean to leave us, then?"

"To leave you..." He seemed to gaze at her face for a moment, but looked away when she tried to meet his eye. "I may be forced to do so. But not to return to London. I doubt I shall ever appreciate the city again, not after this taste of the country life."

"But how shall you be able to have your opera produced? I thought that musicians had to seek the cities in order to make their living? Or shall you seek service with some great duke or earl who loves both music and the country life? I cannot imagine there can be so many of them."

"There are more cities than London in the world. Even in England."

"Yes. Yes, I suppose," she said a little doubtfully. "Well, if there were such a music-master in one of them as would suit me, Grandfather could very well afford to lodge him in Bolventor House for a few years, I fancy. But of course Grandfather would want to be very well assured of my being both serious and capable, you know. I don't know how often he has told us, 'Either a thing is worth any expense, or none at all.'"

"He says that, does he?" For the first time since greeting her today, Mr. Armstrong smiled. "Then perhaps I should ask higher payment for these lessons."

She shook her head. She could hardly tell him that his fees so far had come from her own small savings and what Miss Parsons could lend. Grandmother, although they had won her at last to grant a secret permission and compliance, did not approve quite far enough to donate any of her housekeeping money, and Grandfather still knew nothing of the project. Sally was confident that she might win him over eventually by surprising him some day with a small recital of his favorite pieces, executed to perfection, but until then..."If you hope to ask more," she said, "you must earn it. You must teach me to play as well as you do in despite of my Cupid's bow."

He sighed.

"Well, not so well as you play," she amended, "but so well that my friends will never yawn to hear me."

"But I cannot guarantee that. The composer, you see, may bear the blame for more yawns than the performer. You must learn to choose your music as well as to play it. And, of course, you must learn to play it in order to judge it." Gently, he moved the flute up to her lips once more. "Now, then, perhaps if we were to try varying the embouchure somewhat..."

Edith and Arthur—for already she thought of him as Arthur, not as Mr. Dromgoole nor Artaxerxes nor even that first chosen and soon discarded nickname, Archie—were still near enough the house to hear Sally's struggling notes, but far enough to find them no serious distraction.

Edith closed her eyes for a moment, the better to taste the air's warm fragrance as she inhaled for a sigh of contentment. When she opened them again, the flowers looked yet happier than before. "Many of the country folk consider May an unlucky month," she said. "I cannot think why."

"Odd notion," he agreed. "But if it's so, at least we've less than a week left of it for the year."

"Alas!" Seeing some clover in the lawn, she knelt. "Shall we search out a four-leaved grass? What a chapter it would make for your book if you could write of seeing the Small Folk at first hand! Or ought one to say 'at first eye'?"

"Ten or twenty years ago a plainer cousin than you could've got me down like that, but with my knees and the size of my weskit what they are today, I might prove the month unlucky by not being able to get to m' feet again." He compromised by stirring the clover with the tip of his cane. "But we'll see if my eyes ain't as sharp as ever. There, is that 'un four-leaved?"

"Come down and see for yourself, sir!" Seizing his cane, she tugged.

He could have saved himself by letting go the cane. Instead, he yielded and sat beside her, with more agility than he pretended to in his talk. But in revenge, he came down on the patch of clover they had been examining.

"Dear!" she said. "Well, Coz, it appears we shall never know whether it had four leaves or not."

"Then my eyes' name for sharpness is safe for the time. And with all this around him for a man to look at, why should he want to see the fairies, too?" He winked at her.

She chuckled. "A most unscholarly attitude, Coz. But at least you have proved that the month of May is not unlucky, for if it were, there should have been a bee beneath you in that clover."

"So far, I've found this May a month of great good fortune." He reached across the foot or so of grass between them, took her hand, and went on in a more serious vein, "Suppose I was to try how far my good luck holds?"

She returned the press of his fingers, but said, "It's not yet been even a week since we adopted one another, Cousin. And June is held to be a more fortunate month, in comparison with May."

"There's two reasons I don't want to wait. And neither of 'em's to do with the luck or unluck of the month. Edith?"

"Arthur." She pressed his hand again.

"Well. The first reason's that fifteen years ago I waited a few days too long, and when I did speak out, the lady had made up her mind for another fellow."

"He must have been rather extraordinary. I may well choose no one at all, Arthur, but be sure that with me you're in danger of no rival save resolute spinsterhood."

"Being set in my own bachelor ways, I know better than to underestimate that rival."

She said: "And your second reason for this unseemly dispatch?"

He hesitated before he answered: "I came here on business, ma'am, and not the business I told you a week ago. If you'll give me your help in the real business, I'll be honored. But first I wanted you to know, my feelings have got too deep...Edith..." He coughed. "Dash it..."

She chuckled suddenly, at the same time lifting his hand to her cheek. "Have you read Donne, Cousin Arthur?"

"Donne? At school. Not recently. 'Go and catch a falling star,' 'Ask not for whom the bell tolls,' that sort of thing?"

"'The Ecstasy.' Two lovers sitting together on a grassy bank. 'Love's mysteries in souls do grow, But yet the body is his book,' and much more of the same. I laughed just now because one pictures some tall lord and golden-haired lady, both in the first flush of youth, or the second at very latest, and here we sit, as middle-aged and middle-class a Beatrice and Benedict as one could find!"

She had guessed correctly that a bit of banter was needed to get them over the awkward solemnity that had begun to choke him. He chuckled with her. "More of a Falstaff than a Benedict, though. And Beatrice...you make a fair enough Beatrice, Coz, but...which was that saucy female the Bard put in charge of his Moor's Desdemona?"

"Emilia. Yes, I shall be Emilia, provided you don't mean me to come to a sad end, of course. We may be Falstaff and Emilia, but we'll have no endings but happy ones." Still rubbing his hand, she grew serious. "Now. What is this true business of yours that you fear may get in the way of our happiness?"

He hoisted himself nearer and put his arm around her. "Your promise first. Marry me, Edith?"

"No, first your secret, then my answer."

He hemmed. "I've used you enough already, m'dear."

"You are infamously poor! No, that can't be it...but I warn you, Cousin Arthur, if you tease me like this and then never tell me your secrets after all, you shall ensure that my answer is no." She pulled away and shifted her position so as to sit facing him rather than side by side.

"Very well, then," he said. "To start, I'm a Bow Street man."

"A runner?"

He nodded. "Not here on the Beak's own business. Though it may come to that. Here on a private errand for an individual who wants a relation located. The new Lord Wyndmont."

"The Wyndmont murder?" She quickly cast her mind over what she had read in Mr. Merryn's London newspapers. "The missing brother? You've cause to believe he is here?"

"No cause, no. Not as you'd understand reason and evidence. It was start in the city and follow my nose." He tapped the member in question. "Your local Bart. came in the way of said nose. Your local Bart., as it appears, takes a sharp interest in the case. In which he's probably not much different from a great many other folk, both high and low, but it seemed as good a whiff of a scent as any. If I had a better one, I'd be more sure of what I've found, but as it stands..." He shrugged.

"Mr. Armstrong?" He was the only other stranger she knew of in West Penwith, besides Arthur himself. She made a mental calculation of the dates. "But Lord Wyndmont was killed on the Monday or Tuesday night, was he not? And Mr. Armstrong arrived in St. Finn on the Monday, I'm sure of it...yes, it was the Monday after May Day."

"You seem to've lost a week, Cousin. Wyndmont was killed in the last week of April. And Armstrong arrived here about a sennight later? Time enough for the trip."

"And Sally's music teacher," she whispered, "fits the description of Lord Wyndmont's brother?"

"As much description as I've got, and that ain't much. Dark hair, dark complexion, tall, good looking—uncommon good looking, is Armstrong? I think your sex is the better judge of that in a member of mine?"

She nodded. "Uncommonly good looking," she said without the least desire to see such a face as Mr. Armstrong's replace Arthur's more commonplace features across the grass from her.

"A phiz I might guess to bear some family resemblance to his late Lordship, but the state I last saw him in wasn't flattering. Also, Mr. Anthony Beverton, now Lord Wyndmont, plays the flute. Also, he limps, though my employer wasn't sure which leg."

"And Mr. Armstrong limps in the left leg. And his given name is Anthony—Tony," she said, remembering that he and Robin Jellicoe had very early reached the stage of nicknaming one another.

"Beverton was writing an opera, too. An opera based on our island's mythic history."

"Balin and Balan."

"The brothers that killed each other. Except that this time one of 'em survived."

Edith leaned forward and seized Arthur's forearm. "But surely he wouldn't be so careless as not to change his given name, as well as his surname?"

He covered her hand with his. "As to that, I'd be less surprised if he kept Anthony than if he took a new family name that began with some other letter than *B*. As he may have done, in fact."

"Oh...Poor Sally! Arthur—you don't think there's any danger to her?"

"No. No, that much I don't. The relation who employed me to find him—it's the dowager countess herself," he added, entrusting Edith with even this confidence, "—swears and guarantees he never killed his brother....Well, I won't hide from you that I ain't quite so confident of that, no matter what story we've subscribed so far—and mind you, Lord Wyndmont and the low toby man could still have killed each other, there's no other way we've found to account for that dead footpad. Old Scabcheek Jebby, we wasn't too sorry to see *him* go; been trying to pin him these four or five months. Would've liked to get a few answers out of him, but..." He returned to the musician's case. "Even if Beverton did kill Lord Wyndmont, I don't see he could've planned it overmuch beforehand, or he'd have planned it better."

"Is this meant to reassure me? A man capable of such a temper as can drive him to murder in a moment?"

"By all accounts, the late Lord Wyndmont might have drove a martyr into a temper. Seems that Beverton limps because of a practical joke his older brother played on him when they were boys. I understand that was pretty much the stamp of their brotherly relations." Arthur shook his head. "Never had a brother myself. Nor a sister, neither."

"I had. But not such a brother as that, thank God. But, nevertheless..." She looked at the house, suddenly aware of hearing no more musical or quasi-musical tones issuing therefrom.

Chapter 14

The Dancing Lesson

Sally, her eyes smarting, lowered the flute after a series of particularly unsuccessful attempts to produce a high D. "Oh! I think you must be right, and it is quite hopeless, after all."

"Your lips are tired now, Miss Merryn, as any novice's would be at this moment. Perhaps we've done enough for the day."

"We have done next to nothing, and you very well know it, Mr. Armstrong. I've accomplished nothing at all, and you've wasted your time." As she realized that Uncle Robin was looking up from his book at them, she blushed and turned towards the window. Miss Parsons and Mr. Dromgoole were sitting together on the grass, deep in conversation. Miss Parsons glanced around at the house, and Sally felt tempted to call them in and spoil their tête-à-tête.

"Miss Merryn," said Mr. Armstrong, "after you have shown me such an example of determination until now, will you give up and be defeated by no more difficulty, when all is said and done, than you had experienced before I told you of my fears?"

She tried to blow a B, which ought to have been a simple and easy note, failed even in that, and shook her head, blinking furiously.

"Why not rest half an hour and try again after we drink some tea?" suggested Uncle Robin. "I have heard some very promising notes today."

I am behaving very badly, she thought, but I *will* conquer myself. To raise her spirits, she called a picture of the coming Midsummer Ball to her mind, and glimpsed herself dancing with Mr. Armstrong. That was foolishness, of course, because he would be in the orchestra; but it gave her a hint what to say next. "Very well," she told him, turning back, "I shall not give it up just yet—but only if you agree to learn how to dance."

"Miss Merryn! On the one occasion I attempted it, I made a laughingstock of myself. Do you call this an honorable bargain?"

"No," she said in sudden, mischievous delight, "but it's an eminently fair one! Come, sir, if I am to furnish you an example of courage, you must give me one in return. Here, Uncle Robin, play a dance for us." She dashed across the room and thrust his flute out to him.

He closed his book, smiled, and took the instrument. "Very well, but upon condition...that I am to have the next dance after this."

"Oh, of course!" She looked around, pushed the light tea table away from before the sofa, and judged that gave them ample space. "Well, begin, Uncle Robin. Don't lose a second, or he may take root in your drawing room floor and I shall never coax him out."

Uncle Robin began to play one of the simple country dances they had played at Mr. Botallack's Christmas entertainment, and Sally caught Mr. Armstrong's hands and forced him into a pas de deux in spite of himself. "Now, then, sir, we cannot move up or down through the set, of course, since there's only the two of us. We'll simply have to pretend the other dancers, but that's all to the good, since there would hardly be room for any more, and you'll be astonished how much we *can* do with just the two of us, Mr. Armstrong!"

Edith breathed more easily when she heard the dance music, accompanied by a few peals of Sally's laughter. "Then you truly believe there is no danger, Arthur?"

"The chief danger's that he'll fly Penwith as he flew London, and give us the devil of a job to find him again."

"All the same, I must warn the child."

"Edith." He rubbed her fingers. "Let him get just the breeze of a wind of it, and he'll bolt."

Or grow desperate. Edith could not quite trust even Arthur's Bow Street experience to guarantee that a man who might have killed in hot blood once would be harmless in future; but neither could she trust Sally to keep such a secret without inadvertently betraying her suspicion. Continued ignorance would safeguard her better than knowledge. "Well. I shall warn the child that her grandfather is unlikely to approve of any match with a professional musician. Perhaps I ought to have done so before now, but I was persuaded that a touch of harmless calf love at her age would be rather for her good than otherwise." Of course, she would have to warn Sally very gently, very subtly, in order not to inflame the calf love by opposition. "And then, I suppose I thought, if she must play the coquette for a time, it was better she do so with Mr. Armstrong than with Robin—Mr. Jellicoe. But now..."

"Heartbreakers, the lot of you." He swung round in the grass so as to put one arm around her. "But now, you'll take a little pity on Armstrong, too. Ironic, ain't it? If he is Beverton, he's as good a social match as any young woman below a marquess's daughter could ask."

"Assuming his innocence. And if he is innocent, why has he not declared his identity? It may have been understandable in the first few days, if he were merely running from debt or some such thing, but now, when he must surely know of his brother's death, not to come forward can suggest nothing but guilt."

"Or fear. Or some misunderstanding. Well, now I've had my look at him, I can write off to Lady Wyndmont this evening, leave the identification to her. Meantime...yes, if I was inclined to the match-making game, I think I'd try to steer Miss Merryn over to young Jellicoe. Not that I think she's in any danger," he repeated, "but..."

"But the new Lord Wyndmont may be, from a jury of his peers." She closed her eyes for a moment. "I was not matchmaking, Arthur. Young women, like young men, should be allowed their chance to see something of what the world has to offer by way of mates before making their lifetime's choice. The more particularly as the young women are given only the choice of refusal, not that of proposal. If some hearts must be broken along the way, on both sides..." She thought of her brother and his wife with their over-large and threadbare family... "unfortunately, they may be broken as easily after marriage as before, and more irreparably." But who had Edith Parsons been, to try to suggest to a sev-enteen-year-old girl which of two young men's hearts she could risk breaking and which she should be tender to spare? "At any rate, I have done with all that game forever."

"I doubt you haven't. And glad to say it." He held her closer. "It's all a rare muddle, but there'd be no living together this side of the grave if we didn't tangle each other up sometimes. We're all of us heartbreakers, Coz, men and dames alike," he went on as if in belated apology for his earlier remark. "A pretty lot of good we'd be to anybody if we was not."

"All the same, I have done with their affections. Their bodily safety—that is another matter, of course. Ought we not at least tell Mr. Jellicoe our suspicions?"

Arthur rubbed his chin. "Got rather close to in-timacy, have they? Jellicoe and Armstrong?"

"They seem to have done. I suppose the music has provided a sort of ready-existing bond between them."

"Well, even assuming the worst of Armstrong,

Jellicoe don't seem the kind to drive another man into a murdering rage. And on the other hand, we can't be sure but what if he knew, he might warn his new chum. Then, if Armstrong is Beverton, he leaves and we lose him."

Edith sighed. "I suppose I must try to outgrow the governess instinct. After all, Robin *is* a grown man now, and ought to be able to look to himself."

"Not the surest corollary. If all grown men could look to themselves, where would Bow Street be?"

"Where it is now, I suppose, but without its reputation."

He chuckled. "Be that as it may, I think we can trust Jellicoe's safety for another fortnight, and by then all this business should be tidied up."

"Thank God." Edith glanced again at the house as a burst of laughter issued from it, accompanied by the cessation of the flute music.

It is no wonder that he makes so much of my lip, thought Sally, since he makes so much more of his own limp than anyone else would do. "Splendid!" she cried aloud, enjoying the reversal of their roles as teacher and pupil. "Oh, you're doing splendidly! No—no, wait—the beat, Mr. Armstrong, it's—Oh!"

Alas, he topped what would otherwise have been a promising first lesson by slipping halfway through a *dos-à-dos* and tumbling down—brushing her shoulder, too, in his line of fall so that she came down beside him—luckily, plump on the sofa.

She burst into laughter. Neither of the men joined her at once, though in a few seconds, when it became manifest that nobody was hurt, Uncle Robin smiled. Mr. Armstrong did not. "There, you see!"

"Oh, dear, no!" She tried to check her mirth, out of regard for his chagrin, but only went into a fresh peal. "Oh, no, I'm not making sport of *you,* indeed, I'm not," she went on after a moment. "It was—oh, I hardly know myself, both of us together, the sofa cushions, I can hardly say, but certainly not you! Oh, dear, and Hector Vyvyan always says it's the women who cannot laugh at themselves."

"On a true dance floor there would be no sofa ready to catch us. And you may be sure the mirth of our fellow dancers would be directed at myself, whether yours is or not. Assuming we were so fortunate as to escape injury a second time."

"Neither would there be a carpet beneath us on a true dance floor, to slip us up," she assured him, wiping her eyes. "Well, we've surely found out why they roll the carpets back out of the way before they dance, have we not?"

"The sliding of the carpet beneath our feet did not bring about *your* fall, Miss Merryn. It required my clumsiness for that. You cannot blame it on the carpet."

"I can and I will! Why, look there, one can still see the wrinkle from here. And it wasn't only the carpet, in any case. It was the music, too. Uncle Robin!" She looked up at him accusingly. "You began to play faster all at once, did you not?"

He flushed. "I...may have done, I suppose. When one is the only musician, with neither fellows nor concertmaster to maintain the rhythm—"

"Gammon and patter!" said Mr. Armstrong. "And how is it, then, that every female who plays the pianoforte or every fiddler who takes his stand alone at the end of the dance floor maintains the rhythm very well for any number of dancers?"

"Even granting your generalization," the other returned, "which I do not, for I doubt that even you cannot have heard every musician in England, I conceive that both the pianoforte and the violin are better able than the flute to drown the distractions of the dancers' conversation and keep it from the musician's ears."

Mr. Armstrong stood up. Neither man was smiling, and for a moment Sally feared she might have touched off a quarrel. After pooh-poohing the excuse of the slippery carpet, Mr. Armstrong had seized so very quickly—almost violently—upon that of a faulty beat in the music. And Uncle Robin had responded with as much temper as Sally ever saw in him. She was suddenly aware that, at various times, she had done something with each of them that, if it was not actual coquetry, must be very near to it. Could she have made them jealous, and could the very uncomfortable apprehension she felt be the much vaunted triumph of a coquette at the prospect of having two men fight a duel over her?

Then she saw how overdramatic her thoughts had been, for all that Mr. Armstrong did was to cross the room and pick up his own flute from the armchair in which he had left it. "Very well, Jellicoe," he said, turning, "I believe you claimed the next dance. Try whether your conversation can distract *me* into varying the rhythm."

Uncle Robin laid down his flute and grinned. "None of us ever denied you can play rings around me, Tony. But do everything you please with your rhythm, and we'll see whether I can't cut a caper in pace with it without tripping on the carpet."

"Nevertheless," said Edith, although reassured by the resumption of the flute music, "had we not better be going in to the young people?"

"Let 'em worry a little longer about the propriety of their elders' behavior. Edith?"

She had already begun to rise, but he held her back by one hand. She paused and looked at him. "Cousin Arthur?"

"Well ... will you? Be willing to take such a name as 'Mrs. Dromgoole'?"

She was in a physically awkward position—she must rise all the way to her feet soon, or else tumble over. Bracing herself, she stood, tugging at his arm. Fortunately for both their balance, he rose with her. "Coz," she said, "how many servants could we afford?"

"One or two, I suppose. Three, maybe, depending

on the number of our offspring. That's counting in a boy for the stable and garden. I ain't rich, Cousin, and I don't deny that my fee will come handy if I find Lord Wyndmont, but I reckon if I don't collect it we'll still be able to keep our own carriage even if it's a pony-chaise or a whiskey. I've made some decent investments in my time, saved up a pretty fair nest egg, and not gone hungry doing it. A snug cottage with a romantic name in Fulham or Islington, a servant or two for the house and an income for our old age, and if we don't fatten on truffles and champagne, at least we'll keep up our weight on beef and burgundy."

"And at my age, I am no longer very likely to present us with an unmanageable number of children." She smiled. "By the stuff of your garments and the girth of your waistcoat, Cousin Arthur, I suppose that your bank receipts and account books will bear out your financial statement, but will you mind very much showing them me?"

He bowed, his eye twinkling. "I'll take it as an earnest of your rare prudence and business acumen, dear Coz. Never fear, this time Emilia won't find Falstaff a braggart."

"Why, then, of course I shall endure bearing your surname, as your mother must have done before me."

He reached into his pocket, brought out his silver snuffbox, and offered it to her on his palm. "My pledge, ma'am. For you, I'll give up the worst of my bachelor habits."

"Oh, no, dear. I hope we are both too old and wise to try to reform all of one another's bachelor and spinster habits." She curled his fingers up over the box.

He uncurled them again at once. "I'd really as soon you took it, m'dear. I've been meaning to break the habit any time these ten years past."

"Well, then." Smiling, she took the box and slipped it into her reticule. "In that case, I shall accept it in token of any other engagement gift, with

149

the hope that it will indeed prove the worst habit either of us may want to break for our mutual comfort." She tucked her hand into the crook of his arm and they started slowly back to the house. "And so that was what you meant when you said you had 'used' me? Having got your look at Mr. Armstrong through my introduction. In itself, I mind that no more than I objected to being similarly used when I thought it was for the sake of a scholarly tome. But you might have told me the truth earlier, you know."

"Not before I had your answer, love."

"And if, when you saw Mr. Armstrong, you had known at once that he could *not* be Lord Wyndmont, what would have become of your proposal then?"

"I might have left it for June, seeing it's only a few more days. I couldn't have stopped here very long, without the chance of his being Beverton. Though I wouldn't have minded another interview with Sir Despard. Odd thing, this, his leaving home again so sudden."

"Not so odd, when you know something of his freaks. His uncle, the late baronet, who had the raising of him, was much the same in that respect. You *will* be careful of meeting him alone, Arthur?"

He rubbed her hand. "We don't even know he'll be back before my business with Armstrong is done. But I wouldn't have gone from here without knowing whether and when I could come back for you."

"And you would have told me all this in any case, I trust, when you did offer? For if you had not told me what you suspect of our music teacher, Cousin, I should most certainly have refused you in the end." She sighed, not unhappily. "Well, I had thought to remain with Sally long enough to see her married, but I suppose she is really old enough to care for her own affections. And then, she still has her grandparents, of course. And I certainly do not wish to lose any more time than strictly necessary before starting in to decorate and furnish that cottage in Fulham or Islington."

He acknowledged this assurance of a short engagement by pressing her arm. "There's another reason I wanted to tell you about Beverton, Coz."

"Because you trusted me to help you keep the secret from everyone else? No, that is hardly a reason, unless it were meant as flattery."

"It's part of my work to mistrust my own suspicions. I wanted to be sure the facts pointed the same conclusion to you."

This might also be flattery, but it augured well for the pattern of their married life. If she was to have a husband engaged in such a profession as his, she would much prefer to be kept abreast of the details of his work.

She pecked his cheek. "And now, my dear, I think we really must go in. They seem to be doing safely enough by themselves today, but I shan't be quite easy in my mind to leave them alone again for any length of time until the dowager countess arrives."

Chapter 15

The Rendezvous

Her second meeting with Sir Despard cost Sally much plotting and laying of plans, with the secret enlistment of her friend Diana Vyvyan as accomplice. On the fatal day, Sally was to pay a morning visit to The Gables, during the course of which Diana would propose, as if impromptu, a ride and picnic luncheon along the cliffs. The riding horseback was to discourage Miss Parsons' attendance as chaperon (fortunately, the two young ladies were enough of a size that Diana could lend Sally a riding habit) and the picnic luncheon was to provide a basket for the carrying and temporary concealing of the flute. Once returned home to The Gables, Diana could slip the instrument into the folds of her full riding-skirt in the entrance hall and later bring it forth as if from her room, announcing it as an item Sally had engaged Brother Hector to buy for her on his last trip to Plymouth. This ruse should cause the minimum of comment, since young Mr. Hector Vyvyan always returned from his excursions upcountry with at least half a carriage full of articles procured on behalf of friends and neighbors.

The Wednesday dawned clear, and the visit to The Gables could proceed without postponement, but as it turned out Hector was at home that morning and insisted on riding along with his sister and her friend in place of a servant or chaperon. He had already been taken sufficiently into the secret to ensure that he would not deny having purchased the flute himself; only his extreme good nature and the fact that the three had grown up together in childhood pranks enabled him to trust Sally far enough to agree to this much without fuller knowledge of where, in fact, the item would come from, and now they had perforce to reveal more of the plot to him, which they did not do until they had reached their old favorite picnic site, a partially enclosed stone formation they called Pillicock's Castle because it might or might not be the remains of an ancient settlement.

"So Sal's going to a rendezvous," said Hector, with a trace of brotherly concern but without the slightest trace of jealousy, for, despite or perhaps due to some old notions of the elder Vyvyans and Merryns to unite their two families, Hector had given his heart to Ann Stratton instead. "Not meeting Rob Jellicoe, are you, Sal?" he went on. "No, can't be he, or he would've had me bring him back this flute along with his new canary-bird."

"Perhaps he found an old flute in his lumber-room," Diana suggested. "Or one might even have turned up in old Mr. Crantock's curiosity shop in Penzance."

"Well, dashed if I thought he had it in him to go in for any of this Don Giovanni, clandestine assignation business. Or if I can think *why* he should go it this way with you, come to that. Coming a bit of the romantic in his age, I suppose," said the Vyvyan heir, who had yet to see his twenty-second birthday. "Shall I ride along out of sight and within call, sweet Sal, in case he tries to play the *roué?*"

"Oh, no, I hardly think you need do that!" Sally exclaimed. She and Diana both giggled at the idea of Uncle Robin assaulting anyone. Sally kept her more serious reflections to herself. Not even Diana knew whom she was really going to meet; she had steadfastly cried off telling on the plea of the other party's reticence. Truth to tell, so strong were old habits of thought even in face of personal experience that the adventuress might have accepted Hector Vyvyan's offer were it not for the fear that curiosity was mixed with his concern for her welfare. She supposed that when she came back she must tell her friends that Uncle Robin had not been her rendezvous, or Hector might mention something to him and she would be faced with a still more complicated tangle of deception. But until she returned to the picnic, she might as well let them believe they had guessed the riddle.

So she reasoned when she bade them adieu and set out alone. As her borrowed mount neared the field where she had met Sir Despard a fortnight ago, she began to feel less pleased with the idea that her friends were unlikely to follow her at a distance. But then, Sir Despard might not be able to come, after all. As of this morning, she had still heard no reports of his return from this latest mysterious journey. In one way, of course, that worked to her advantage, for not even Hector and Diana would have been inclined to let her ride away alone if the baronet were known to be in his own country. Perhaps he had realized this and come home in secret, late at night, so as to facilitate her task.

Or perhaps he had only been making sport of her that other Wednesday a fortnight ago, and never intended to meet her at all! For a moment this idea seemed almost welcome. Then the relief was overwhelmed by indignation that he should use her so. She half made up her mind that if he were not already waiting for her in the appointed field, she would ride back to the picnic at once.

When she came in sight of the field, however, she saw that all these thoughts had been idle, for Sir Despard was there waiting. He had tethered his mount to a little wooden stake which, though driven so deep as almost to have disappeared in the grass, seemed hardly adequate for holding the great black mare—surely an animal from his own stables, this time. But the horse was in something of a lather, as if she had been galloped along the seashore in the sand, and so she appeared content enough to stand

and browse, her muscles twitching now and again, her tail whisking round her flanks. Her master was striding up and down the field, not as if impatiently or apprehensively, but still from time to time flicking his riding switch against the top of his high, polished Hessian boots.

He must have been deep in his thoughts, for she saw him before he lifted his head at the sound of her approach. "Sir Despard!" she called when she was near enough to hail him without shouting.

He turned and stood facing her, his riding switch now held behind his back. "My Lady Pisky. I was unsure until this moment whether I might expect a second visitation or whether I must content myself with a reverie of the first. Indeed, I am not yet sure whether you are manifest in the flesh this time, or a mere illusion wrought by my desire."

"Here, then." She rode to within ten or fifteen yards of him, stopped, and held up the light stake she had brought along for tethering her mount. "Tie up my horse for me, if you please, and see whether that does not persuade you of our reality."

"It will persuade me, at least, of the reality of the horse." He covered the ground between them in long, unhurried strides and helped her dismount before tethering her horse at some little distance from his.

Whilst he completed this operation, Sally walked about in circles, taking consciously dainty steps and flicking her borrowed riding switch at the wildflowers until she realized that by hitting she spoiled them. "You had promised me a flute, sir," she said, "but I do not see one. You did not fail to lay hands on it, after all?"

"Lady Greed," he remarked. "For a few moments I had assumed that your asking me to tether your mount indicated some intention on your part of remaining in my company for a little while, but now I see that all your interest lies in collecting your gift."

"Oh, no, of course it does not. How can you speak so?"

"I breathe again. But then, I had forgot. The second half of your motivation will of course be concern for our Midsummer Ball."

"I—I confess I had begun to worry a little. You've been away so long, and nobody has said anything, so it seemed you'd left no sort of instructions..."

"I assure you, it will be the talk of four hundreds by tomorrow week, with invitations sent to all the gentle families of Kirrier, Powder, and Pyder as well as Penwith."

"Oh...Oh, I shall be quite outshone," Sally replied, less from vanity than from a lack of anything else to say.

"I think not. It is to be a masked ball, if you remember, and even with the lower part of the face left bare, it is rather difficult, in lantern light, to adjudge one dominoed female fairer than the rest."

"You do not flatter me, sir."

"I beg your pardon, madam. I believe that I paid you a fair enough bit of flattery on your arrival, and I was unaware that you wished for a continued deluge of such fulsome praise as any shallow fop can, with a modicum of study, bestow upon any equally shallow dame. Very well. You need have no fear of being outshone, my lady fair, for you yourself must in all certainty outshine the very lanterns and illumine our poor pavilion more brightly than sun, moon and stars; and, far from fearing the competition of the beauties of Kirrier, Powder, and Pyder, I should have thought you would welcome the opportunity of having so many more luminaries of lesser brightness to offset your own charms, as foil is used to show off a diamond to its best advantage." Having tethered her horse, he approached her, made an elaborate bow, and took her hand. "Now. Shall I kiss it or shake it? Which does my lady prefer?"

She giggled and closed her fingers round his before he could lift her hand to his lips. "Oh, shake it, by all means. But will it really be so dark in the dancing pavilion?"

"The moon will be waned to a sliver, and the bonfire far below us on the beach, where the commoners' coarse songs will not disturb our gentler revels. Nevertheless, as you once suggested, we will create our own Vauxhall in miniature, with a hundred Chinese lanterns to keep the shadows at bay. Candles, of course, we must not count upon, lest the souls passing to and fro that night puff out their fragile flames; but the hundred lanterns and perhaps a few torches should suffice to illuminate the refreshment tables. No, it need not be so very dark in our pavilion. As for the banquet tables, those, I think, we shall raise up on trestles at the proper time, in the medieval fashion."

"I see I needn't have worried a bit. My dear, you must have been thinking about it a great deal all the time you were from home."

He smiled in such a way that she wondered what she could have said to amuse him. "Did you call me 'my dear' because it's a common enough pattern of speech in the West country," he asked, "or because you feel the true stirrings of friendship for me, little love?"

"Why, I . . . I have come to meet you here, have I not? What does that show if not that I trust you, and there certainly cannot be trust without friendship, sir."

"You think not?" He shook his dark head. "Child, child, I may trust my enemy to do his utmost to slay me. I may trust some man of honor to abide by his word, though I feel neither liking nor animosity for him, any more than he for me. Or I may love a gallows'-bait as a bosom friend, yet know that, given the opportunity, he would bilk me of my last farthing. The emotions of friendship and trust are neither interdependent nor yet mutually exclusive, as you may someday learn at first hand."

"But, however, trust is surely one base for friendship. Surely you must admit that much, sir?"

"Very well, ma'am. To please you, I admit it."

"Oh. Thank you." Her easy victory might be no real victory at all, but it did put a period to that particular debate. "But perhaps it will be a very calm evening, you know, and admit of candles."

"You cannot imagine that mere candles will furnish us more light than lanterns and torches?"

"No, of course not. But candles would look so very elegant on the tables. After all, the dancers themselves must cause so many drafts in a regular ball room, and then in the warm weather they open the windows, too, so if it should be a calm night, there ought not be that much greater difficulty in keeping the candles alight."

"I did not say the natural winds of heaven would endanger the candle flames, my dear, though they are hardly like to be perfectly still for very long at any time upon a sea-cliff."

"No, you said 'the spirits passing to and fro,' I think. But I took it you were speaking poetically—"

"I was speaking in deadly earnest. Have you never heard that on Midsummer Eve the souls of all those living persons who are so bold as to fall asleep leave their bodies for an hour and pay their nocturnal visit to whatever place they are doomed to meet the final separation?"

"Oh, you cannot be serious, sir!"

"So the ancient Celts believed, and until it can be proved otherwise, I see no reason for discounting the theory. I myself, on such Midsummer Eves as I have dozed off to sleep, have almost invariably dreamed of the place in which I am like to meet my death."

"That have I not, and I have never watched all the night through on Midsummer Eve."

"And can you swear to it that all your Midsummer slumbers have been dreamless, or that, having dreamed of some particular site, you have not simply failed to take note of and remember the fact?"

She shuddered a little. "I know that if one watches all night in the church door on Midsummer Eve, one is supposed to see the souls of everyone who will die that year, all coming past in procession. But Miss Parsons says such stories are only nonsense and superstition, so I have never been tempted to try it. Besides, all the people who are supposed to have tried it always see themselves in the procession."

"Then we will prudently avoid all church doors on Midsummer Eve. And have you never turned your shift inside out and hung it over your chair on that night, to see your future husband enter and turn it rightside for you at midnight?"

"Oh, yes, I did try that once, last year," she confessed. "It was the first time I had a fair chance of doing it without fear of Miss Parsons finding out... You won't tell Miss Parsons I did it, will you? Not that she would give me such a severe scold, she would only laugh and call it foolishness, but..."

He laughed. "I assure you, child, that I have not the slightest ambition to make the acquaintance of this Miss Parsons, whom I assume to be your dragon of a duenna, let alone inform her of your harmless experiments."

"She is not at all a dragon, and I trust you *will* make her acquaintance, sir, because I know that Grandfather and Grandmother will never allow me to come to the ball unless Miss Parsons accompanies me, and besides, you'll hardly be able not to meet her if you ever begin to pay us proper visits at Bolventor House."

"Very true," he agreed. "Well, don't deprive me of that most important part of any experiment, its result. Did your future husband manifest himself, or did he not?"

"He did, I think, but I could not quite see him clearly. I thought... I thought he might not even be anyone I had been introduced to yet. But then, in the morning, my shift was still inside-out, so it must have been only a dream."

"Ah, but the fortunate lover comes only in apparition, and one can hardly expect an apparition to make a thorough job of turning a garment, though he may try and even seem, at the moment, to succeed. And you've only met me this year. Had he my height, perhaps? My complexion, or the breadth of my shoulders?"

She glanced down to hide the blush that she did not feel, but guessed she ought to feel. "Why, sir? Did you doze off last Midsummer and dream of coming to my room?"

"I dreamt of entering some young lady's chamber and turning her shift," he replied, a smile flickering around his face. (Sally saw it because she had not been able to keep her gaze modestly on his boots for very long.) "Among other, less pleasant dreams," he went on. "But not all previewings of the future are grim. I did not recognize the young lady. I saw that she had golden ringlets and was delicately pale and daintily slender, and I guessed she was of some estate by the fine quality and excellent workmanship of the garment—"

"It was one I stitched myself," she interrupted eagerly.

"Was it? But you see, at that time, I had not met you."

"No, and nor are you the only gentleman I've met this past year, sir," she added, recollecting herself. "I have also met Mr. Armstrong, and now I consider it, the man I saw last Midsummer Eve could just as well have been he as you."

"Ah, yes. Mr. Armstrong—your music-master, as I recall? The professional musician in whose opinion your mouth is misshaped for blowing a flute?" Sir Despard shrugged. "Some common sense, I believe, should be applied to the interpretation of these portents. Wealthy and gently-born young ladies do not commonly marry struggling young professional musicians of the unemployed-servant class."

She felt tempted to retort that they did on occasion

marry amateur ones; but all she said was, "Well, Sir Despard, you really must have a chat with Mr. Dromgoole. He's come to our country in search of just such old tales and superstitions, you know, to make them into a book."

"Mr. Dromgoole? I shall make a note of it to welcome him on your recommendation, should any party of that name seek me out. Meanwhile, I regret that this year our ball must prevent your repeating the test of your shift and possibly obtaining a clearer look at your future husband. But perhaps we shall be able to replace that imperfect prophecy with one at once more natural and more plain."

Sally hardly heard these last sentences, because something was perplexing her about Sir Despard's reaction to Mr. Dromgoole's name, and after a few seconds she realized what it was. "But have you not met Mr. Dromgoole already, sir? He is Miss Parsons' cousin, and he must have arrived in St. Finn on the same day you did, two weeks ago today... Yes, for he first came to visit us that Thursday, when I was being kept in, and she had met him at the mail coach the day before. And she saw you descend from it, too—it must have been at the same time, for she was only in St. Finn the once that day, and..."

Sir Despard shrugged. "Well, the thing is possible. So this Mr. Dromgoole was my traveling companion? But the chance sharing of a mail coach, like other temporary associations of mere convenience or necessity, does not constitute a true introduction, nor obligate the parties to recognize one another afterwards."

She could not quite understand how he could have forgot a man with such a surname, even if Miss Parsons's cousin had not turned out to be one of the jolliest old gentlemen she had ever met. But she decided to let the matter drop. "We have not been regularly introduced, either, Sir Despard," she pointed out with a touch of mischief.

"Alas, no. But that will be rectified within these

three weeks at the uttermost, and I trust that the originality of our first meetings will not prevent you from cultivating my acquaintance when we have descended to more everyday and conventional social intercourse."

"Of course it will not! But I must pretend, just at first, never to have met you before, you know."

"The masks," he said, "will help to ease us over any initial awkwardness in the transition. Masks free their wearers to some extent from the need for propriety in the strictest sense."

"Is that why folk light bonfires and dance round them on Midsummer Eve, Sir Despard?" she asked suddenly, in a slight shift of the subject. "To keep from falling asleep and dreaming of the places where they are going to die?"

"In part, perhaps. And in part, I fear the bonfires have a still more sinister origin. The word, you know, derives from 'bone-fires,' or fires fueled with bones."

For a moment she seemed to glimpse Sir Despard as if he might have been an olden Druid. She shuddered again, and the illusion was dispelled. "Well! Well, sir, if you have indeed brought back the flute you promised, had you not best give it me? I fear I cannot remain much longer, or my friends may begin to worry after all, and come in search of me."

"Your friends? The agreement, miss, was that you were to come alone. It's a cheap trust that relies upon friends out of sight and within call."

"But they are not within call, Sir Despard. They are fields and fields away, and they haven't the least notion that it's you I've come to meet. Why, did you think I would be able to get away so easily a second time without making at least a show of propriety about it? We are supposed to be on a picnic—in fact, we are on one, and I am beginning to be very hungry for my share of the basket," she finished with a little laugh.

"And who might these accommodating companions be?"

Something—she could not have said what, unless it were that brief vision of him as a Druid of ancient times—prompted her to reply, "I am keeping your name secret from them, sir, and they are keeping the secret of my having slipped away from them for this rendezvous. It seems only fair that I also keep their names a secret from you."

"I see. My accursed reputation again." He laughed. "Well, it seems I must respect your confidence and rely upon your unknown friends' discretion. Now, the flute."

He crossed to his horse. She put up her head, nickered, and stamped at his approach. He stroked her nose and neck, saying, "Now, now, my Nightmare. For this moment have you been guarding the treasure," and she quieted, only twitching her ears once or twice as she lowered her head to continue browsing.

Sir Despard went around to the horse's other side, where she hid his actions from the young woman's sight. Unable to contain herself, Sally also walked round, careful to make a wide circuit of Nightmare, and at length reached the other side, just as Sir Despard was fastening up his saddlebag again, having taken out a bundle that now peeped from beneath his right elbow.

He turned and shook his head at Sally. "Go to the horse, thou creature of impatience; consider her ways, and learn restraint."

"Yes, but I think you have rode her very hard this morning, have you not, sir? So that it's small wonder if she is very patient to stand still now and rest."

"I have rode her to London and back within this past fortnight, with time enough spent in the city for a workman to fashion the box you are about to hold. If I have whipped her into a lather this morning, it's no more than she's accustomed to. Yes, I know how to ride my mares well and long and hard." Giving Nightmare a final pat on the flank, he returned to Sally and held out the bundle. It was longish, oblong, and looked rather bumpy, being wrapped up in canvas and bound with twine. "I would have removed the outer coverings before presenting it," he told Sally, "but now, madam, for your impatience, you must perform that office yourself."

The knots, though tight, were simple, and she had them undone almost as soon as she could stop her fingers from quivering with excitement. The canvas wrappings came off to reveal a smooth zebra-wood box, polished to a high gloss and decorated with its own natural markings. It was hinged, and the back hinges were to her. Seeing this, Sir Despard discarded the canvas and twine with a graceful sweep of one arm and turned the box, presenting her with the catch. She sprang it, lifted the lid, and looked down at a creamy white porcelain flute, painted with sprigs of dainty flowerets in blue, rose, and pale green, and nestled in a bed of green satin.

"Oh-h-h," she breathed, staring at it for some moments before she dared actually touch it. "Oh, Sir Despard, I did not even know they made such lovely flutes!"

"A previous owner called its name Meadowsong. Well, child," he said, sounding amused, "lovely as it may be to the eyes, I presume it was crafted to be at least equally lovely to the ears."

With the utmost care, she plucked it up from the satin, held it to her lips, and tried to play a scale. B and C came out tolerably well—as well, at least, she thought, as she had played them on Uncle Robin's more commonplace boxwood flute—but the other notes ranged from troublesome to unproduceable, and it was not that she did not know them, for by now she could finger the entire scale quite surely. "Well...Well, I daresay it is the newness," she explained, feeling an unfeigned blush as she returned the flute to its case. "Its newness to me, I mean. Mr. Armstrong says that every musician must learn his own instrument as every rider learns his own favorite mounts."

"Whatever Mr. Armstrong's opinion may be of your playing, I have no more objection to hearing you become acquainted with your instrument than I would have to watching a blossom unfold its petals for the honeybee."

"Oh, but—but I have, sir! No, I shall play a concert for you when I can do it well, but until then, I must have my time quite alone with—with Meadowsong, was it?" He nodded, and she hurried on, "After all, some privacy is absolutely requisite for the growth of any intimacy with a friend, is it not? Even if the friend is only a musical instrument."

"Perhaps especially if the new friend is a musical instrument," he agreed, "and one as delicately constituted as our Meadowsong. I believe that the olden folk ascribed souls even to inanimate objects, and, since the soul is sometimes associated with the breath, an instrument that is animated with its player's breath must have a great claim to be considered as possessing a soul."

"Yes—Oh, I do like that! But your arms must be growing tired." She closed the box over its precious contents and clicked the catch. "It *will* hold, will it not? You are quite sure it's a very sturdy catch?"

"Had I entertained the least doubt, I should have had the craftsman employ three catches to fasten his box, not merely one."

Nevertheless, she tested it several times, shook the box a little—very, very gently at first—to satisfy herself that the padding was tight and sufficient, and then insisted on bundling up the whole again in its canvas and twine, lest any harm should come to the zebra-wood between here and her picnicking friends. "Oh, I hope our basket will be long enough to carry it back in...Yes, I'm sure it must be." At the last, she threw her arms around Sir Despard and kissed his brown cheek, out of pure gratitude.

"And now," she said, a little embarrassed by her impulsive display, "I really must be getting back, or they will have eat up the entire luncheon and left nothing for me."

"True. There is some limit to the fortitude of even the staunchest friendship, when balanced against a well-laden picnic basket." He untethered her horse, helped her into the saddle, handed up the flute in its ample wrappings, and shook her hand once more before they parted.

"Poor child," he murmured as he watched her ride away at a walk, carrying the bundle as carefully as if it were eggs tied up in a kerchief. "May you have pleasure in your new toy for three weeks, at least, since you may wish to shatter it over my head on Midsummer Day....Still, it's a long enough time, three weeks. The novelty of any new plaything may wear off of itself in a fortnight and a half." With this comforting reflection, he untethered and re-mounted Nightmare. "But our third meeting," he remarked, with one backward glance at the young horsewoman, who was almost out of sight by now. "Our third meeting, and then will my patience be repaid. Until Midsummer Eve, Miss Merryn. Until Midsummer Eve."

Chapter 16

Cynthia

On a wet Friday morning in mid-June, Tony Armstrong hired old Tremiggan's donkey Jinny, wrapped his manuscript and his flute in linen and oilcloth before stowing them in the saddlebag, and rode up to Oakapple Farm. He and his librettist had adopted the custom of meeting to work on their opera when the weather discouraged outdoor employment. The agriculturist had offered to come down to Pennyquick on such days, but the musician preferred temporary escape from his village lodgings, which became drabber with drab daylight.

The work progressed to neither man's satisfaction this morning, and it was to both their credit that, with the help of an urn of coffee and several conversational forays into other topics than the opera, they kept their artistic tempers for the best part of two hours.

As the clock struck ten-thirty, Robin held up a sheet of manuscript music and said, "This is not the sort of melody I had in mind when I wrote the Lady of the Lake's aria."

"No more are the words you wrote the sort of lyric *I* had in mind for that particular aria." The composer plucked the sheet from the librettist's hand. "But listen to it as it ought to sound."

Tony played several bars on his flute, while Robin tried to listen impartially and still found the tune wanting. Then his new pet canary, Pirripip, burst into an aria of his own, as if desiring to add his small assistance to the composition of the musical drama.

"And Pirripip has done it without the benefit of a quarter-dozen keys in his throat." Robin had never stopped maintaining the basic superiority of the simple, single-keyed flute.

"Quite true, but neither has Pirripip half a dozen fingerstops in his silvery windpipe." Tony sighed. "I fear that enharmonic differences are a refinement that must forever escape Miss Merryn's skill, even if it were not for her Cupid's bow, as long as she persists in trying to play upon that porcelain toy. I wonder at young Vyvyan's being gulled into bringing her back such a fallal in preference to a real instrument."

"That lad never did have an ear for music, unless it's Miss Stratton's singing. He must have bought it for its appearance, without so much as thinking of having it tested for tone."

"But Miss Merryn, too—determined to squeeze melody out of a pipe that's only fit for a china shepherdess. It's unlike her. She had seemed..." Leaving this statement unfinished, Tony heaved a deeper sigh. "She does not...have a predilection for Vyvyan, does she?"

"Hector Vyvyan? No, hardly for Hector Vyvyan, I think!" Robin attempted a chuckle. "Besides, he and Miss Stratton have been as good as engaged this twelvemonth and more. No, I believe that Sally's—Miss Merryn's—infatuation is all for...all for her preposterous porcelain pipe," he finished, catching himself just as he had been about to say, with a probable touch of bitterness, all for Mr. Anthony Armstrong. "It does have a sort of quaint prettiness, you'll have to admit."

"Oh, yes. Prettiness. But not her kind of prettiness. Not, at least, in my judgment."

"Oh?"

"I should call Miss Merryn far too resilient, too natural for a trinket of prettified porcelain."

"It is always of interest," said Robin, "to hear the opinions a comparative stranger may develop in a short time concerning a young lady one has oneself known for years."

For a few moments they sat silent, and Pirripip began to sing again. Tempted to voice some envy of Armstrong's gift for winning a young lady's affection, or some sarcastic advice to approach her grandfather and see how far he might succeed in winning permission to pay his addresses in a more regular manner, Robin managed to hold his tongue by avoiding the other's gaze until the effort seemed to become a reversal of that old game of trying to break one another down by staring directly into one another's eyes. Struck at last by the ludicrous aspects of this comparison, he stole a glance, and was surprised to catch, in the instant before Tony looked away, an expression that almost suggested Tony had been regarding *him* with something akin to envy.

"Well," said Tony, rising and stretching his limbs, "back to work." He lifted both their cups, returned one to the table when Robin shook his head, and refilled his own. "I think the chiefest difficulty is that you have yet to draw the relationship between the brothers correctly."

"We had agreed, I seem to recall, that it was to be mixed with a certain degree of rancour."

"Yes, but..." Reseating himself, the composer swallowed some coffee and shuffled through the manuscript. "Here, take the penultimate scene, for instance. The climax. The battle."

"I thought it rather an original touch to have Balin recognize his brother at the crucial moment and strike home—in retribution for a thousand small old grievances—before realizing the conclusiveness of his act."

For an instant Tony seemed on the verge of crumpling the paper, but instead he slapped the manuscript down on the table, causing Robin's cup to rattle in its saucer. "Well, I find it out of character. Besides, Balin is the older brother. If either of them had borne the greater brunt of the relationship, it would have been Balan as the younger."

"Oh, you think so, do you?"

For a moment Robin wondered what deep chord so simple a retort could have struck; his friend seemed actually to pale. "I take it," said Tony, "that you have never had a brother. Forgive me if I touch upon a tender subject."

The tender subject, of course, being Robin's orphanhood.

"Balin shall *not* recognize his brother," Tony went on. "Come to that, though, where is it actually wrote in Malory's book that Balin is the elder?"

"Bless me, you may be right. We may have merely assumed it because Balin's the more prominent. Now I suppose you'd prefer him the younger?" Robin shrugged and picked up the manuscript. "Well, I'll see whether we can't rearrange their respective ages without doing too much violence to the poetry. And if Sir Thomas does anywhere state Balin to be the older, it won't be the only detail we've diddled a bit." He scribbled "Balin the younger??" on the slate he used for such revisatory memoranda. "Have you any further changes to demand of me today? You'd best have a little pity, for my slate's all but filled as it is."

"Your choice, Rob. Use a sheet of foolscap for once and damn the extra expense, or be content with the knowledge that what revisions I don't request today, I'll save up for another time."

"And find more in the interim."

"Most like." Tony drained his cup. "I could wish there were some worthier damosel in the tale. If we were to make the principal soprano more lovable, more of an innocent lily-maid, and thus heighten the tragedy when the castle falls upon her..."

"I find that lady perhaps too lovable for the best dramatic effect as she is—I modelled her on our dear Miss Parsons, you know. Any more so and her death in the fourth act would overshadow the tragedy of Balin's and Balan's in the fifth."

"I trust you didn't model her slain lover upon Dromgoole?" After sharing a chuckle, Tony went on, "But I had in mind some role... some role that might suit Miss Merryn. If she could sing."

"What, you'd have a castle fall on Miss Merryn?"

"No more than you'd have a real one fall on her good governess!... But a pure young being... golden and innocent..." Tony shook his head as if to clear it. "No, not in this opera, but I think perhaps my next shall be the story of Elaine, the Lily Maid of Astolat, and dedicated to Miss Sally Merryn."

"Then you'll want another librettist, for I cannot by any stretch of my imagination picture Miss Merryn allowing herself to pine away for the love of a single gallant, not even if he were the peerless Lancelot."

"No, you may be right. Fortunately for Miss Merryn. Very fortunately for Miss Merryn..."

"There's the tale of Sir Alisander and his Lady Alice," Robin suggested, having dipped his way through a considerable portion of Malory's book whilst preparing his own text. "There might be a promising role in that for someone like Miss Merryn. The damsel who buffets the knight half off his horse?" Robin wished he dared give Tony a buffet or two. Let the talk turn to Sally, and the musician's mood fluctuated to a sort of melancholy earnestness that his friend misliked for more reasons than one, and for all their sakes. "Of course," he went on, "Dame Alice's tale might be most fit for an *opera buffa.*"

By now, however, Tony seemed no more than half listening. "Will she want her lesson as usual on Tuesday? With the ball following the next day? I believe that young ladies want as much time as possible to prepare for a ball."

"Well, she'll want her lesson tomorrow, in any

event, unless this rain continues. We can settle the question then."

"What may be more to the point, will you wish to spend your hours hosting us again? With that officious scoundrel FitzNeil having called us to an extra rehearsal Tuesday night, as if one were needed."

Neil FitzNeil was the sort of whom it was difficult not to speak unpleasantly. Robin was glad that Tony had bestowed the epithet and saved him the trouble. "Well, he may be driving us on his master's instructions. Sir Despard is paying us handsomely enough to justify some solicitude for the quality of services rendered, and young Killigrew does tend to let his violin squeak at times."

Tony shifted his legs. "Has the rain let up a bit? Think I'll pay a visit to the dunegan."

"Take the bone-handled umbrella from the stand by the kitchen door." Going out through the kitchen cut in half the walk to the necessary house at the bottom of the garden.

"Thanks, old fellow." Tony cocked his head, listening to the rain. "Should I swing on the old cloak, too? No, it sounds slacked off and steady."

"If you fear dissolving in the elements, you can always use the closestool."

Tony clapped one hand on Robin's shoulder. "Gammon! The stroll will do me good." He crossed the room, but paused at the door long enough to say, "All the same, Rob, if I had your means, I'd think again about fitting a nice little closet into that cubbyhole beneath the stairs."

Tony's suggestion did bear some pondering, though not, probably, for the reasons he had had in mind. If anything were ever to come of certain hints Sally had seemed to be dropping this spring, then Robin must plan on enlarging his bachelor home, bringing it more into line with what she was accustomed to at Bolventor House.

But this depended, at least for the present, upon whether Sally's behavior towards him had indeed been what it had sometimes seemed earlier this year, or whether, as had seemed the more likely these past few weeks, he had been building himself an air-castle. He sighed and, partly to turn his thoughts, fell to studying Tony's flute where it lay in the armchair, just within reach if one stood and leaned across the coffee table.

Robin had been more swayed than he would so far admit by his musician friend's arguments in favor of the many-keyed instrument. But whereas a skilled musician like Tony Armstrong could master the use of four keys to help him achieve sharps, flats, and enharmonics without loss of tone purity, would it be so practical for a dilettante? Robin had often been tempted to experiment with Tony's flute, and now, his head still half muddled with Sally Merryn, indoor waterworks, and Pirripip's warbling, he stood up, leaned across the table, and got Cynthia into his hands almost without remembering her master's jealousy. The musician had not, after all, had occasion to remind them of it for some weeks.

A sudden increase in the sounds of rain and wind coinciding with Robin's touch upon the flute caused him to start as he lifted her. But now that the deed had been perpetrated, would it so much compound his guilt to essay a few notes in Tony's absence? Robin both hoped that Tony had gained the shelter of the dunegan before the fresh downpour, and guessed that the new violence of the weather would keep him there until it subsided again. No better opportunity might ever present itself.

Robin put Cynthia to his lips and blew. The tone sounded clear enough, but—perhaps it was only his old fascination with the unusual length of the head-joint above the blowhole—it seemed to him a trifle sharp. He tried to adjust the tuning-screw, but—as he now remembered Miss Parsons having discovered and Tony having explained some time ago—the knob at the tip of the headjoint was a mere decoration, made to resemble the small tuning-screws of such other flutes as possessed this convenient feature. On Cynthia, the entire hand's-breadth above the blow-hole constituted the sole tuning mechanism.

A slight twist produced no noticeable flattening of the tone. Robin tried a second twist, then a third. The fourth, somewhat more drastic than the others, did a strange thing indeed to the sound—it became a toneless soughing, as if Robin were the rankest beginner, or as if there were some obstruction in the tube of the instrument.

Sitting, he looked into the blowhole. Was there indeed some sort of foreign object? Where, then, had it sprung from? The hole was too small to admit his fingertip, so he inserted his pencil and found that there did seem to be some sort of thin blade inside the flute. He gave the tuning-screw another turn, and the thing inside moved with it, catching the tip of the pencil. When he extricated it, it seemed to bear a little scar, as of an encounter with a knife.

He continued to turn the overlong tuning-screw. Eventually it loosened...but did not come off in his hand, as the small screw on his own flute would have done. He drew the two sections of Tony Armstrong's instrument apart. A foot or so of oiled steel followed the tuning-screw out of Cynthia's body. He turned it back and forth a little and noticed its shape. Gingerly he put one thumb to its edge and found it keen.

He became aware that the sounds of rain and wind had died again. He looked up. Armstrong was standing in the doorway.

"So you've found out our secret," said Tony.

The other flushed and grinned. "So this is the secret of a sharp tone?" He reinserted the blade a little jerkily. "I...er... wonder what sound a flute might produce if it were made entirely of metal. Not simply...not simply cored with metal, so to speak."

"Brassy. And we have brass enough in our orchestras already, I believe." Tony reclaimed his former seat beside the other on the sofa and deliberately extended his right hand.

"No, not brass, of course. We would hardly want the flute to become a—a sort of smaller bugle or trombone. But if a bit of—steel, is it?"

Tony nodded and moved his hand closer. "Toledo steel. And even at that, the devil to keep free of rust. Perhaps you noticed a few flecks of brown despite all my care?"

The farmer shook his head and began screwing the handle-headjoint into the body again, but continued to ignore Tony's hand. "I take your point. Not steel, then, neither, no more than brass. But silver, perhaps? Or gold, for the prosperous and elegant..."

Tony wiggled his fingers all but beneath the other's nose. "Cynthia is sufficient as she is for a man of my own mettle. Don't turn her screw too tightly, there! You may crack the wood."

Jellicoe moved farther toward his end of the sofa, away from Tony's hand. He looked down at Cynthia, tested her screw once more with a nervous touch. "Well, well, there are aplenty who carry swords in their walking sticks and umbrellas—why not in their musical instruments?" Slowly he laid the flute on her master's palm. "But why keep it secret, Tony? You might start a fashion among musicians?"

Tony closed his fingers round her smooth wood. "She reminds me," he said, "of death concealed in a wood coffin. Who would eagerly display the contents of his brother's coffin?"

Robin stood, refilled his coffee cup, and strolled as if casually to the far side of the armchair. "But if a man lets it be known that he carries such a weapon, you see, he's less likely to be put to the need of using it. At least, that's the favored theory in these parts."

Tony shrugged as casually as he could. "I hope you'll refrain from telling anyone of this? You see, as Cynthia is, I believe she may be unique among musical instruments, and likely jealous of the distinction. I doubt she would not appreciate becoming one of many. Should we set a Cornish fashion with her, she may demand we cut short our stay."

Robin lifted his cup and drank, demonstrating the eyes' potential lack of expression when the lower half of the face was covered. Tony regretted having let slip such a term as "cut short." Fortunately, however, his host seemed to have taken it in stride, for on lowering his cup again he smiled and replied, "If that's your wish, Tony, yes. I'll respect your notions and keep Cynthia's secret. Word of a gentleman. Now, shall we send for a bite of luncheon?"

Tony would have liked to call for brandy, but thought it more prudent not to do so. "When you had your cup to your mouth just now," he remarked, "it put me in mind of an old thought of mine. When only half the face is masked, why does custom make it the upper half?"

Robin laughed. "Probably so that the revellers can eat and drink freely before unmasking. But we can thank Comus it is the custom, for I much question whether all we of the orchestra would have been granted our dominoes for this ball if they were fashioned to mask the mouth instead of the eyes."

It had been Robin's own suggestion that musicians as well as revellers wear masks at the forthcoming Midsummer Ball. That was a stroke of luck for Tony. He might have been safe enough tucked away in the orchestra at the end of a fitfully illumined pavilion; it was not overlikely that any of the Cornish gentry from "upcountry" would be well acquainted with him by sight, though some of them might have been with his brother. But the orchestra was not large, and the flutists sat in the front rank, so Tony had privately rejoiced at the idea of masking and its adoption by the rest of the players. Remembering this now, Tony felt more at ease in his friend's house. The librettist did not seem to have made any connection between Cynthia's concealed blade and Lord Wyndmont's death—indeed, Robin had ever shown himself perhaps the least interested of all West Penwith's inhabitants in what news of the London murder reached this little tip of England, so his unsuspicion was plausible. Tony might be able to remain here awhile longer, after all. At least long enough to collect his share of Sir Despard Rudgwerye's money. Perhaps long enough to finish his opera...though in his soul Tony understood that the opera had become a pretext for drawing out his stay in order to see Miss Merryn as often as possible. He had even come to relish any and all ineptitudes in the libretto, in that they helped prolong the work.

But all this might be changed within the week, Robin's discovery aside. Here, where social events on a large scale were rare, he conceived that each single ball might be made to serve as a proportionately greater marriage mart. And, even though Miss Merryn was but seventeen, and even though her grandparents, by Miss Parsons' testimony, were in no undue haste to find her a husband, still, if the young lady herself were of a more eager mind, if she had indeed been practicing her skills of flirtation with the material at hand in order to sharpen them for the gentlemen to come, and if some petty but personable and untainted country squire should make his entry into her affections on Midsummer Eve...would Tony Beverton then have the strength of will to pocket his musician's fee and use it for immediate departure toward Wales or the north before passion conquered reason and goaded him to pit himself against that country squire?

God help us! he thought, feeling a touch of the mystic, What dreams shall we all be dreaming this Midsummer's Night?

Well, maybe it would rain on Midsummer's Eve.

Chapter 17

The Last Music Lesson

Saturday dawned bright and clear. Edith Parsons could have wished for a continuance of the rain.

On Friday afternoon Robin Jellicoe had braved the still mizzly weather to drive to Bolventor House. Thank God, thought the governess, that he mentioned his business first to me. (Mr. Merryn had been keeping to his study, deep in perusal of his neighbor Mr. Botallack's new mining scheme.)

"I am very much afraid," Robin had confided shamefacedly, "that I may have made a rather serious mistake in giving Mr. Armstrong a good character to you."

Had he, also, come to suspect who Mr. Armstrong might be? Impossible to discover, for he would not confide the grounds of his new misgiving, and Edith, remembering Arthur's words, dared not reveal what she knew, not even when Mrs. Merryn was out of the drawing room for five minutes to find another skein of worsted for her knitting. If the young farmer's doubts had a different basis than theirs, to put the idea into his head of Armstrong's being Anthony Beverton might produce doubly unfortunate results. She did gather that his fears concerned Mr. Armstrong's character with her sex. He left it a moot point whether and how far he would break off his own acquaintance with the musician, but he was of the firm opinion that Sally ought not receive any further musical training from the man—he was so firmly of this opinion that he actually offered to put aside his former hesitancy and take over Sally's instruction himself, if she were still bent upon learning the flute.

Robin obviously remained unaware that Mr. Merryn had not only never given his permission for these flute lessons, but had never been informed of them. Edith's thoughts had darted over the probable consequences of her employer's enlightenment at this point. Edith's part in the deception must cripple her influence with Sally's grandfather, at least for a time; Arthur Dromgoole's entrance into her life made her employer's opinion little threat to her own future happiness, and between Robin's tact and that of Sally's grandmother, they might at last succeed in winning Mr. Merryn's consent to the girl's continued study, under the tutorage of her old friend and adoptive uncle. But in the meantime, to punish his granddaughter, Mr. Merryn would almost certainly forbid Sally's attendance at the Midsummer Ball. His permission had been hard enough to win as matters stood, and Sally would have been heartbroken for a fortnight to lose the treat now.

Mrs. Merryn must have realized this as well. Sally's grandmother and her governess, working together though without benefit of special private consultation, managed to keep Mr. Jellicoe unaware of the state of Mr. Merryn's ignorance. Mrs. Merryn guaranteed to settle the matter with her husband so that he should write Mr. Armstrong a dismissal at once; and, when Mr. Merryn and Sally (who had been upstairs construing Latin in her room) joined the others for tea, the two older women had contrived to steer the conversation clear of dangerous topics.

After Robin's departure, Mrs. Merryn had penned the letter of dismissal herself, in her husband's name, enclosing a banknote in recognition of past services rendered; and Edith had slipped it to Jan the houseboy for delivery that same evening. But everyone, Edith mused with some disgust, remained in the dark as to some greater or lesser aspect of the affair. Poor Sally, for instance, was still unaware that she would not be taking her next lesson from Mr. Armstrong. Her grandmother had left it to her governess to impart the knowledge, but Edith had not found opportunity coincide with resolve that Friday evening, and Saturday morning Sally chattered so, chiefly about the ball, all the way from Bolventor House to Oakapple Farm, that Edith had not a chance to get in half a dozen words together.

"Good morning, Pirripip," was Sally's first utterance on entering Robin's parlor, and she whistled a few notes as if urging the little canary on to more complicated arpeggios than he was already warbling forth. Then the young woman laughed and looked around. "Oh—Where is Mr. Armstrong?" He had never so much as been two minutes late, let alone missed a lesson; indeed, he had once or twice come up in vain on mornings when nasty weather kept his pupil in Bolventor House.

Edith returned Robin's reproachful glance with a smile of apology and a small shrug. "I'm...afraid he won't be here today, Sally."

"What, he's not sick, is he? We've warned him against riding out in the rain and dirt..." Sally's expression puckered into a frown as she gazed at her old mentors, probably struck with the thought that if Mr. Armstrong had caught a cold, the news should have been Uncle Robin's to impart to both ladies at once.

"Well," said Robin, "the truth of it is, it's rather more serious than that...you see...that is to say, I very much fear..."

He coughed and Edith, in a burst of compassion, tried to make up the duty she had left undone. "I ought to have told you last night, Sally. The truth of it is, Mr. Armstrong will not be teaching you any longer. We have learned that his character is—is less satisfactory than we had been led to believe."

Did Sally refrain from throwing her flute case out of concern for its contents or out of confusion which of her mentors to hurl it at? "How can it be less than satisfactory? Have you ever seen him in the least disrespectful? Well, have you? You've always been here to watch us—if you chose. Has he ever—"

"I must take full blame," said Robin, twisting one of his coat buttons until Edith thought she heard threads begin to pop. "It was...something yesterday...when he was here alone with me. I saw at once—I had never suspected before—"

"No? Well, perhaps you should not now, neither! It must have been something—something he said in joke!"

"My dear," said the governess, "surely we can trust Uncle Robin to take all such things into account."

Sally plumped down on the sofa, turning the zebra-wood case in both hands and looking down at Robin's flute, laid ready on the tea table before her. "Well...Well, and who is to teach me now, then?"

The young farmer crossed the room, sat beside her, took his flute from the table and held it out to her. Pirripip sang on in his polished brass cage, and for a few seconds Edith envied his blissful bird indifference to human contretemps.

"It's not because I met him alone that day, is it?" Sally looked up, and Edith noticed with a pang that she was on the verge of tears. "That was only the purest chance that we met—truly it was—and he was as respectful as he could possibly be, as anyone could desire, he was the very...very model of respect. And I have never gone out to meet him at any other time—never! And it was all my fault that day anyhow, it was not his idea at all, so you cannot blame him for it!"

Edith attempted gentle reason. "Sally, dear, if it were anything at all to do with your mischief that day, do you not think we would have forbade you further association with him long before now?"

The girl dropped her flute case into her lap, fumbled for her handkerchief, wiped her eyes, blew her nose, and blinked. "Well, I think it is hideously unfair

181

and unjust. After all your promises about the day when I would begin to meet young men, and now when I have met one—and just when we were getting on so famously, too! But I suppose it is because he's a mere professional musician?" she added with a touch of sarcasm that almost transcended the childish. The look she cast at Uncle Robin suggested it was only through heroic self-control that she stopped short of accusing him of jealousy. "No, thank you," she said, pushing away the boxwood flute he had all this time been holding out helplessly. "I do have my own flute now, you know. I hope you will not try to tell me I must not use Meadowsong any more, either. It was not Mr. Armstrong's gift to me, after all."

"No," said Edith. "Of that, at least, I am sure, or he would not have tried so consistently to persuade you it is a mere porcelain toy." Yet even in her exasperation, the governess could not but feel a little pride in how Sally was carrying herself. Yes, thought Edith, my scholar and protégée is growing up.

And perhaps Robin had deserved that accusing glance. Well as she thought she knew him, Edith still could not be sure whether he really had learned something material against Mr. Armstrong's character, or whether he had at last been teased to jealous desperation. How would Edith herself have reacted to Robin's extremely vague charges, had her Bow Street beloved not shared his intelligence with her?

Sally opened the case and brought out the fragile instrument she had—rather foolishly and prematurely, in Edith's opinion—enlisted Hector Vyvyan to buy for her. "At least," said the young woman, "we need have no more discussions about how many keys a flute is best to have, since mine has but one, also. Very well, Mr. Jellicoe, teach me."

He looked down with a perplexed face at the boxwood flute in his hands. He glanced around the parlor. Trying to send him a look of encouragement, and wondering how much of the expression was actually legible in her eyes and how much it could help him in any case, Edith sat in an armchair and listened to Pirripip. The canary was silent now, but not in anticipation: glancing up, she saw he was preening his feathers.

Robin raised his flute to his lips, more as if at a loss what else to do with it than as if meaning to demonstrate some technique. Then he seemed to change his mind and lowered the instrument without playing a note, although he kept it in his lap with both hands on it, like some sort of buckler or quarterstaff between him and his new student. He coughed. "Well...er...perhaps if you could...I mean if you would...kindly play a...er...the scale in A-flat?"

"Oh," said Sally, "am I permitted to remember what Mr. Armstrong has taught me?"

"Miss Sally Merryn!" said the governess.

"I am very sorry, Miss Parsons." Sally lifted her flute and began to play notes almost as toneless as her voice had been, except that the notes sometimes squeaked and more often wheezed as they shuffled their way upwards.

Edith closed her eyes. She heard Sally begin the descent of the scale, and stop with a gasp in midnote. She opened her eyes and caught her own breath.

Mr. Anthony Armstrong stood in the parlor doorway.

His plain, threadbare brown coat was brushed, his neckcloth tied with even more care than usual, the points of his collar folded down—in deference to the summer heat and dearth of starch in his bachelor laundry—with particular neatness, his hair was combed to a shine and he must have rubbed the journey off his boots just outside the door...and the glower on his face suggested that all this had been done in a cold fury.

Robin and Sally had both sprung to their feet, Robin positioning himself between the young woman and the newcomer, but at the same time keeping his distance. Flexing her leg muscles, Edith slowly eased down her right hand to slip off one of her shoes with its leaded heel.

"You will pardon my letting myself in in this manner," Armstrong stated to the room at large, holding out a folded letter. "I wished to ascertain the meaning of this, and I had received the impression that were I to knock in the customary fashion, I might be turned away at the door without a hearing."

"Oh, Mr. Armstrong!" cried Sally. She stepped towards him, but Robin interposed his arm.

Having barred Sally, the farmer took a step or two forward. "Tony..." he began.

"I believe my more immediate business is with our good Miss Parsons, Jellicoe." As Robin took another step, Armstrong held up his leather flute case. "One shake," he said inscrutably, "and Cynthia is out of her sheath and into my right hand."

Robin stepped back, sweeping Sally farther out of the way at the same time with his outstretched arm.

"Oh!" Sally exclaimed. "Have a care—you almost made me break my flute."

"Miss Parsons," Armstrong went on, striding toward the governess.

She rose, holding the lead-heeled shoe in her right hand, hid behind the folds of her cotton skirt. With her left hand, she accepted the letter from him and flipped it open. It was the same Mrs. Merryn had penned last night. "I should think the meaning of this quite clear, Mr. Armstrong. My employers see fit to terminate your services as their granddaughter's music-master. I believe you should have found a banknote enclosed, equal to what you would have earned during the next fortnight."

"Damme, Miss Parsons, one don't dismiss a man like this without so much as a reason stated, on the same morning when he's dressing to give a lesson!"

"This same morning? You only got it this morning? Who brought it you?"

"I think it was your page, or gardener's boy, or some such. Having been kept out of your house, I can hardly be expected to know your every servant by sight. Oh, don't worry for his sake, madam. I packed him off home again quite unharmed."

"You were meant to have received it last night, sir, but the lazy young brat appears to have feared a wetting in the rain."

"Last night!" He laughed shortly. "I thought as much from the date, madam. Allow me to point out that a few hours' difference hardly deadens the blow—except that had I read this yesterday evening, I would have been here awaiting you this morning, rather than stewing about in my own rooms for half an hour until human endurance could stand no more."

"It was our opinion that human endurance could perhaps better endure a polite dismissal in tactfully vague terms than one stated with full particulars already known to the party concerned," said Edith, aware she might be entrapping herself but able to think of no other reply. "If we were mistaken, so be it. I trust you will at least be content to await a more particular explanation in the privacy of your lodgings, rather than endure the embarrassment of having it out in Miss Merryn's hearing?"

He stared at her a moment, then turned and started back across the room toward the other two. Robin gave Sally a little push and murmured something in her ear. Edith guessed he had urged her to hurry to her governess, but the girl only half obeyed, beginning across but stopping at the far end of the tea table to gaze from one to the other of them.

Armstrong, meanwhile, paused at the near end of the tea table to deposit his flute thereon, still in its case. At this deliberate gesture, Robin stopped retreating and waited just behind the sofa. Can it be, thought the governess, that he supposed Armstrong likelier to strike him with his flute than with his fist?

"I did not break my word, Tony," said the farmer. "Believe me, I did not break my word."

There followed a discussion in low, rapid mutterings between the two men. Edith could not catch more than a word or two; she thought that an accusation of jealousy came into it, and some promise Robin had made to keep a secret of Armstrong's, but Sally destroyed all possibility of her overhearing more by coming to her at last, putting one arm around her in a tacit plea to be hugged and comforted, and whispering, "Oh, Miss Parsons, how could he? He has told you some lie of Mr. Armstrong, has he not? So that we should not see each other anymore. Oh, how could Uncle Robin do anything so mean?"

"He told no lies, my dear." The governess put one arm around the girl and tried to keep one ear on the men's talk (but in vain, for Pirripip chose this incongruous moment to break forth in fresh song). "We have no reason to believe that what little he told us is not true. Indeed, Mr. Armstrong himself is—"

At that second, he was turning to face her again. "Very good, Miss Parsons. You offered to state particulars. If you would be so good as to state them, I will risk the consequences."

"They may be more damning than you expect, sir."

"I might request to hear them from you in private, but I misdoubt you would stoop to so unrespectable an action as being alone with me for even a few moments, so I will accept your witnesses."

He had braved her dare by challenging it, perhaps unconsciously, with a dare of his own. If he had guessed what she and Arthur suspected, if he thought that might be the reason for his dismissal, would he not already be packing to quit Cornwall? Unless he were innocent...but what other secret could he have shared with Robin, if not that he were the new Earl of Wyndmont? No, she thought, I must remember Arthur's practice and question even my own theories. This deep, wicked secret may be no more than some old gambling debt unpaid. Nevertheless, if I were to throw it all in his teeth now, what we believe and why we believe it, *that* would pay him in the coin he is taunting me for. Yes, and it might send him scuttling indeed, as well—a fine thing that would be! *Why* does not Lady Wyndmont come to identify him? I'm sure Arthur wrote her long enough ago.

Aloud, she said the one thing left her to say, under the circumstances. "I fear we owe you a deep and sincere apology, Mr. Armstrong. The fault is not in you, but in us. You see, Sally's grandfather never gave his permission for her to learn the flute; he had never been informed of these lessons."

Robin came round to the front of the sofa and sat heavily, staring at the two women.

Armstrong began to laugh. "That's it? That is it, is it? You have...You've..." Laughing harder, he collapsed beside Robin on the sofa. "And I thought...I thought...Well, never mind what I thought! Oh, lud, what fools we males be!" He slapped the other on the back, then withdrew his arm. "Yes, but I forgot—you're not entirely absolved yet, are you, man? You did put as shabby a trick on me yesterday as was in your power, didn't you? 'Consistent with the word of a gentleman'?"

"Have a care, Armstrong," said Robin. "Make a mock of my word of honor, and I may consider your laughter to have released me therefrom."

Armstrong sobered somewhat, though remaining cheerful. "Well, mesdames," he said, rising and bowing to them. "I see no reason why you should not continue duping the good old gentleman as well now we are in the secret with you as when we were in the dark."

"I see three," said Robin, holding up that number of fingers and folding each one down in turn. "Firstly: that he *is* a good old gentleman, with what he considers his granddaughter's best interests at heart. Whether we consider him correct or mistaken, it is our part to persuade him with reason, not to go behind his back. Second: Where is your pay to come from? It cannot be from Mr. Merryn's purse, and I conceive, if the ladies will forgive my saying it, that their own funds may be—"

"We have managed very nicely so far, have we not?" said Sally.

"Hush, child," the governess put in. "Uncle Robin is quite right. Our funds *are* growing thin, even if Hector Vyvyan did so kindly agree to await indefinitely his repayment for the flute."

"There's the money for my ball gown and—or, no, I don't mean—"

"It is already spent. We cannot draw back now that your dress is ordered. Nor, I think, do you really want a makeshift gown for this grand event."

"Tush!" said Armstrong, waving his hand. "I'll waive my fee."

"That you will not, Mr. Armstrong," Edith told him.

"And lastly," said Robin, having waited some moments to turn down the third finger, "Neither I nor my home will continue a knowing party to the deception."

"Why, you overscrupled old puritan!" said Armstrong.

"Not Puritan. Methodist." Robin glanced again at Armstrong. "I rather think that I could produce another reason or two, if I put my mind to it."

"Can I not at least have my lesson today?" said Sally. "Now that Mr. Armstrong is come up and all..."

"No," said Edith, who was only surprised that Robin had listed his personal scruples last. "We have imposed quite sufficiently for one summer upon these gentlemen, your grandfather, and ourselves. But I see nothing to prevent our enjoying half an hour's visit," she added, noting with private unease how Sally's face brightened again at the words. "But put your flute away at once now, child, so as to have temptation out of the way."

"Oh, very well, then." Sally obeyed, sitting beside

Robin on the sofa and taking her flute case from the tea table. "But if you and Grandmother and Mr. Armstrong and Uncle Robin and I were all to come at Grandfather at once, don't you think we could finally persuade him? I'm sure if he were only to hear Mr. Armstrong play as he's played for us, he *must* be won over."

Edith sighed. "Well, if the gentlemen will bear with us so far, perhaps we may attempt it. But not until after the ball. I think that will keep us fully occupied next week, without additional complots. You know we'll be putting up the Trelawneys and the Gifflets at Bolventor, and I hardly think your grandfather will be more of a mood to hear our arguments, or your grandmother to join our effort at such a time."

Armstrong's sigh was to Edith's as a fresh westerly to a zephyr. "Well, I had meant to have enquired this morning whether Miss Merryn would wish her lesson next Tuesday. I am answered."

"Oh, but I would have wanted it, Mr. Armstrong! But we'll approach Grandfather so soon as the Gifflets are gone home again—Mr. and Mrs. Trelawney may stay on for a week, but Grandfather gets on very well with them, so if we can persuade them to aid us, too... oh, I'm sure it will come out well, and you'll be teaching me again within the fortnight. Cupid's bow and all."

Edith sat, gave Robin a nod to tell him she would keep an eye on the others whilst he arranged for refreshments, and began the process of returning her shoe to her foot as unobtrusively as possible.

"After the ball," said Armstrong. "Yes, Miss Merryn, if you are still of a like mind after next Wednesday evening..."

"But I will be! Of course I will be."

Armstrong sat beside her, though at a respectful enough distance to cause no more than a momentary tightening in the cords of Edith's neck.

"Do you know," Sally went on, "until now, I do

not think I could even imagine anything after the ball. It was as if life would stop there and we would all go on dancing forever, as if we must all be translated somehow directly into Heaven."

"That sounds rather blasphemous," Edith commented. "As well as not quite comfortable."

"But now I shall have something to go on looking forward to, after the ball! If only all goes well with Grandfather...oh, it must! Promise me you will persuade him?"

The governess thought Armstrong was about to take Sally's hand, but he refrained. "I promise I will approach him and do my utmost, if you make the request of me once more when the dancing and frivolity is done."

So the morning seemed to end amicably, but Edith's relief was fragile. Armstrong might be satisfied with the explanation she had given him, but were the others? Robin might have accepted her ploy for the protection it seemed to offer him against Armstrong's wrath, or he might have been too shocked at learning of the deception they had practiced on him to examine matters more closely at once; but he was certainly aware that his own warning of yesterday afternoon had more to do with the attempted break than Edith had admitted. And from what she had heard of the words that passed between the two men, she was convinced the farmer did know something new and potentially alarming about the musician.

As for Sally, her doubts surfaced that same morning on the drive home. "But has Grandfather really found us out, Miss Parsons? And not read me a rare lecture?"

"No, he does not know of it yet, but he soon will if you don't employ a little more caution with that pretty flute of yours about the house."

Sally made some further attempts to pester her governess with speculations about the situation, but

Edith copied Robin's reticence and put her off with evasions and vaguenesses. She might have had a harder time of this had the younger woman's thoughts not still run, childlike, to the impending Midsummer Ball.

Meanwhile, in the following half week, Edith contrived several private interviews with her betrothed, and he with the young farmer, but all Arthur could report to Edith was that Jellicoe still continued so close-tongued that it remained ticklish to take him into their suspicions. "Bless us," said Arthur, "her ladyship of Wyndmont's a strange woman, and maybe she's made a trip abroad and not got my letters yet, but if she don't come soon, we'll demand she give us the extra days she's lost us here before she breaks off her bargain. I don't take to being diddled out of my work and my pay, not even for a countess and her whims."

Edith wished she could retreat into Sally's old whim of being able to anticipate nothing beyond Midsummer Eve. A great many things, thought the governess, are hanging over our heads to drop upon us like the sword of Damocles, immediately after the ball.

Chapter 18

The Midsummer Masked Ball

On the day before Midsummer Eve, a young stranger in rusty black descended at the Ship and Castle in Penzance, and hauled his luggage—a small, light, shabby trunk and a small, neat, heavy portmanteau—up the stairs himself. The following afternoon he hired the best horse to be had, packed the saddlebags in his own rooms, and set off overland alone.

Though his silence and his alternate displays of frugality and plentiful means aroused much speculation among the locals, none had suggested he might be a widow and a countess. But when, near dusk, he came within sight of the pavilions on the cliffs, he chose a shelter in the rock formations, hid his horse, and transformed himself into a tall, dark woman in brown silk dress and cloak. Her mask, more than a simple domino, was made to resemble an owl's face, in brown and white feathers with a small, lacquered beak; it dipped down to cover her cheeks and shadow her mouth and chin. Instead of fan or reticule, she carried a thing which suggested some ceremonial club of obscure priestly function, but which had a core of solid iron beneath the flowerets and silken streamers.

Mr. Dromgoole had mentioned the forthcoming country ball in his second letter to Isabella, Lady Wyndmont; but she had already learned of it from Sir Despard during his latest trip to London. She had also got Sir Despard to confide in her that by the time this ball was over he would have initiated another young country gentlewoman into the ancient phallic mysteries. He seemed to take for granted that Lady Isabella would view this matter in much the same light he did.

"I have also," she murmured as if reminding herself, "to try for a look at this young musician of my Bow Street runner's."

Dusk fell late in midsummer, even this far south. In the largest open pavilion, the musicians were tuning, and some of the earliest and most eager guests seemed already in process of soliciting partners for the first dances. One of the smaller, enclosed tents that flanked the dance floor was glowing very faintly from within; no doubt this was the card room, illuminated for the shufflings and dealings of the first players.

As the twilight deepened, the card tent glowed more brightly, while in the more outlying tents lights came up to make moving forms visible in silhouette, and the striped canopy of the main pavilion took on the appearance of being set about with jewels. But for the fact that these jewels were Chinese lanterns, the scene might have looked more like the Middle Ages than an imitation Vauxhall. The common folk must have kindled their bonfire on the sands below by now. Lady Isabella sat amongst the ancient rocks, waiting for full dark.

Mr. Merryn was amongst the card players in their closed tent. The strictness of his principles did not extend to denying himself the comparative excitement of picking up and throwing down rectangles of printed pasteboard, even for money, when the alternative was watching younger people, got up as human peacocks, weave in and out amongst one another on a dance floor while their elders sat in a flow of idle chit-chat around the edges. He chose a table where the play was for trifling sums, and left Sally's supervision to her grandmother, the governess and her spark, and those of their neighbors who were present. Although the upcountry regions seemed better represented than Sir Despard's own immediate neighborhood, there were still aplenty of Penwith gentlefolk attending, and Sally's grandfather, who still thought of her as a guileless and transparent child, had no fears for her safety in all this press, surrounded by friends and well-wishers.

Sally's grandmother, watching from one of the chairs set round the edge of the dance-floor scaffolding, grew less and less at ease as the evening went on. Her eyes were not so sharp as they had once been, nor was this place so well illumined as a true ballroom ought to be, with wax candles set in mirror sconces at a reasonable level, rather than colored lanterns swinging high overhead, and with walls and looking glasses to help hold the light, rather than drafty nothingnesses to let in the surrounding dark. The assemblage, moreover, had something the effect of an Aesop's fable, with many of the men and a few of the women, not content with simple dominoes, sporting headgear and occasionally full costumes designed after fanciful beasts and demigods. Even amongst these Sir Despard was easy enough to pick out, in his green satin court dress and red mask like a fox's face; but Mrs. Merryn's granddaughter, in simple white muslin with a pink satin mask, was not so distinctive.

"Look there!" the grandmother whispered to the governess during the fifth dance. "She is standing up with him *again*, is she not, my dear?"

Edith peered at the long sets. Sally's partner for the first pair of dances had been Hector Vyvyan. That was arranged beforehand, almost from the time of the Merryns accepting their invitation. Then the baronet himself had come to solicit Sally for the next two dances. Though not entirely pleased, her chaperones could hardly withhold their consent from a host and neighbor who was behaving above reproach in their sight; but Edith and Cousin Arthur had joined that set themselves without loss of time. Inconveniently, it had been impossible for them to overhear more than a few snatches of Sally's conversation with her partner, but all of these had been innocent. The girl had not returned to her family party between the fourth and fifth dance, but this need not betoken danger. If young people formed groups of their own for laughing together at such entertainments, that was healthy enough. When the musicians struck up the fifth dance, however, Sir Despard's partner was certainly a slim figure in white muslin, with golden curls and a pink domino.

"There are three yellow-haired young women here tonight, at the very least, in pink dominoes and white gowns very much like Sally's," Edith reassured Mrs. Merryn. "Besides four or five others with blue or green or purple masks." Nevertheless, she looked around for her betrothed, who had gone to fetch the ladies some punch and cake.

Others of Sally's friends had a better opportunity to see the dancers. It was by now full night, but the lanterns above the musicians' dais, high as they were hung, seemed all the brighter against the dark, and the flutists, sitting in the front rank with an unobstructed view, had a close look at Sir Despard's partner, the lace trim on her gown and domino, the pearls in her golden hair, each time the two dancers reached this end of their set and stood out for a few moments.

"The devil!" Tony muttered, dropping Cynthia from his lips long enough to lean over and nudge the second flutist. "He's dancing with her again!"

Robin nodded. Neil FitzNeil frowned and dipped his violin bow at them. On Sir Despard's authority, he had usurped Mr. Killian's glory as concert-master, and the entire Musical Society followed him with resentment.

Tony and Robin finished the tune with outward obedience, but in the brief pause between the fifth and sixth dances they had their heads together again at once. "It *was* she," Tony repeated. "I could see the very bow of her upper lip."

"I know it was—I can see as well as you. I can also see there's half a dozen other young ladies who might be mistook for her at a little distance."

"I trust it's not your country customs for an unengaged young lady to go on dancing all the night with a virtual stranger, even if he is the local nabob?"

Robin shook his head. "At least there's no one else who could be taken so easily for him. There's some hope in that."

FitzNeil rose and crossed the front of the platform to them. "You are meant to rest your lips in this interval, not to exercise them, messieurs."

Behind his back, Mr. Killian shook his bow. Sir Despard had reminded the musicians beforehand that they were to consider themselves neither more nor less than paid professionals for the nonce; some of them were lower class and actually gained a little by the pretense, while those who might otherwise have claimed their place among the guests had in the baronet's opinion freely chose to forfeit their social position for the night by remaining in the orchestra and accepting his pay. Nothwithstanding these strictures, the little apothecary, for all his fuss when he led the Musical Society, would not have been such a stickler as FitzNeil about whispering on the dais between dances.

Tony glared up at Sir Despard's valet. "You overstep yourself, man. What in Lucifer's name do you know of either gentlemanly or musicianly behavior?"

"Quite right, I did forget myself." FitzNeil made a mock bow to his first flutist. "I had forgot for a moment that we do in fact have a true professional in our midst." Turning in time to quell Mr. Killian with a glance, FitzNeil lifted his instrument and signalled the start of the next dance even while returning to his seat.

Meanwhile, Lady Isabella had come at last to the revels. She had spent the fifth dance circling the outskirts of the main pavilion, neither quite mingling with the fringes of the crowd nor yet strolling far enough from the shelter of the canopy to make herself conspicuous by her aloofness. Three tables of light refreshments, one on each of the pavilion's long sides and one at the end opposite the musicians' dais; rows of folding chairs arranged between these tables for the non-dancing elders and the wallflowers of both sexes...Lady Isabella passed behind them all, sometimes pausing to study the more rotund of the gentlemen, until she found one not unfamiliar to her, stolidly awaiting his chance at the punch bowl and cake trays. She glided round to his side of the table, laid her hand on his shoulder, and drew him out from the press and the cast of colored lights.

Dromgoole had borrowed an old black satin coat and breeches from Mr. Merryn, put on his flowered silk waistcoat, and added a plain black half-mask. The borrowed duds were thirty years or so out of fashion and not a perfect fit—well enough to get by when the ball was masked and partly in fancy dress—but he had looked in the mirror at Bolventor House before setting out, and when he saw that the woman with her hand on his shoulder was not Edith (who wore blue muslin and a plain white domino with only a small trim of feathers), he could hardly be other than surprised. Having followed her several yards into the darkness outside the pavilion, he sounded her with the statement, "Beg pardon, ma'am, but I think you've made some mistake. I'm an engaged man."

"Indeed? You had not mentioned that, neither in your conversation nor your letters. Is she someone you keep tucked away in town, or have I played Eros by engaging you to chase about the countryside in my employ?"

"Lady Wyndmont?"

"Mr. Dromgoole. Yes, I thought I had succeeded in recognizing you by your figure and the lower half of your face."

"Egad, ma'am, you've chose a pretty time to join us," said Dromgoole, blinking at the dim outline of her owl's mask. "The musicians are wearing their masks too, y'know, but if you can identify your brother-in-law so neat—"

"Your flutist can wait, Mr. Dromgoole. We've other business tonight. Sir Despard Rudgewerye is that lover of whom I once told you." As Dromgoole made no comment, Lady Isabella went on, "He and I took each other in full knowledge and consent. But he means to take another tonight in all her unwitting innocence."

"You wouldn't know whom, your ladyship?"

"I do not know her name. It would have meant little to me even had he mentioned it. But I have reason to believe he has presented her with the gift of a porcelain flute."

Dromgoole started. "What a rum little widgeon!"

"I take it you know of such a child. Perhaps she is less innocent in the matter than I had assumed. But I misdoubt it, or he would not need to take such elaborate pains. Now, then. He means to spirit her to his castle for the deed."

"He's like to have some trouble there. The young lady's not so easy to pick out in this crush, but the Bart. is."

"I know his mind, but not his present appearance. Which is he?"

"There." Dromgoole pointed Sir Despard out as best he could across the dark and the distance. "Green satin with a fox's face. In the far set."

"Ah! My red man-dog...I thought that might be he. Depend on it, he has some henchman concealed about, of much the same build and with a like costume, ready to take his place on the floor and befuddle these ballgoers when the moment comes. Your best plan, Mr. Dromgoole, is to wait on the path to the castle."

"And your ladyship?"

"I shall mount watch on them here and, with the help of the gods, join you in time to alert you of his coming. Trust me. I know him as a lover, you only as a chance acquaintance. Now that I have seen him in this costume, no other is like to deceive my vigilance, no matter how similarly attired. Nor need you have any fear that I came unprepared to look out for my own safety." She stroked her beribboned mace.

Dromgoole accepted his new commission with a touch to what would have been the brim of his hat had he been wearing one, repeated, "Your ladyship," and strode away.

Lady Isabella smiled and went on stroking Masher. "So now I have you safe out of harm's way, Bow Street...out of my way, for this next hour."

She could not follow him far enough with her eyes to see him stop on the far side of the pavilion and draw his betrothed apart for a hurried consultation. She continued her circling of the pavilion and came to a fourth table of refreshments, set up in a little striped tent, open on one side, that stood some yards behind the musicians' dais. She helped herself to some punch, drank it and concealed the cup in the rocks before mingling once more with the revellers.

After the sixth dance, the musicians had an interval for rest and refreshment. Most of them, leaving their instruments on the dais, made for the three-sided tent. The two flutists stood as if to stretch their limbs, but did not follow the other players. Tony stared steadfastly into the throng of dancers dispersing en masse to their punch bowls, while Robin glanced back at the departing concertmaster. Probably not even FitzNeil would have insisted they leave the dais before entering conversation now; nevertheless, Robin waited until Sir Despard's man was at a safe distance before he spoke. "I must insist you leave your instrument here."

Tony's fingers did not loosen from round his flute. "You should be aware that I would sooner turn the blade on myself than on Miss Merryn."

Robin regarded him a moment, started to say something, checked himself and murmured instead, "We may have been divided and conquered, Armstrong—divided her attention between the two of us until we left the way open for him."

"Now!" said Tony. "He's leaving her side for the punch bowl."

"At least tuck Cynthia up your sleeve or beneath your coat," said Robin as they quit the dais and slipped round the outer edge of the pavilion. Tony ignored the advice. Robin could only shrug and follow him to where Sally waited, near one end of the table.

"Miss Merryn!" Tony called softly, over the heads of two or three dowagers. He had concentrated on keeping her in sight throughout the dance and its immediate aftermath, but it was still a relief to find that this particular pink domino was indeed she.

"Mr. Armstrong!" She turned and pushed her way around chairs and guests to him. "Oh, and Uncle Robin, too!" Breaking through to the uncrowded periphery, she threw her arms first around the older friend, then, after a moment's hesitation, around the newer one. A few of the revellers looked at them curiously, but either they recognized none of the trio, or else they were more involved in their own jokes and flirtations, for their interest soon waned and they turned away again, leaving Sally to retreat farther into the night with her two gallants. "Oh, it is just beautiful!" she was repeating. "Is it not beautiful? And your playing—your lovely music—oh, I really think I must be in the Elysian Fields!"

Robin cleared his throat with a cough. "Well, but...but in fact, Sally, you're not," he said in his best uncle-ly manner. "That is, tomorrow you'll be back in West Cornwall again and...and hasn't Miss Parsons ever told you, my dear?"

"Oh, no, she never told me it would be as wonderful as this! But then, how could she? How could anyone ever describe it?"

"She should have told you," Tony prompted, "that one don't dance—"

"No more than a single pair with any one gentleman, Sally," Robin went on. "Not...not without some definite...er...connection or...people will

200

think there is one, whether or not, you see. You must give the other lads their turn, too," he finished in a rush of happy inspiration.

"Oh, but that rule does not hold at masked balls. He's explained it all to me, you see. Besides," Sally went on, "there's no one else I'd rather dance with, who's not already playing in the orchestra and so cannot—"

"Who are your friends, my dear?" Sir Despard came up to them, a cup of punch in either hand. "You'll present me, of course..." His glance fell to the lantern light reflecting on the flute in Tony's hand. "One of my musicians, sir?"

"Two of them," Sally began proudly. "And—"

"I think," said the baronet, "you fellows have your own belly-timber elsewhere? Do you find it unsatisfactory, or is your concertmaster allotting you so lengthy an interval between dances that you attempt in boredom to mix with your betters?"

"Sir!" cried Sally.

Tony was clenching his fist. "I think it is you who forget yourself, sir. These are amateurs, some of them your own close neighbors; and good enough to—"

"Tony," Robin whispered in his ear, simultaneously tugging at his arm. "It's all right, Miss Merryn," he went on in a louder voice. "It's only for tonight..." And again to Tony, "In Heaven's name, let it go!"

"Some of them may be good enough to call me out tomorrow, if they wish," said Sir Despard, "but I notice by your use of the third person plural rather than the first in referring to your fellow players that you seem not to consider yourself of their exalted number. And you, sir?" He turned to Robin. "Perhaps, beneath your present guise, you may be of a rank to challenge my bidding you begone to your own place?"

"No, sir, not at all...(Tony, *come!*)...We were

just going. Don't worry about us, Sally—I mean, Miss Merryn. But remember—"

"We stand in a somewhat different relation to this young lady in daily life, sir," said Tony, still clenching and unclenching his fist, "than you would relegate us to this evening. I would be advised, were I you, that a man may throw off his mask and appear more than your equal to issue his challenge."

With a mighty effort, Robin tugged his friend around and a step back toward the musicians' table. "Remember your friends, Miss Merryn!" he called back over his shoulder. Had he paused to say more, all the work of getting Tony under momentum and out of Sir Despard's way might have been lost.

Even as things stood, it was touch and go whether Tony might not turn back at any moment and issue his challenge. "To snub us in that high-horse manner! To behave as if he were the Prince of Wales himself, and not some petty provincial lordling. To dress me down like a mere paid musician in front of her!"

"Come, Tony, if the rest of us don't mind it, why should you? He *is* paying us, after all, and very handsomely, too. None of us precisely thought to snub the fee when he offered it. If he chooses to ask us to play the role for one night, I'm sure Miss Merryn will understand."

"Yes, *you're* playing the role very well, are you not? I swear you all but pulled your forelock for the man! Thank God I still have some pride left."

"It's hardly a question of pride," Robin said wearily. "It's a question of humoring one who, for all you may despise him as a provincial lordling, is still perhaps the most powerful man in Penwith...for good or ill...and who has already, for generosity to his tenants, for magisterial leniency to petty lawbreakers hailed before him, and for—"

"And for treatment of women? You can really feel comfortable to leave Miss Merryn in his company, can you?"

Robin flushed beneath his half-mask. "Well, we must hope and pray...we are not, after all, the only friends she has about her tonight. Far from it. And he's capable of great good as well as..."

"My God!" cried Tony. "Are you an entire countryside of cringing lickspittles? I'm wearied to death of hearing his sins excused on every hand with a reference or three to his balancing benefactions. Very well, Jellicoe, let's hear it—what great good deed has the man done for you, that you should be ready to thank him for his insults and beg him for more?"

Robin hesitated. "Put it...Put it that a rich man should extend a very large sum to a young orphan with no references and no material resources. Put it he should ask no interest, demand no sudden repayment, and thus enable this struggling youth to acquire freehold lands, build up a prosperous farm, become, in short, in a few years' time a substantial and respected member of society, all owing to the rich man's generosity. Even if the original loan were subsequently repaid, would not every sentiment of human reason and Christian gratitude keep that once impoverished fellow forever in his benefactor's debt?"

"So that's your story, is it? Well, you've been damned close-lipped about it," said Tony, not quite with the best of logic.

Instead of asking why he should have revealed all this, unsolicited, to an acquaintance of less than two months' standing, Robin added, "Put it further that the rich man, practicing that parable which enjoins us not to let the right hand know what the left is about, had sworn the poor one to eternal secrecy in the matter."

"He's hardly secretive about other of his great benefactions to man and beast," said Tony. "But he only came into his title about a year ago, didn't he? If he did all that for you, it must've been when..."

"He was still little more than a boy," the other

answered. "Though already possessed of considerable personal resources—how strict soever the old baronet might have been in other respects, he did not tighten the pursestrings for his heir—and of a taste for dabbling in the grandly charitable pleasures as well as in debauchery. He might not even know my face again at once. Such memories tend to blur without constant brushing of shoulders."

"Hmm. Well, I wouldn't want to brush shoulders with him, either, if I was so hellfired much in his debt. I'll give you credit for that. But there's still a difference between honest gratitude and toadying."

Robin was no longer entirely attentive to his friend. "Listen," he said. "Over there."

Snores were issuing from a cranny in the outlying boulders. "Just some gentle guest who's already tippled more than he can stomach," said Tony.

Nevertheless, with only a few yards to cover, they went for a closer look. They found a bulbous-nosed fellow of near middle age, snoozing peacefully beside an empty bottle. The cut of his fancy satin dress resembled that of Sir Despard's, and its color, as well as they could make out in the bad light, was green. A red fox mask lay not far from hand.

"George Bosweega!" whispered Robin. "He'd do any office for Sir Despard, in return for being taken back as tenant after—"

Bosweega snorted and partially wakened. "Maester Neil? 'S't time a'ready?"

"Not time, no," muttered Tony. "Sleep on, you drunken oaf." For a moment he seemed about to ensure Bosweega's slumber with an even stronger soporific than gin, but Robin pulled him away.

"And the women?" said Tony. "All the golden-haired damsels in white? Are they here by chance, or has he any number of fair slaves as ready as Bosweega to do him any office?"

"A little of both, I fear."

"But how would he have known what she would wear?"

"White muslin and a simple domino. More than one young lady would have been sure to wear something similar. He may not even have...have had designs on Sally in particular."

"Or he may have bribed the dressmaker. But that fat fool pass himself off for your baronet?" Tony went on as they left Bosweega and his snores behind.

"No doubt they'll pull him up with stays, and instruct him to hold his tongue..."

"When it is the time. And when will that be? During the supper? Or between dances?"

"He could best play the part in dumb show during the actual dance, I think," said Robin. With this logical assurance, both men turned back at once to try to get the real Sir Despard in sight again.

"Oh, Sir Despard, how could you?" Sally had burst out when he banished her two friends.

"Not with the greatest ease, my dear." He held out one cup to her. "The press is rather severe around the punch bowl."

"You know perfectly well what I meant. How could you drive them away like that? I'm sure they've as much right to be here as...as Mr. Dromgoole. And I don't want any punch now. You've spoiled everything."

"My dear, sweet child, if you were to step round behind to the musicians' table, you would find it heaped with refreshments equally tempting as our own, and in proportionately more plentiful supply, therefore in less danger of being mobbed. The musicians' table must be a very model of sufficiency and decorum when compared with those 'round which swarm our fellow gentry. Moreover, it is only for the duration of a masked ball."

He continued offering the punch. That pride might be false which would persist in refusing liquid refreshment after the thirsty business of the dance. She accepted the cup. If the cleanliness of his white glove seemed to belie his difficulties in procuring the beverage, a glance at the crowd around the table did not.

Sally sipped the punch. It contained champagne, and she softened a little. "Well, I cannot imagine anyone's refreshments being nicer than these, Sir Despard, and I cannot imagine they will run short...but I suppose it might really be more peaceful at the musicians' table, after all."

"I misdoubt you've any great experience of the true well-bred glutton, if you suppose the refreshments in no danger of depletion. Fortunately, supper should intervene in time to save the crush from starvation. Meanwhile, being disbarred by my own arbitrary rules from the comparative peace of the musicians' tent, shall we seek a modicum of quiet by strolling out to look down on the bonfire?"

She took another sip of punch and put her free hand through the extended crook of his arm. "But, however, it was still too bad of you to speak to them like that, sir. I think you are quite heartless."

"Then you are in grievous error, dear child. Did I lack that organ, all bodily functions would cease." He shook his head. "Oh, no, be assured that I possess a finely-tuned and most energetic heart. But too much emphasis, I have long thought, is misplaced upon the heart as the supposed seat of the emotions, when it is in fact no more than the servant and slave of passions originating in other parts of the human frame."

"What other parts, sir? Do you mean the brain? Or the stomach, perhaps. I know I do feel very queasy sometimes in my stomach when I'm anxious or unhappy."

Beneath the fox muzzle of his mask, he smiled. "Let us call the brain one such seat of the emotions, the stomach another, the blood yet a third—often, and not without reason, equated by the ancients with life itself. The brain, as the house of mind and intellect, must be counted the highest such seat, the blood the most all-pervasive; but in many the stomach may lie nearest of all to the most dearly cherished passion."

"I suppose you mean your gluttons, don't you? And the lungs, they'd be another seat of emotion, too. You told me once, did you not, that breath used to be considered the same as the soul?"

"And the lungs, too. But here, I think, we will leave off our listing of bodily members, at least for the time."

This might have been a tactical error on his part, for with the game ended, she returned to her former plaint. "All the same, poor Mr. Armstrong!"

"This is the same Mr. Armstrong who so callously informed you that the shape of your lip must forever bar you from mastery of your chosen instrument?"

"Yes, but..." She sighed. "But I'm beginning to be very much afraid he must be right. I still cannot seem to catch the trick of it, not even with that lovely flute you gave me. And, anyhow, he really has been very gentle... very gentlemanly with me, so he did not deserve such a snub. Nor Uncle Robin, neither."

"I shall endeavor to make it up to them. Perhaps by inviting them to dine with me some day. Look there!" He gestured with his free arm.

"Oh, how lovely!" She gazed down at the bonfire, surrounded by tiny, dancing figures which seemed to be silent because their songs were so distant and the noise of the revelling gentry so much nearer.

"In olden days, young men and maids were used to leap through these bonfires whilst the flames rose about them high as their heads. Even now, you may sometimes see their more cautious descendants dance and dash through the glowing embers."

"Indeed, I cannot think why!"

"As a fertility charm, my dear. Have you any notion what that may mean? It was an ancient and venerable fertility charm, and not, I fancy, a bad one, as the heat of the flames raised an answering fire in the blood, animating and enlivening all the vital members."

Shifting uncomfortably, she returned to the subject of the flute. "I fear your beautiful gift has been wasted, Sir Despard. Your finding Meadowsong for me. I'm afraid I may never be able to play you a proper concert, after all."

"The gift that brings any pleasure soever, no matter how brief, has not been wasted." He put one arm about her. "Come, child, shall we descend to the sands?"

"I... I'd much rather dance where there's no flames and embers, sir. Hadn't we best be going back to the pavilion now? I—I think it must be nearly time for the next dance..."

Edith Parsons had been keeping Sir Despard in sight since her betrothed shared Lady Wyndmont's warning with her. Because of the similarly clad female figures, she could not always be sure that the one with the baronet was indeed her charge; but she could reason that if Sally were not with him, she would be safe, and therefore the distinctive costume was the one to watch.

The matter of the porcelain flute put an especially nasty light on the affair, and Edith muttered vague threats of some rare chastisement in the morning; but meanwhile she mentioned nothing to Sally's grandmother, loath to disturb what peace of mind the old woman might still enjoy. To have informed Mr. Merryn would have necessitated slipping into the enclosed card tent and thus losing Sir Despard for a dangerous length of time. She might have worked her way around to alert the Vyvyans, Robin Jellicoe, even perhaps Mr. Armstrong... but she could not quickly recognize any close friends and neighbors in the masked figures amongst whom the trail led, and she found she could not have reached the musicians without leaving Sir Despard and his companion unwatched at an uneasy distance from the pavilions.

She crept close enough to recognize Sally's voice

and to overhear words confirming the provenance of the porcelain flute. She also overheard enough to evidence that the child had embroiled herself innocently in the intrigue. When Sir Despard put his arm around the girl, the governess saw it was high time to intervene, even at the risk of putting him on his guard.

"Sally?" she said, stepping forward.

"Miss Parsons!" said Sally, with a little start suggestive both of relief and of a mildly guilty conscience.

"Oh, forgive me, sir," Edith went on. "We've been looking for her everywhere, you see. Sally, my dear, you must come back and let us introduce you to a very genial young man who requests the honor of the next dance with you."

Sir Despard bowed to the governess. "But suppose she is already bespoke, madam?"

"By whom, Sir Despard? Not by you, surely, for whom else do people commonly take refreshment with afterwards, if not their partners of the set just finished?"

"I bow to the voice of social nicety," he replied. "If the young lady is not to be given her unfettered choice, then your protégé, ma'am, no doubt takes precedence over mine."

Thus he left Edith with the problem of enlisting on the spur of the moment some young gentleman from the masked crush who could, unrehearsed, play the solicitous stranger she had invented. Her task was doubly ticklesome in that Sir Despard insisted on accompanying them until he saw Sally partnered. Edith's only advantage lay in the dominoes, which enabled her to address gentlemen without naming anyone's name, and to pretend mere mistakes in identity when the first two men she accosted (choosing those in simple ball dress and plain black half-masks) proved to have partners already.

On her third try, with the musicians actually

playing the opening measures, the stranger on whom she seized showed himself more amenable.

"Pardon me, sir, but are you not he who desired to stand up with my young lady?"

"Charmed," said the youth, trying to conceal a hiccough as he took Sally's hand.

Sir Despard smiled and bowed away from Edith's side. She watched with not overmuch cause for triumph as the stranger led Sally to a place in the set. No doubt his tipsiness had a deal to do with his complaisance. Still, he appeared harmless and genial enough, and if he could only hold his liquor sufficiently well to stay on his feet...

Then she saw Sir Despard lead another slim, blonde woman in white to a place near Sally and her partner in the same set.

Tony and Robin had not been able to observe this interchange, taking place as it did on the far end of the dance floor. When Sally and her partner worked their way up through the set to the musicians' end, however, Tony nudged Robin and dropped his flute for a moment to mouth the word, "Who?"

Robin shrugged and smiled to indicate he had no idea with whom she was dancing this set, but at least they should be glad it was not Sir Despard.

In the next few steps, the baronet and his partner reached the top of the set, and he seemed to nod at FitzNeil. The concertmaster improvised a kind of *gruppetto* gone wild, with high and low tones a whole octave apart. Mr. Killian and several other musicians grimaced, but continued to play. Perhaps it was a quirk of just such misplaced virtuosity as Mr. FitzNeil permitted none of the others, but he had executed it with skill, never faltering in the rhythm he set them.

Sally and her partner, Sir Despard and his, blended back into the set in their turns. As they worked their way down, Robin nudged Tony. Continuing to play, or at least mimic playing, Robin pointed with his instrument. Beyond the dais, yet another white-clad woman was disappearing toward the place where they had left Bosweega asnooze in his green satin. It might well appear that FitzNeil's freak of notes had been a signal.

Tony continued holding Cynthia to his lips, but not to play with his usual perfection. Bit by bit, he was unscrewing her body from her headpiece, with a quarter twist at the end of every measure, every phrase. Robin did his uneasy best to carry the burden of the flute part.

This time, working their way back up through the set in conformity with the complicated figure, Sir Despard and his lady reached the upper end and stood out before Sally and her gentleman. The baronet nodded again to his concertmaster.

Just as Sally and her partner reached the top of the set, but while they were still involved in the figure, FitzNeil went off into another fit of embellishment—this time in the nature of a ragged, half rhythmed cadenza better suited to the moody concert hall experiments of such moderns as Beethoven than to the ballroom. Musicians and dancers alike were thrown momentarily off their beat, and in the confusion Sir Despard snatched Sally out of the figure, whilst his own former partner slipped into her place opposite the tipsy stranger.

Sally opened her mouth, but Sir Despard laid his fingers on her lips, shaking his head and showing her a smile of mischief beneath his fox-mask nose. Whether he was urging her to slip away with him at once, or reassuring her of the impunity with which they could now continue the dance together, Tony could endure no more.

One last twist, and Cynthia's blade was free. Dropping her body on his chair, Tony sprang down from the orchestra dais to confront the baronet.

Not all the musicians saw at once what was happening. Many of them continued to play for a few measures, and the dancers at the far end of the sets to attempt dancing. But FitzNeil sprang up and started to his master. Robin thrust out a foot and brought him down on the dais. Killian and two or three others gleefully jumped forward to sit on their fallen concertmaster, and the last strains of music came to a halt.

Meanwhile, Sir Despard looked down at Tony's blade. "Ha," he remarked. "Threatened by one of my own hirelings, eh?"

Tony reached down to take Sally's free hand in his. She clasped his fingers readily, but Sir Despard held fast to her other hand.

"I am unarmed, fellow," the baronet went on.

"You are also without honor, sir."

Sally's erstwhile partner was not too tipsy to take a leading part in pushing the other guests back, leaving a clear space around the glint of the dagger. But Lady Isabella, who had ever kept the baronet within sight, pushed to the front of the crowd.

"Despard!" She held up her mace. "I brought Masher to use upon you, but now instead I offer a trade. This weapon for that child!"

Sir Despard released Sally's hand and accepted the mace. The young woman drew close to Tony, still clinging for a few seconds to his hand, until Lady Isabella gathered her away from them, out of the arena. Edith Parsons had by now gained the top of the dance floor. Though the two older women had not been introduced, it was obvious to the eyes behind the owl mask that this newcomer was dear to the trembling girl, and Lady Isabella relinquished her into the arms of her governess.

Dromgoole joined them, George Bosweega in tow. (The runner suffered enough sense of chivalry to have allowed the female accomplice to slip away in the crowd.) "You'll forgive me, your ladyship," he said to the owl mask, "but I didn't quite see my way to waiting on the path." He would have pushed on through to try to separate the antagonists, but it was even now rather late for that.

Tony and Sir Despard had been circling one another. Sir Despard raised the iron club and closed the distance, aiming for the musician's head. Warding the blow with his left arm, Tony stabbed his blade deep between the baronet's shoulder and chest.

Sir Despard staggered back, his green satin already drenched with blood. "Damnation," he said, "I think I'm killed by a musician."

"By an earl, sir." Tony removed his mask. "By the Earl of Wyndmont."

"Wyndmont?" Sir Despard sank to the dance floor. "Damme, Wyndmont..."

Robin jumped from the musicians' dais and knelt by the unconscious baronet, cradling his head, pressing his own handkerchief to the wound and muttering old Cornish charms to staunch the blood—

> "Christ was born in Bethlehem,
> Baptized in the River Jordan,
> There he digged a well
> And turned the water against the hill,
> So shall thy blood stand still....

Killian!" he cried up to the apothecary. "For the love of God, Mr. Killian!"

Chapter 19

Lady Isabella and the Elf-Knight

The youth who had partnered Sally through the last set now remembered that his father was a medical man and fetched him from the cardplayers' tent. By the time this upcountry doctor arrived to claim Sir Despard's treatment from the St. Finn apothecary, Lady Isabella had torn most of her long cloak into bandaging.

Robin wiped his hands on a spare fragment of cloak and turned to Sir Despard's manservant, who still lay watching the proceedings from a prone position beneath the combined weights of old Tremiggan the oboist and young Pendruck the trombonist. "Say," said the farmer, "would your master not wish the ball to continue?"

FitzNeil shrugged. "Lud knows what else we'll do with the supper. But I'm damned if I concertmaster for you coves again."

In the end, while FitzNeil was let up to help bear his bandaged master home to Rudgewerye Castle, under the supervision of both doctor and apothecary, Lady Isabella made herself a local legend by marshalling, more or less at random, Mr. Botallack of Carnsew to help her host the shards of the ball. The third fiddle, Dan Killigrew from near Centry, did his best to concertmaster the remaining musicians through a last few dances for those guests still of a mood to join in a set before the supper tables were set up, rather earlier than scheduled.

The upcountry physician pronounced Sir Despard's recovery not improbable, prescribed a balsam and a palliative, and returned to the pavilions to find Mr. and Miss Atwill of Ardensaweth, whose house-guest he was, secure in the assurance that he would be sent for if needed again before midday. Mr. Killian set off for his shop to prepare his own preferred versions of the stranger's medicines. Most of those who had helped carry the baronet likewise dispersed.

Robin, lingering, intercepted FitzNeil on his way to watch by Sir Despard's bedside, with a bottle of spirits in each hand and another beneath each elbow.

"Is this how you propose to tend your master?" said the agriculturist. "Pickling yourself with the best of his cellar while he lies senseless?"

"Why not? If he dies, he'll never know the loss, and if he lives, he'll keep me on regardless."

"Sir, you are a rogue and a scoundrel."

"Of course I am," FitzNeil agreed. "What other type would his nabs employ in my capacity?"

Robin pushed FitzNeil aside and put his own hand on the latch of the bedroom door. Although accepting this displacement cheerfully, FitzNeil left with a parting shot: "I may be a capital rogue, but at least *I've* took off my mask."

In the press of the emergency, Robin had never got round to that detail, nor did he spend the time to do so now. He entered the bedchamber, poured a very little brandy into a tumbler (few rooms in Rudgewerye Castle lacked a decanter or two of some kind of spirits ready to hand) and took a seat beside the bed to watch, if necessary, through what remained of the short summer night.

Some time later, the door opened quietly and Lady Wyndmont stepped in, minus owl's-head but recognizable by her gown and her bearing. The farmer stood. "My lady?"

"They say he will recover. In your estimation, is it likely?"

"He is resting easy enough now, ma'am."

"Has he wakened?"

"Once, briefly...among other things, he spoke somewhat of Lord Wyndmont."

She poured herself a generous draught from the crystal decanter. "Would you not watch in greater comfort sans domino?"

"Indeed...absent of me." He put up one hand to remove the mask.

"Not that you need watch any longer." She waved as if to dismiss him.

He tapped nervously on the mask. "If you'll pardon the observation, my lady, I think you mentioned something earlier to the effect that you had brought that mace to use it upon him?"

She opened the hand that did not hold her brandy glass. "I had. But now the honor of your country maid is saved and the edge of my jealousy dulled, even though I myself was not the one to strike the blow, I think you may trust me to play the gentlest of nurses to my sometime lover."

Sir Despard stirred, his left hand groping towards the wound. "Bella? Isabel?"

Robin stepped back. Lady Isabella slipped into his former place at the injured man's pillow. Lifting the dampened cloth, she stroked Sir Despard's forehead, and Killian's preparations not having arrived, tipped her brandy to his lips. "Sleep on now, Elf-Knight. Take your rest."

Robin, satisfied with her credentials, bowed himself out of the bedroom. She stayed on, stroking Sir Despard's face between applications of freshly wetted cloths. Once or twice she moistened his lips with brandy or water. It seemed to sweeten his dreams. Perhaps another half hour went by.

Then the door opened again. Edith Parsons came into the room.

"I will not let this vigil be taken from me so easily as I took it from my predecessor," said Lady Isabella.

The governess shook her head. "I came to sit with you awhile, not in your place."

"You are my Bow Street's affianced, I think, by the way you and he stood together a few hours ago?"

Nodding, Edith pulled up a chair and sat across the bed from Lady Isabella.

"I misdoubt you've come out of any overgreat concern either for him or for me," the countess went on. "That leaves concern for...is it for Tony?"

Edith nodded again. "Once owning his true identity, he has gone on and made a complete breast of it to Mr. Dromgoole."

"Has he?" Lady Isabella raised one eyebrow.

"He has confessed to killing your late husband."

"Has my young brother-in-law so strong and sudden a desire to cry cockles in a silken collar? Does he fear that Sir Despard will baffle his ambition to dance on air by not dying, or that no jury of his peers will call it murder to defend oneself against a man who is trying to strike one's head into one's ribcage, no matter which started the fray?"

"No, I think that the present Lord Wyndmont truly believes he killed his elder brother that night. But Mr. Dromgoole tells me you are firmly convinced he did not." Edith leaned forward. "I shan't disguise my purpose, Lady Wyndmont. I came here hoping to learn why you have maintained his innocence."

Lady Isabella smiled and bent over Sir Despard. "Hark, how on every side they hem us in...No, he sleeps. Hark, love, how I could yet destroy you with a blow."

"Lady Wyndmont...as one woman speaking frankly with another..."

Lady Isabella looked up at her interlocutor. "You love our Mr. Dromgoole?"

"Dearly."

"As for me, I am not sure I know what it is to love. But in certain ways this man lying here so unaware of life and death is more a husband to me than was Wyndmont. Perhaps you consider Mr. Dromgoole your husband already?"

"That depends—"

"No, my dear, I meant in the matter of secrets shared between husband and wife. Which, though not perhaps to be guarded with such strictness as the seal of the Romish confessional, have still their own measure of solemn privacy. Has it occurred to you that the line of direct descent must die with either of these two men, and their respective titles pass to some third or fourth cousin? Of course, I have already suffered the claims of a few distant pretenders to Wyndmont's title and estates, but in the case of Rudgewerye, it must take some probably unsuspecting distant relation quite unawares."

Edith reached over the bed for the other woman's hand. "Your ladyship, not a few of the countryfolk regard their baronet with some affection. As a stranger here, and one about to leave the West country, I should not wish to bequeath them some unknown and perhaps worse landlord in his place. But your husband's brother has been in mental agony for two months now, and the future happiness of a young woman whom I regard as very nearly a daughter may also be at stake."

Lady Isabella took Edith's hand and smiled. "Very well, then. In the close confidence of two women and their two near-husbands..."

Chapter 20

Sally

Mrs. Bosweega, George's mother and Sir Despard's housekeeper, made her own abode not in her employer's castle, but in his gatehouse, which equalled many a country parsonage for comfort and roominess. Hither Tony had accompanied Mr. Dromgoole in an ambiguous position: although the Bow Street man did not call him a prisoner nor lock him in, he put him on his parole not to run away.

Hither also, with some difficulty, Mr. and Mrs. Merryn had been persuaded to bring their granddaughter, for it was much nearer than Bolventor House, and Sally had some arguable right to learn as soon and accurately as possible the fates of both her would-be abductor and her rescuer.

As for George Bosweega, since nothing that could be proved had come of his part in the affair, Dromgoole let him off. Mrs. Bosweega did not stop to assimilate the idea that it could hardly concern Bow Street if a man chose to get himself up in whatever outlandish dress soever for purposes of mingling with his betters at a provincial masked ball; in her gratitude, she could not do too much for any of Mr. Dromgoole's party who chose to wait in the gatehouse.

So she plied Mr. and Mrs. Merryn with as substantial a supper as they would have got at the ball, while Dromgoole and Edith proceeded on to the castle and Sally lay down in an upstairs bedroom, as if to sleep. In fact, when sure that she was left alone and her elders all safely occupied, she had sought out the room where Mr. Armstrong's—Lord Wyndmont's—honor held him prisoned (it was easy to locate, by the sound of pacing within) and joined him there, intentionally lightening and unintentionally embittering his vigil.

"I shall break Sir Despard's flute, if that would be best," she was saying when they had reached the stage of sitting with arms around each other. "Indeed, I had no idea what he meant by it."

"I think it would be extreme to break the thing. Send it back by some messenger, if you scruple to keep it...though he owes you more reparation than a porcelain flute. But you should have a true instrument. Let me bequeath Cynthia to you...but you must have the blade removed..."

"Don't talk so!" Wiping away a tear, she stretched upward to kiss him. "I've needed such a great while to learn my own mind, but I know it now. It is you I have loved all this time."

He tried to remove her arms from about his neck. "I will not ask any woman to be my bride and my widow within the month."

"I'd be your bride if it were only for the rest of tonight. I shouldn't be content to have it over so soon, but still I would..."

"And when you were the widowed countess of a felon earl who died with a halter round his neck, even though the halter had been silk...would your farmer have you then?"

There was a cough from the far side of the room. They looked up to see Robin standing in the doorway.

"He might," said Robin, "though the match would be considerably above any reasonable social pretensions the farmer could claim, and a proportionate topple for the countess. Is a silken noose really more comfortable than one of hemp? A purely rhetorical question; in the event, we have no cause to look for any such untimely shortening of his lordship's earthly pilgrimage."

Robin stepped aside and let Edith and Dromgoole

precede him into the room. Dromgoole nodded to the governess, who crossed the floor to take one of Sally's hands and one of Tony's.

"My dears," she said, "it was an unlucky coincidence. On the same night when our Mr. Armstrong was attacked by a footpad—merely and simply a low robber of the streets, sir, one Scabnose Jebby by name, and struck down in just and honest self-defense—Sir Despard and Lady Wyndmont had met for a rendezvous in those very inn fields, as many other lovers have done through the years. The late Lord Wyndmont had grown suspicious, and he followed his wife. The two men fought, and it was Sir Despard who killed the then Lord Wyndmont, your late brother."

"We only know this under the rose," said Dromgoole. "Her ladyship hired me to find Wyndmont's heir, not to bring in her gallant. She swears it was a fair fight, even if it didn't go strictly according to the duelling Code, and as long as it can stand officially that his late lordship and the low toby man killed each other, I don't see the profit to anyone in making a stir of the real story at this point. Handy thing your lordship waited until we was private to out with your confession."

"No one outside this room, aside from Lady Wyndmont and Sir Despard, of course, has any reason to think otherwise than that we brought you here in simple custody for the unpleasantness with Sir Despard this evening. Lady Wyndmont," Edith added, "plans to take Sir Despard to Italy for half a year to convalesce. She says she may stay on in that climate even after he has returned to Cornwall, and leave the new earl in complete enjoyment of all his English property." The governess briefly joined the two young hands she held, then separated them with a smile of encouragement. "But now, dear child, if we are to clear the way for his lordship's applying to pay his addresses in a more regular fashion, we must get you back to your room for now and make you promise to give over your naughtiness, at least until you are Lady Wyndmont."

As Edith drew Sally away from Tony, Robin came forward again, bringing out from behind his back a hinged case covered in old, faded baize. "I would have had the box recovered, had there been time," he said, holding it out before Sally and lifting the lid to disclose a cherrywood pipe nestled in blue velvet padding.

"What is it?" said Sally. "Some sort of antique clarinet?"

"A recorder. Also called a *flûte d'Angleterre,* to distinguish it from the German flute or *flauto trasverso* that we've been using."

"Yes!" Tony interjected. "The principle of tone production is much the same, the air passing over a sharp edge. But in the German flute—"

"Do you mind, Armstrong?" said Robin, between annoyance and whimsy. "If you were not an earl, famously rich and obviously the man of Miss Merryn's choice, I warn you I might have put up a shrewder struggle for her; but as it is, at least allow me this last moment. Where the lips have all the work of it with the German flute, you see," he went on to Sally, "in the *flûte d'Angleterre* the upper part of the mouthpiece channels the air for the player—"

"So that not even my Cupid's bow can stop me from mastering the *flûte d'Angleterre!*" she exclaimed, and he did not object to her interruption, but went on with a smile,

"The recorder's been out of fashion for some years now, but the sound should still be as sweet as when it was the rage. You'd best oil this one well before you play it. It has been in Sir Despard's family for several generations...it was last played by Sir Despard's brother, the one who was lost or drowned. He wants you to have it now."

"And if it's so long out of fashion," cried Sally, "then I shall have a truly unique instrument to play!" In almost a single movement, she snapped the case shut to keep its contents safe, snatched it up in her hand, and threw her arms around him. "You must—You must thank him for me. And oh, Uncle Robin, will you forgive me for—for flirting so desperately with you?"

It was only a moment before he replied. "I should have begged the honor of giving you away at the altar, as an uncle, of course, if you did not already have a grandfather to perform that office."

She kissed him on the cheek, let him go, and turned back to Tony, her hand twitching to reach out again for his.

"Well," said Edith, "you've been alone together for Lord knows how long already this evening. It can hardly do any great harm for you to escort her back to her own room, your lordship, provided you go quietly and prudently and come back within five minutes."

"And should you return to visit the Cornish relations after the honeymoon, Tony," said Robin with a handshake, "bring along the music, and maybe we can finish *Balin and Balan*."

As Tony and Sally disappeared on their short journey down the passage, Dromgoole clapped Robin on the shoulder and said in an undertone, "Well done, lad. Afraid I can't say I took it so noble when I lost out the first time 'round."

"Thank you, Mr. Jellicoe," murmured the governess. "May it turn out as well for you in the end as it has for us."

He shrugged. "Oh. Don't fret for me, Miss Parsons. I'll yet make some fortunate young lady the finest husband in the West country." He then took his leave on the tacit assumption that the senior pair of lovers, like the junior, would not object to five minutes alone.

Strangely, the governess and the runner spent their first moment or so of privacy peering down the passageway to where they could make out Sally's white ball dress, Lord Wyndmont's white collar points and shirt ruffles in the shadows.

"And that young pair?" Dromgoole whispered. "Pretty green still, maybe. Think they'll do as well as us, Coz?"

"They will do as well as themselves, Cousin Arthur," Edith said softly. "What marriage can do more?" And she drew him back into the otherwise unpopulated room.